DATE DUE

Late Bloomer

 Late
Bloomer

DAVID A. KAUFELT

Harcourt Brace Jovanovich

New York and London

Lyrics from "Get Me to the Church on Time" by Alan Jay Lerner and Frederick
Loewe copyright © 1956 by Alan Jay Lerner and Frederick Loewe; Chappell &
Co., Inc., owner of publication and allied rights throughout the world;
international copyright secured; all rights reserved; used by permission.
Lyrics from "The Lady Is a Tramp" by Richard Rodgers and Lorenz Hart
copyright © 1937 by Chappell & Co., Inc.; copyright renewed; international
copyright secured; all rights reserved; used by permission.
Lyrics from "I'm Gonna Live Till I Die" by Al Hoffman, Walter Kent, and
Mann Curtis copyright © 1950; copyright renewed 1977 by Al Hoffman Songs,
Inc., a division of Music Sales Corp., New York; all rights reserved; used by
permission.
Lyrics from "Side by Side" by Harry Woods copyright © 1927 by Shapiro,
Bernstein & Co., Inc.; copyright renewed; all rights reserved; used by
permission.
Lyrics from "April Showers" by Louis Silver copyright © 1921 Warner Bros.,
Inc.; copyright renewed; all rights reserved; used by permission.

Printed in the United States of America

Library of Congress Cataloging in Publication Data
Kaufelt, David A
Late bloomer.

I. Title.
PZ4.K199Lat   [PS3561.A79]   813'.5'4   79–4591
ISBN 0–15–148792–8

First edition

B C D E

For my wife, Lynn

Author's Note

To my knowledge, there is no
Marie Antoinette Suite in the
Fontainebleau Hotel in Miami Beach.
The hotel called the Monte Excelsior
is a pure invention, as are all the
characters and events in this novel.

Late Bloomer

One

She was disappointed. She had expected the back of the limousine to be luxurious, to make her feel aristocratic and rich, coddled and protected. Sitting between the hefty bodies of her husband's sister and brother, she felt as coddled as an egg in a Mixmaster. Staring at an overflowing ashtray in front of her, she had a near irresistible urge to empty it.

Meyer's hand, hairless and huge, distracted her. It patted his knee in a continual and probably unconscious attempt to console himself. He smelled of expensive cigars and obsessive cleanliness. Ruth put her small, soft, and no longer young hand on his, hoping to stop the constant movement. Meyer misread the gesture, placing his free hand on top of hers. She wondered if they were about to begin the children's game in which the players pile their hands on each other's, quicker and quicker, until it turns into a smacking match. She removed her hand. "I'm getting hysterical," she told herself.

She turned to Frieda. A cascade of tears was flowing down the grooves of that woman's face, circumventing the small warts, flooding the minute wrinkles and somewhat deeper grooves both nature and forty winters of Miami Beach sun had put there. The sisters-in-law's eyes met. Frieda gave out with a sound that was halfway between a hiccup and a convulsive sob. Ruth patted her on her round, strong shoulder while Frieda held a once-white handkerchief to her nose and slowly turned back to her reflection in the green-tinted window.

"Everyone seems to be doing an awful lot of patting," Ruth thought. She took her hand from Frieda's shoulder and resolutely placed it in her lap. "What is the matter with me?" Ruth asked herself. "Why am I thinking of everything but what I'm supposed to be thinking of?" Before she could come up with an answer, she noticed that Meyer was at it again, his hand keeping time to music played by some orchestra only he could hear. She forced herself to stop watching his hand and looked up at his face. His heavy eyelids were half closed. There were tears in the corners of his eyes.

"There is something the matter with me," she thought. "There is something definitely the matter with me." She crossed her legs, the black silky material of her dress making an unpleasant sound. She felt rather than saw Meyer look at her for the twentieth time that day with that annoying, endearing cocker spaniel expression of his. His pale, round, teary eyes were looking for some answer. "I don't know the question," Ruth said to herself, "much less the answer."

She purposely didn't return his gaze. She stared straight ahead of her, through the glass partition, concentrating on her daughter, Audrey, and her son, Nick.

Audrey was keeping up a steady flow of conversation, aiming it at Nicky, who, like the chauffeur, was keeping his eyes focused on the road ahead. The depressing, factory-lined highway was all there was to look at. That and the sleek black vehicle in front of them, leading the way.

"I won't think about him now," Ruth resolved. "I'll think of other things. Audrey. Hard to believe she's only forty-six. Per usual she's wearing a dress with one too many *chatchkas*. That white collar makes her look like the witch in *Snow White*. She should never let them dye her hair such a dark color. It looks as if it's been permanented permanently. For once I'd like to see her with a hair out of place. *Oy,* why can't I be a little more charitable? My own daughter yet and I'm ripping her apart like she's my favorite enemy. It's that expression on her face like she's sucking on a large lemon.

"And what's she saying to Nicky? Most of the time she gives him a hello, a how-do-you-do, and a that's that."

Ruth looked away, wishing she liked her daughter more, wondering not for the first or even the hundredth time why she couldn't. "What went wrong? Where did this sour, mean person spring from, this woman with all that anger? Where did the anger come from?"

Nicky, the *maven,* had explained it to her many times. "She was a girl, Ma. The Meyers aren't fond of girls. When I was born, you dropped her like a hot potato. I was the prince, Ma. Audrey was yesterday's *blintza.*"

"That's not true," Ruth had protested. "You weren't a prince."

"Of course I was. I got everything I ever wanted. You waited on me hand and foot. Dad pranced around with me on his shoulders as if I were a conquering hero. Even Grandma was obsessed with flashing my photograph. And Audrey? She was detailed to take care of me. Who the hell, I'd like to know, was taking care of her?"

"Me. Who else?"

"You didn't, Ma. You didn't know she was alive."

"If you feel so sorry for her, how come you're so mean to her? Your only sister?"

"Because she's a hostile, emasculating bitch who's tried to do me in from the day I was born. I understand her. I feel sorry for what you did to her. Doesn't mean I like her."

"You have an answer for everything, don't you, big shot?"

"Ma, at some point in your life, it would be nice if you took a little responsibility for . . ."

"Besides," Ruth non-sequitured, "you weren't a prince."

"Then what was I? You were still cutting my meat for me when I was ten years old . . ."

"You weren't a prince," Ruth had insisted. "You were a king. Nichlaus *Amaelich*. Nichlaus, the King. The first son to be born into the Meyer family after all those years of girls. They had given up, already. You should have been at your *bris*. The fuss, the hoo-ha they made. How they loved you and . . ."

"And Audrey the Goose Girl was sent to the kitchen to mash my potatoes. You wonder why she hates my guts?"

"Nichlaus the King. Do you know that when your Grandmother Meyer (may she rest in peace) saw you for the first time . . ."

Nichlaus the King turned and looked at his mother through the glass partition. "He doesn't have the Meyer eyes," she said to herself, pleased. "They're big brown eyes, plaintive and long lashed, just like my father's." There were tears in them.

And again, unbidden, there were tears in her own eyes. She found herself remembering her father's funeral. A cramped cemetery in Queens crowded with rich people's mausoleums. A little rabbi standing on his toes in front of the narrow grave. "It's too small," she wanted to cry out. The rabbi's pinched, high voice read the prayer for the dead, his small body bobbing back and forth. She had been afraid the rabbi would fall in. She had been afraid of so many things.

"Father," she whispered aloud. "I haven't thought of him in such a long time. A good man. So kind. So patient. And so lost after Mama died from the influenza that killed so many in nineteen eighteen." She remembered his dying in a great brass bed, calling out for his Ruthie. "I'm here, Father," she had said, "I'm here." She had been his baby, the child of his old age. At the end, he hadn't been able to see her.

She couldn't stop crying. Meyer, awkwardly, put his thick

arm around her. He had had a crush on her from the day his brother had brought her home. Poor Meyer. Her face was pressed up against the smooth material of his dark suit, so different from the rough tweed her father had worn nearly fifty years before.

And, as she lay there in her brother-in-law's arms, smelling the really terrible smell of Palmolive Gold, she allowed herself to face what she had spent the past twenty-odd hours avoiding.

It was not her father who had died. She wasn't being driven to the overgrown, undercared-for cemetery in Queens. She wasn't twenty years old. Her life wasn't just beginning as her last remaining constraint was being lowered into the earth.

No. It was her husband who had died. And they were going to a monumentless golf course of a cemetery in Metuchen, New Jersey. "And far from my life beginning, at sixty-six years old, it's almost over."

She cried as the limousine pulled into the scrupulously modern grounds of the Gates of Israel Resting Place. She cried for her husband, for her father, and most of all—"I have to admit it"—she cried for herself. "I never dreamed that this is what would become of me. Never. I always thought that something would come along to save me, to make me special. I'm not special. I'm ending my life as a businessman's widow, as Harry Meyer's wife, Ruth. As my father used to say, it's a fine how-do-you-do."

While she wondered where her dreams had gone to, what had happened to the miraculous intervention she had expected, the terrible defeating sense of loss hit her with its full impact. "Harry is no more." She felt hollow, as if some limb had been removed during an unsuccessful operation. "He was everything to me," she said out loud, for the first time using the past tense.

"I know," said Meyer. "I know, Ruthie."

"How will I live?"

"Like we all do, Ruthie."

The limousine stopped. Meyer got out and she saw Nick reaching in for her. She tried to stop crying as she grabbed his hand. "Nicky," she said. *"Totela."* They stood there in the wing created by the door and the body of the car, holding on to each other, until someone with a disembodied voice asked them to "please step this way."

The services had been scheduled for ten A.M. to give the New York contingent time to drive in. They began promptly at eleven as Ruth was led to her seat in the first pew in I. R. Silverman's immodest funeral parlor on Elizabeth Avenue in downtown Elizabeth, New Jersey.

"Why do they always call it for ten when they always mean eleven?" she could hear Harry's cousin, Sam Monosoff, saying at the top of his voice. "Why do they do it every single goddamned time, I'd like to know?"

He was shushed as the recessed lights dimmed, indicating that the service was about to begin. The curious objectivity that had come over her in the middle of the night, after the hours of chaos stemming from the moment the doctor had called, was still with her. Everything seemed so clear, outlined in sharp detail, like a cartoon in a coloring book.

Straight ahead was an enormous wall mosaic depicting the Tree of Life in stones of pale blue, gray, and tan. On a bier in front of the mosaic, flanked by two burning candles, rested the closed coffin. It was made of polished poplar, a Star of David carved into its lid. Lit by overhead beams, it resembled a stage set. A drama was about to take place. Serious, but still theatrical.

The rabbi hired for the occasion stood behind the podium, looking at the mourners in the first row, shaking his head from side to side, as if he were denying Harry's death. He waited until the room was silent before he gripped the podium with both hands and began the now familiar prayer.

"*El Moley Rachamin* . . ." "O God, full of compassion . . ." She turned once, during the service, to "case the house," as Nicky put it. Three hundred people were crowded into the paneled chapel. She picked out the face of her niece (well, Harry's niece, but they had never made that kind of distinction), Summer, and a man named Frank Frankomano, a salesman for United Cigar whom she hadn't seen in twenty years, not since Harry and Meyer had started expanding the business.

The rabbi, finished with the prayer, launched into his eulogy, an unmoving but satisfying message listing a number of Harry's real and imagined virtues. Lou Feinberg and the boys from the Masons, dressed in white satin aprons and red hats, performed their acutely silly dance. Harry really hadn't been much of a Mason. The rabbi said a few concluding words and then Nicky was helping her up, guiding her through a side door onto the macadam parking lot, into the limousine.

She just had time to take one last look at the coffin. She suddenly understood the reason, the need, for open coffins. It was too difficult to believe that Harry was lying inside the neat, ugly box.

"There's been a mistake," she said.

The unreal quality of the day continued at the cemetery, its Astro-Turf lawn spreading in all directions. Discreet brass plates indicated the "last resting places of loved ones." A narrow lane called the Lion of Judah Way bisected the fake greenery. In the background, a yellow bulldozer stood behind the open grave, a giant toy left overnight on the lawn.

The day was faultless, warm for early October, the blue sky filled with what looked like hand-painted clouds. The cars,

new and shiny in subdued metallic colors, had lined up neatly
behind the limousines. "It looks like a television commercial,"
she thought, no longer crying, once again in her lucid,
objective mood. "A television commercial for perfect funer-
als."

The mourners grouped themselves around the open grave as
if they had been practicing all morning. The coffin was
lowered into the earth by a noiseless, metal contraption. When
the coffin touched bottom, the rabbi began to intone. "Eternal
God, our Creator, who makes and takes, You have given, now
You have taken away Harold Jacob Meyer, may he rest in
peace . . ."

She turned and found Meyer standing behind her, weeping,
putting a crumpled tissue to his eyes. His wife lay under one of
the insufficient brass plates at the outer edge of what Nicky
called the Meyer Family Plot. "I'll be buried next to Harry,"
Ruth thought. "But I won't like it. I don't want to be buried
in this fake, plastic place, overlooking Route Number One. I
want to be buried under a yellow moon and a sheltering palm
in Tahiti." The thought, so irreverent and inappropriate,
made her laugh.

"What's the matter with you, Mother?" Audrey, startled,
asked.

Ruth looked at her daughter and in that moment, the
worrying objectivity was once again gone, giving way to
feelings and behavior over which she had no control. "No,"
she cried out, holding onto Audrey's arm, shouting into her
shocked face. "It's a mistake. A big mistake." She felt Nick's
arm around her. "It's a mistake, Nicky." She leaned against
him, afraid she would fall into the hole, on top of the ugly
coffin.

"It's no mistake, Ma," Nick said, holding onto her.

She stopped talking, allowing the service, the burial, to

continue. The image of Harry as she last saw him came into her mind. A thin, ivory-white body. She hadn't known where the man began and the tubes and machines left off. She erased the ugly image and created a new one: Harry, when he was young, a cigar in his mouth, his muscular body clad in a dark, double-breasted suit, one foot on the running board of his black Studebaker, his expression cocky, all here-I-am.

She held onto that image as the rabbi began to read "The Mourner's Kaddish." His voice, for a moment, lost its glistening, broadcast quality. Five thousand years of collective suffering broke through his thick, prosperous suburban facade. "Extolled and hallowed by the name of God . . ."

Her knees buckled. She pitched forward but was caught by Nick and Meyer. They held her up until the rabbi finished. Then she was led away from the grave to the limousine, walking between the crowd of relatives who stood in small groups, gossiping, renewing acquaintance, feuds, affection.

This time Nick sat in the back with her. He hadn't given her time to turn around, to watch the patient bulldozer fill in the hole in which the coffin lay.

"You didn't give me a chance to say good-bye," she said to her son. "I'll come back soon, by myself."

 Two

"Listen, Ruthie: I put the white fish on the pink platter from my good set because if I put it on your platter it would look like *dreck*, not that I have any doubt it would go uneaten if I served it on waxed paper, knowing your family. The cake is on the back porch, sitting on the bridge table, and I beg you, please, don't ask if I used a tablecloth. (P.S. I did.) I got *ruggelah,* sponge, and that seven-layer you don't care for though I, personally, will never know why. I also picked up four pounds of dietetic cookies for those of us who have to worry. They weren't your freshest so that bitch, Martha, gave them to me for a dollar less. I'd like to take her head and ram it into a wall, perferably brick. Such a nasty, miserable excuse for a— You've been crying. Nicky, get your mother a Valium. They're in that little plastic bottle . . ."

"April," Ruth said, removing her gloves, putting them in her good bag so they wouldn't get lost. "April, I just want to go upstairs for a minute."

"I'll come with you."

"No. Please. I want to be alone for a few minutes. Before they come."

"You okay, darling?" April asked, looking down at her friend, putting her arms around her. They had been more than best friends for nearly thirty years, from the day they had spotted each other laughing at a speech the president of some forgotten Jewish organization had been giving. They felt they complemented each other: Ruth had good looks and sincerity; April had a healthy irreverence and a filthy mouth. "You okay, *mamala?*" April repeated, kissing her friend's forehead.

"Sad," Ruth said, enjoying the comfort of April's unyielding body.

"You're entitled. Believe me, Ruthie, you're entitled. There's the bell. The descending hordes. Don't worry, Selma will answer it. She was the first one here. I'm going to get the lox out of the refrigerator. I put it on a platter from your everyday set. With lox, I figured it doesn't matter so much. I bought Nova Scotia even though that little bastard behind the counter . . ."

"I'll be down in a minute, April," Ruth said, walking up the gray carpeted stairs. "Thank God for April," she thought. "What would I do without April?" She stepped into the comfort of the pink bedroom. "Pepto Bismol Pink," Harry had said when he had seen it.

"You don't like it?" she had asked, worried.

"Did I say I didn't like it? I only said it was Pepto Bismol Pink."

"You still haven't said you liked it."

"I like it. I love it. It's the most beautiful color I ever saw in my life. Next time I have an upset stomach, I'll come in here and lie down."

She sat in the chair upholstered in blue and yellow chintz and studied the French Provincial bedroom suite with the Queen Anne legs they had bought when they were first married. She remembered how nervous she had been going into the luxurious store on Grand Street and how Harry had spent more money than they could afford, proving how not nervous he was.

"Daniel Jones!" her sister-in-law Frieda had said when she had heard. "Daniel Jones, yet. You mind if I ask a little question just to satisfy my curiosity? How much?"

Then Ruth had thought it beautiful, worth every penny of the eleven hundred dollars it had cost. ("Eleven hundred dollars," Frieda had said, growing pale. "Somebody get me a chair.") All that honey-colored wood. Those brass drawer pulls in the shape of roses and cherubs. Now she recognized the lunacy of its design but still, "I love it. I love this room."

What she didn't love was the hospital bed with eight different positions and a swing-out tray that stood off in the far corner like a malevolent boarder, unwanted but necessary. Harry had slept in it (and eaten in it and cried in it) for the past three years.

She turned away and looked at the two closets which framed
the bed that had come with the furniture. One held her
clothes. The other held Harry's. Even though he hadn't worn
any of them for the three years of his illness, she had kept them
"just in case." Now she would have to do something about
them. "But what? What am I going to do with all of his
clothes? That's what I want to know. What am I going to do
with them? Did you ever see a man who loved clothes the way
Harry loved clothes? And shoes! Did any man in the world
have as many shoes?"

She tried to get up from the chair to go to his closet but
found she couldn't. "I don't have the strength." She didn't
attempt to summon it. Instead, she sat where she was and
looked at the framed photograph which stood on the top of the
double chest of drawers. It was of the two of them, taken on
their twenty-fifth anniversary at the Hotel Alamac in Lake-
wood, New Jersey, all one hundred and fifty of its rooms hired
for the occasion. "We did it right," she thought, not for the
first time. "We put every single one of them up and gave them
three meals to the bargain. Not to mention a party with a live
orchestra they're still talking about.

"What I look like in that photograph. Nineteen fifty-five
wasn't one of my red-letter years. I wonder what happened to
that gold dress. The same exact color of my hair, then. But
Harry looked well. So big and alive in that Witty Brothers
tuxedo. He was a high liver, my Harry. A big-time sport."

There was a knock on the door. She knew who it was.
"Come in, *totela*."

"You okay?" Nick asked, opening the door.

"As okay as I could be under the circumstances."

He went to her, handing her his handkerchief. She hadn't
realized she had been crying again. She dabbed the handkerchief at her eyes. Everybody else in the world carried Kleenex.

Her husband and her son had to use handkerchiefs. Initialed handkerchiefs. Selma always complained bitterly when she had to iron them. "They ain't sanitary, Mrs. Meyer. Now, tissues, they're sanitary."

"Everyone here?" she asked, folding the handkerchief, putting it in her pocket, making a mental note to have Selma wash and iron it before he went back to California.

"Just about."

"I'd better go downstairs."

"Sit for a few minutes."

She stood up anyway and surveyed herself in the mirror over the chest of drawers. "I'm surprised," she told herself. "I look, if not my very best, at least not my very worst." Her short hair, "windblown" and heavily sprayed, was silver gray now, as neat as if she had been to Gina's Golden Jewel Salon of Beauty only that morning. Gina had been at the services. She had worn her dark blue taffeta, which Ruth knew she saved for very important occasions.

Ruth applied a light coat of dark lipstick but she was not one, she knew, to need makeup. "Even the black dress doesn't look so terrible," she said, out loud.

"It looks fine, Ma."

It was only around the eyes where the sorrow and fright showed. Her lids were red and puffy. She ordered herself to stop crying.

Nick came up behind her. In the mirror she saw herself looking up at him. "Your father always hated when I cried."

"Today," Nick said, "he'd forgive you." They stared at each other in the mirror for a moment. "It's best that he died, Ma."

"I know," she said, looking away, the tears starting again.

"He suffered for three years, Ma. The man we knew died three years ago, Ma."

"I know, Nicky. I know. But knowing doesn't help."

The door opened, Audrey coming into the room as if she
were on official business. She looked at her brother, a decade
younger than she, with distaste. "Do you think you could put
your tie back on?"

"Do you think you could shove it?"

"Everyone is here, Mother," Audrey said, ignoring Nick.
"Everyone's wondering where you are."

"We'll be right down," Ruth said.

"Well, everyone is asking."

"Fuck 'em, then," Nick said.

"I'm not staying in a room where that word is used."

"No one's sitting on you, Audrey."

She turned and left, shutting the door firmly behind her.
"Not today, Nick," Ruth said. "Not today."

"Did you hear her on the way to the cemetery? Talking
about her country club and her sisterhood and her mother-
hood? Did you—"

"Not today, Nick. Please."

"Has she ever said anything real in her life? Has she ever
confessed to one genuine emotion, one—"

"Nicky . . ."

"Okay, Ma. Okay."

He held her arm as they went down the stairs into the large,
pale yellow living room. "Not one soul here from my own
family," she thought, looking around her. "They're all dead,
may they rest in peace. Truth is, the only one I miss—besides
Papa—is my sister Helen. Poor thing. She didn't have much
of a life."

She allowed herself to be kissed by half a dozen members of
her husband's family. There were only two surviving from
Harry's generation: Frieda and Meyer. But the next generation, the first Americans, were all there—eating, drinking,
laughing, crying, fighting. "Not exactly Yankees yet," she
thought to herself. "Good, kind, and not very sophisticated

people. Harry's family. *My* family for the past forty-odd years."

"Aunt Ruthie," someone screamed, and before she knew it Ruth was being embraced by Harry's eldest niece, Summer. She towered over Ruth on too-high heels, holding her favorite aunt to her too-ample breasts, her tears raining down on Ruth's recently sprayed hairdo. "I'm so sorry, Aunt Ruthie. So sorry. He was a wonderful man, my Uncle Harry. A wonderful man. I'll never forget when I was a kid and my father wasn't feeling so hot how he took me up to South Fallsberg . . ."

It was an afternoon of reminiscence. Summer continued with her memories and the others—the nieces and their husbands, their children and their spouses—joined in. The memories, the anecdotes, went on through the early evening as April served food, as Selma poured soft drinks and iced tea because the weather continued to be warm.

It was the Meyer family's way of mourning: by remembering.

Audrey couldn't join in. She and her husband sat on the brown velvet sofa, their two daughters and their two husbands surrounding them as if for protection. "My granddaughters," Ruth thought and shook her head.

Nick stood on the other side of the room, listening, holding his wife's hand. Linda, his wife—so beautiful, so smart, so gentile—kissed him and went to help with the food and the traffic.

And Ruth listened to stories she had heard before as if they were fresh and wonderfully interesting. The stories softened her own memory of Harry, made him suddenly a great joker, a witty and avuncular man.

". . . and Uncle Harry took the seltzer bottle and, aiming it very carefully, spritzed it all over the waiter," Esther from Utica was saying. "How we laughed. And that poor *schlemiel* of a waiter. Drenched."

*

It was on the second afternoon when Frieda, the reigning matriarch of the Meyer family, cornered her. ("She's just like Mama," Harry used to say. "When she wants something— always for the family, never for herself—she gets it, that Frieda.") "Do you think that maybe you and I could have a tiny conference, darling?" Frieda asked.

"Right now?"

"As your husband's only living sister, as the eldest member of the Meyer family, I don't have a right to ask? Okay. I don't. I'll go stand in the corner and close my mouth. A little thing to ask but if it's too much, tell me right away and I swear I'll never open my mouth again."

Checking a desire to put her hands around Frieda's throat ("providing I could find it under her chins"), Ruth followed her through the dining room, greeting friends, relations, Selma's husband and son, through the kitchen, and into the dinette. Frieda's husband, Saul, was there, eating a lox and cream cheese sandwich, drinking a Dr. Brown's diet black cherry soda from the bottle.

"Get a glass, Saul," Frieda told him.

"I don't need to dirty a glass."

"Go into the kitchen and get yourself a glass, Saul."

"I won't drink it." He pushed the bottle away from him.

"I want to talk to Ruthie alone."

"You're alone."

"Saul . . ."

"I won't listen. My ears are stopped up. Frieda, please! For once in your life, let me enjoy my food in peace. Don't nudge me. How often do I get Nova Scotia?"

"Frieda," Ruth said, "people are leaving. I have to say good-bye."

"All right. All right. I'll say exactly what I have to say and not one word more. Saul can witness. You listening, Saul?"

"No. I'm eating."

"What is it, Frieda?" Ruth asked. "Out with it, already."

"Just remember, you asked for it, Ruthie. I very purposely didn't say anything yesterday. It was the first day, you were feeling maybe a touch sensitive, and I didn't want to start something. You know me, I never like to start something. Usually I let people do what they want and I sit quietly out of the picture, counting my blessings. Be well and be happy is my motto.

"And I know I shouldn't be asking this question. It's none of my business and far be it for me to stick my two cents in where they have never been appreciated. Still, since my baby brother is no longer alive to say anything, I thought just this once I would open my mouth and ask one question: where, I should like to know, are the orange crates?" Frieda put her plump hands on her plump hips and looked at her sister-in-law.

"Orange crates! Are you crazy?" Ruth asked, surprising herself. In her relations with Frieda, she had always taken her husband's cue, treating her as the head of the Meyer family, a mother manqué, not to be crossed.

"I know you come from a family that didn't observe," Frieda said, magnanimously, "so there's some excuse. But by this time, Ruthie, you must have realized that the Meyers are different. In our family, when a man dies you're supposed to remove the furniture and put in the orange crates."

"With or without the oranges?" Ruth heard herself say.

"What's more," Frieda went on, "it says in the Bible that you must cover the mirrors, that you shouldn't take a bath for at least ten days after a man dies. Doesn't it, Saul?"

Saul, who didn't work because he was a non-card-carrying Communist and didn't believe in the capitalist system, had two answers and gave them both: "Religion is the opium of the people," he said, studying his sandwich. "And don't ask me, Frieda, and don't put me in the middle of anything. I just want to eat my bagel and lox."

"You thought," Ruth said, "that I wasn't going to take a bath for ten days? That I was going to have orange crates and covered mirrors?"

"It was a terrible shock, believe me, when I walked into this house and saw people sitting on chairs. I almost had to sit down myself. I'm sure you haven't noticed but I've been standing for the past two days. And my legs aren't what they used to be."

"They never were," said Saul.

"Frieda," Ruth said, standing up very straight, putting her hand in her pocket, happy to find Nicky's handkerchief there. "I wouldn't have wooden crates in my house if I thought God was personally going to come and pay me a condolence call. And Frieda, for the past forty years I have kept my mouth shut when it came to the subject of you and your famous Jewish laws. I did it because of Harry. Now that Harry is no longer here, Frieda, I'm going to tell you something and I'm going to tell it to you in plain English: you're a royal pain in the *tuchas*, Frieda."

Frieda sat down next to her husband on one of the chrome-and-vinyl dinette chairs, looking as if she had been shot. "I'm the oldest in the family. No one talks to the oldest in the family like that."

"I do. I did. And I will. As long as you keep trying to run my life. Now I am going back to my guests. Feel free to go on sitting in my dinette chair or in any other vacant seat in the house. If you want an orange crate, I'll send Nicky over to Foodtown and get him to set one up for you in the finished basement."

Head held high, Ruth sailed into the living room where Leona LeVine (orginally Levine) was making her entrance. "It

was a blessing," that woman shouted, elbowing her way across
the living room, taking Ruth by the shoulders. "A blessing.
What that man suffered! I only heard this morning, on the
golf course at the club. Why didn't you call me? Heaven and
earth couldn't have kept me away from that funeral."

Ruth allowed Leona to press her new nose against her cheek.
Her mind was operating on several levels. At the top, she was
wondering what perfume Leona had bathed in and how much
an ounce it had cost. In the middle was the hollow space where
she mourned her dead husband. But at the very bottom and
slowly working its way up, she was experiencing an odd but
exhilarating feeling. She didn't recognize it and she couldn't
name it but it seemed to her as if some seed of happiness that
had been planted a long time ago had suddenly begun to grow.

As she responded to Leona's cross-examination ("What were
you doing when they called to tell you?"), she tried to ignore
that new, odd feeling. "It's not negative," she thought. "It's
definitely positive. I should be ashamed of myself. But
somehow I'm not." She wished there was time to examine just
what she was feeling.

There wasn't. She said the right things to Leona and to
Clara Weltcheck and to Rose Novick and the two Minnies and
Miriam Rakin (such a lovely, nice woman). She helped Molly
and Lou Holtz find their respective ways to the bathroom,
made sure that Meyer got coffee and that Linda, her too-thin
daughter-in-law, ate something. She allowed her two granddaughters to attempt to comfort her.

But all through the long afternoon and even later, when she
had gotten into the lonesome bed and cried, that odd / good
feeling was still there. She tried to find a word for it and did,
pushing it out of her mind almost before it had slipped in.

"For the first time in my life," she thought, "I do not have
an authority to report to. There is no one I have to answer to

for my actions or beliefs or rude remarks to Frieda. For the first time in sixty-six years, I have what I have heard so often guaranteed to everyone else: freedom.

"It's too much to think about now. I'll get all involved. I won't be able to sleep. I'll put it away for the time being, I'll take it out and look at it some other time."

She tried to think of her husband, of his long illness, of his quick death, of his eventful and fulfilled life.

Still, some television station deep down in her psyche continued to send out the subliminal message: freedom.

 Three

It was the afternoon of the last day of mourning. It had remained October warm throughout the long/short week. There had been people in the house each day, from early morning to early evening. People Ruth was used to seeing in other clothes, in other capacities. Like Mr. Diamond who ran the newspaper delivery service and came in through the front door, ill at ease with his wife and his Dacron sports jacket.

And there were people she hadn't seen or thought of in years. Like Martin Gornisht (poor thing, such a terrible name) who used to play pinochle with Harry when they had first moved to Elizabeth. They came with cake and candy, with sorrow, memories, curiosity.

"They keep me busy," she said to April. "They don't give me time to think."

"Never one of your strong suits, Draisal," April said, wiping up the gravy a guest had spilled on the dining-room table.

"You know something, April? You got a sandpaper mouth on you."

"That's not what the boys tell me," April said, hugging her.

Nick had surprised them all, going to the synagogue on Murray Street each night, being patient (it was reported) with old Rabbi Kauffman, who had shown him how to read the prayer for the dead, who had turned up early one morning and hugged and cried with Ruth. She was sorry Rabbi Kauffman hadn't been able to officiate at the funeral. But he was Orthodox. They were Conservative.

Nick hadn't been in a synagogue since his *bar mitzvah.* "I'm only going because Dad would have wanted me to," he said, feeling an explanation was needed. "And besides," he went on, looking at his sister officiously patting one of the pillows on the brown velvet sofa she coveted, "it gets me out of the house."

"Those two," April said, her powder-blue eyelids half closed so that she could see them better. "More like cat and dog than brother and sister."

"Thank you for your astute analysis, Mrs. Freud," Ruth said, handing her friend a stack of dirty coffee cups. "Next time I want my children's characters charted, I'll make an appointment."

"You want to know something, Draisal? You couldn't afford it."

"You always have to have the last word?"

"Yes."

"But she's right," Ruth admitted to herself. "They hate each other. They were born too far apart. That's the problem. It's a pity the middle one, the one that lived only a day, didn't survive."

But she didn't want to think about that. She left the wing chair Harry, when he had been well, liked to sit in and went

into the dining room. "The wallpaper has to be replaced," she
thought. "The stripes are disappearing." She picked up the
silver (plate) platter, half filled with slices of turkey, but it was
pulled away from her.

"No you don't," Frieda said. "You go back in there and sit
yourself down, Ruthie. I'm in charge of putting everything
away. I shouldn't want you to wake up tomorrow morning and
curse me."

"No one's going to curse you, Frieda. We all thank you for
being such a help."

"Don't thank me so much. What's a sister-in-law for,
anyway?"

Frieda had recovered from her compunctions concerning
covered mirrors and wooden orange crates. She had become,
almost overnight, a kind of playful, obedient puppy, calling
Ruth "Ruthie," bringing her cups of tea, plates of cookies.

"I wonder what she's up to?" April had asked.

"For once in your life, April Pollack, try and be a little
charitable. Maybe she's changed."

"And maybe man is good and we'll have peace in our time."

"You know something, April? You're a very cynical
person."

"And you know something, Draisal? So are you."

Ruth went back to the wing chair in the living room,
allowing the new Frieda the opportunity of carrying the turkey
platter into the kitchen. She could hear Saul, sitting at his
headquarters—the Formica dinette table—complaining. "You
put butter on my tuna sandwich? You trying to kill me?" A
Reader's Digest article had made him conscious of the dangers of
cholesterol.

"There was no mayonnaise," Frieda said, wrapping the
turkey in tinfoil, inserting the tinfoil into a plastic Baggie,
wrapping a tie around the neck of the Baggie, and carefully

placing the package in the refrigerator. "I've never been in a house where there was no mayonnaise."

"Mayonnaise?" Saul said. "Just as bad as butter. If not worse."

"So sue me," Frieda said, preparing to wrap several slices of tongue. "When the case comes to trial, I'll throw myself on the mercy of the court. 'I didn't mean to do it, your honor. I didn't know the mayonnaise was loaded.' "

"You won't be making fun when I'm in the hospital," Saul said, aggrieved. "Believe me, you won't be making fun."

They were scheduled to leave at sundown. "One more hour," Ruth thought, closing her eyes. "Meyer's already gone, back to his Miami Beach, to his condominium, to his Cadillac Coupe de Ville." She refused to think of their last conversation, of the "serious requests, you might even say proposals" Meyer had implied he would be making in "the not too distant future. You know," he had said, taking her hand, "it says in the Bible that when a man dies and leaves a widow, his brother (if not attached) should step in and marry the woman?"

"You and your sister Frieda read a very peculiar Bible," Ruth had said. "I doubt very much if it says that in the Jewish Bible. And if it does, I bet you a dollar it doesn't say anything about unattached."

"Why not?"

"They were allowed to have more than one wife in biblical times. So a man wouldn't have to be unattached to marry his brother's widow."

"Good thing we're not living then, no, Ruthie?"

"Yes. Since we wouldn't be living now. Have a wonderful trip, Meyer. My regards to one and all." She had kissed his cheek, he had kissed hers, and then he was off, getting into the front seat of the taxi with difficulty, turning to give Ruth one last wave, one more "when-the-time-is-right" smile. The family had a backlog of jokes about Meyer's crush on Ruth. She knew he did care for her and always had.

For a solitary second, she wished he wasn't going. Then she was happy he was gone. She wished they all would go. "I want to be like Garbo," she thought. "Alone. To think." But who could think with those mutual antagonists, April Pollack and Leona LeVine, sniping at each other from either side of her living room. True, the war had been brewing all week. But why did hostilities have to break on this, the last afternoon?

"What I could never understand about Nicky," Leona was saying innocently, "was how he had the gall to be ashamed of his father's accent. So Harry had an accent. So what? He gave that kid everything. Everything! I can remember sitting in this room in front of a dozen strangers and that kid correcting his father's English. Imagine, that *pischer* ashamed of his father's accent."

Leona LeVine was right. Harry *had* had an accent and Nicky *had* been ashamed of it. Harry was born in Poland in nineteen hundred and seven and he spoke every language he knew (English, Yiddish, Polish, a little German) with an accent. He had come to New York when he was fourteen, but his English was never the King's. So Nicky was ashamed of it. Kids go through funny stages. He had outgrown it. "Who could have been a better son during these past years?" she asked herself.

She was about to ask the question aloud, to defend her son against Leona LeVine's cutlass *yenta* tongue, but April, dear April, was first with a counterattack.

"What I never could understand about you, Leona," April said, pausing to pat her thin red-brown hair into place, "is why you were so ashamed of the nose your parents gave you, you had to have it cut off (at age fifty, yet) and replaced with Sandra Dee's. We all knew your husband—that runt—was running around with a *shicksa,* but getting a new nose wasn't going to win him back."

Leona sucked so much air into her lungs in a gesture of
ultimate outrage, Ruth was afraid that when she expelled it,
her girdle would go. They all waited for her reply. "You got
some hell of a nerve, April Pollack," Leona said at last, letting
the air out to no evident detriment to the girdle. ("Even if she
is a doctor's wife," Ruth had said to April, "she's not so choosy
when it comes to girdles. Spends a lot of money on clothes and
cosmetics, yes. But concerning foundation garments, she's a
very careful shopper.") Leona stood up. "You and that loser
husband of yours . . ."

That was it. Nuclear war had been declared. April could say
what she wanted about her late husband (and often did), but
Leona couldn't. And calling him a loser was too close to the
mark to be taken lightly. Ruth sprang out of her chair,
intending to stand between them, but April Pollack was
already in center ring, tears in her eyes, her face within
snapping distance of Leona's. "You fat-assed, *curva* bitch. I'll
give you my loser husband. I'm going to take that nose and
make it look like the one you were born with, you . . ."

Nick, thank God, came in from the synagogue at that
moment. He looked at the two women, put his arm around
April, and led her away, at the same time calling, "Sundown,"
like a referee at the end of a match.

"About time, too," Leona said, straightening her silk dress,
giving a tug to her inexpensive girdle. She strode the length of
the room to where Ruth was standing. "Now, don't be a
stranger," she said in her machine-gun voice. "You come over,
dear. I'll take you to the club. We'll have lunch. I'll introduce
you to a very nice class of people. We'll go shopping in
Milburn. Don't bury yourself alive," she said, looking over her
shoulder at April, "like others we could both name just
because your loser of a husband is dead."

"You bleached-blond bitch," April said, trying to break out
of Nick's bear hug. "You low-life *yenta.* Why, for two

cents . . ." Nick reached around, took her clenched fists in his hands, and led her through the living and dining rooms into the kitchen. He sat her down with Frieda and Saul, who liked to give April a pinch every now and then when Frieda was otherwise occupied.

Nick went back into the living room to help speed Leona on her way. "You tired, *mamala?*" he asked his mother, after putting Leona into her Malibu.

"A little."

"Where is everyone?"

"The kitchen. The bathroom. Upstairs. I don't know." She *was* tired. Tired and muddled.

"You want a cup of tea?"

"A cup of tea would hit the spot, Nicky."

"Sweet 'n' Low or you want to go all the way?"

"Tonight, all the way. Two lumps."

He went into the kitchen where Frieda was creating a care package for herself. "Ruthie will never eat all this up in a zillion years. There's a whole roast beef in that refrigerator."

April, recovering from her encounter with Leona, was putting Saul on. "When's the last time you got it up, comrade?"

Ruth rested her head against the solid upholstery of the wing chair, wondering where that freedom feeling was now. She decided, after a moment's thought, that it still had to grow. "Besides, that's not what I need right this minute. Right this minute I need the comfort of familiar things." She touched the arm of the chair where Harry had liked to rest his hand, a long cigar held between his index and forefingers, the ash dripping, as intended, into the ashtray below.

And once again she began to think of her life with Harry.

 Four

After the stroke, everyone counseled her to put him in a rest home. "You'll never be able to care for him," they said. Even Nicky thought she should "put him someplace comfortable."

Slowly, because she didn't want to, she began to visit rest homes. Most of them fell into one of two categories: converted Victorian houses with thin, paneled wood dividing the old rooms, making what was once grand and ugly, tawdry and ugly; and computerized motels with Plexiglas solariums and programmed nurses in pale blue uniforms. Of the two, she preferred the first, but only slightly.

Once, left alone for a moment by the bearded director of a modern rest home, she wandered into a large, white, tiled auditorium. Sitting in a wheelchair behind the last row of seats was a very old woman with wispy white hair. She was screaming, in a soft voice, "Get me out of here. Get me out of here."

Ruth had run from the place, refusing to listen to the director's explanations, getting into the Chevrolet Harry had bought her when he was well, speeding back home to him.

He was aware of who he was, where he was, only on occasion. Sometimes two or three hours in a week. Sometimes for entire days. When he wasn't aware—when he was "out," as April put it—he would call her Ma. "Ma," he would shout, like a child. "Take me home, Ma. Take me home."

Which home did he want to be taken back to? The farmhouse in Poland where he had been born? The tenement

on the Lower East Side of Manhattan where his family had all
lived, the eight of them in two rooms, when they had first
come over? Or the top floor of the two-family house in
Flatbush where he had moved with his mother, later? She
would ask him. She wanted to help him. She would have taken
him anywhere if only she knew where he wanted to go. But all
he could say during those tormented moments was, "Ma, take
me home. I want to go home, Ma."

And when he wasn't "out," when he did know who he was
and where he was and what condition he was in, he would say
more terrible things. "I want to die," he told Nick once. "A
man shouldn't live like this. Help me die, Nick."

Before the stroke he had weighed two hundred pounds.
After, he went down to one hundred and twenty. His body
had become thin and small and his skin had turned a terrible
ivory white. He looked as if he had been shrunk.

She hired nurses. Because of course she hadn't been able to
put him in a rest home. What if he had woken up and known?
What if he had shouted, "Ruth, take me home," and she,
Ruth, hadn't been there for him?

"We, the nurses and I, worked hard," she thought. "We
had to feed him, a man who had no appetite. We had to take
him to the bathroom, wait for him, clean him." They had, in
the beginning, tried to get him to walk by himself; or at least
with the walker. He wouldn't. He developed a relentless
dependency upon her. Even when the nurses were there, he
would call out, "Ma. Ma. Ma." "If I were gone for an hour, to
the beauty parlor, he would spend the hour calling out for me.
What could I do?"

The nurses quit regularly. "It was a revolving door full of
nurses. I paid them what they asked. I treated them like minor
royalty. But every one of them, after a few months, left. Was
it too much, watching the grown man turn into a child, a

baby, a fetus? They all had excuses. A sick child. An ailing mother. A full-time job in a doctor's office, a hospital.

"But I stayed on." At times she had felt like a character in a Greek legend, one doomed to spend eternity rolling a stone up an endless hill. There was never any relief. He never got any better.

Moving from the chair to the sofa, listening to April *kibbitz* with Nicky in the kitchen, she wondered, "What penance did I have to work out during those years? What crime was I atoning for? Was it a case of this for that? Because he cared for me for all the years of his health, some divine plan called for our roles to be reversed?

"But he had insisted on taking care of me. The Wife Isn't Supposed to Work. So I stayed home. Though in the beginning, when he couldn't afford a bookkeeper, who did the books? Me. I had to do them at home so no one would see that Harry Meyer's wife worked. And I cooked. I took care of the kids. I learned to be a good shopper. I learned to be concerned with small things."

Early on she had known that wasn't what she wanted. Though what she did want was elusive. "I only knew what I didn't want. I didn't want to be a *balabuster*." For Ruth that word—*balabuster,* Yiddish for "good housekeeper"—was the sentence the judge imposed for a crime she couldn't remember committing.

"You'll grow up, you'll meet some good man with a nice business, please God, and you'll be a fine *balabuster*." *Balabuster* meant cleaning bathrooms and baking sponge cakes and wrestling in the night with your husband. Her Aunt Hannah had always made it sound like a reward. "Some day, Ruth, you'll be just like me, a *balabuster*." Aunt Hannah, with the sweet disposition and the cherry-red cheeks, had spent her life dusting: under beds, in corners, over doorway moldings.

"If it's clean then I'm happy," she'd say while scrubbing the
kitchen floor on her hands and knees. She was, in everyone's
estimation, "some *balabuster*." She made up for the years of
dirt and filth endured by her family first in Russia, later on the
Lower East Side.

Ruth had become, perforce, a *balabuster*. She did what she
had to do. Yet when she received her allowance each week,
from Harry, she felt both over- and underpaid.

"What made me," she wondered, "so unhappy?" Harry had
given her what he, as a Jewish husband, had contracted to give
her: a house; a mink coat; a diamond bracelet, pin, and
engagement ring; her own car. Her friends were envious, the
ultimate *yenta* satisfaction. Still, the knowledge that something was missing, that something was out of focus, off kilter,
that something wasn't "quite right," was always there, a faint
echo of reproach.

"First of all," she thought, "we were so different. Right
from the beginning. I was born in America, Harry didn't get
here until he was fourteen. My father was well-to-do for most
of his life (until that skunk, his partner Rastanovitch, ran off
with so much money). Harry's father refused to work when he
got here. 'I worked long enough. Now it's your turn,' he told
his children."

And then she had been bookish, "a regular bookworm."
Too pretty, however, to let her reading get in the way of her
social life. "I wasn't exactly a vamp like my sister Helen (may
she rest in peace), but my Saturday nights (the only night Papa
let me go out) were filled months in advance." They'd take her
to movies and Chinese restaurants (always upstairs) and dances
in hotels. Once in a great while, if the boy were especially fast,
they'd go to a speakeasy. The other evenings of her week were
spent reading, listening to the windup Victrola with her
father. Amelita Galli-Curci and Caruso sang as if by magic on
records a quarter of an inch thick.

"Harry never read a book in his life," she thought. "Not that I could blame him. When he was young he didn't have the time. Too busy working. Later, he didn't have the inclination. He liked, God bless him, nightclubs."

She thought of all the nights she had spent in the Copacabana and the Latin Quarter. She remembered the emcees with their collarless satin jackets, greasy hair, endless patter. She remembered the conga lines, kicking girls in fishnet stockings, translucent pasties, their high-heeled voices shrieking some popular, suggestive song as the pancake makeup cracked and the heat from the klieg lights caused beads of perspiration to form on their foreheads. "Why had Harry always demanded a table in the front row?" Any illusion the shoddy, gimcrack acts might have gotten away with was instantly destroyed by proximity.

She hated those nights. "Those boy singers! Those cigarette girls and hatcheck girls and bar girls and boy girls!" The transvestites seemed to have the most fun, blatantly imitative. The real girls had to pretend it was genuine.

She remembered the smoke. "It's a wonder we all didn't come down with lung cancer.

"But Harry loved it. He loved everything. The risqué jokes, the insult routines, the production numbers straight from the 'world-famous Folies Bergère,' the distressing stand-up comics." Every time she heard one of their names—Buddy Hackett, B. S. Pulley, Henny Youngman—she would get nauseated. Not Harry. He had laughed. At the comics. At the girls' bare bottoms. At the ventriloquist with the pornographic dummy. He liked "the atmosphere." It was a playground for big boys to romp in. And he wasn't fooling. He so evidently and honestly had a good time.

In the beginning she would sit still, a fixed smile on her face, wondering what on earth everyone was so amused by. Occasionally she'd escape to the ladies' room with one of the

other women—wives or "friends" of Harry's business associates, men who sold or bought or hijacked cigars and cigarettes.

She didn't drink, which might have made it at all bearable.
She had tried but she couldn't stomach the taste of alcohol. It
was as if she were tasting the event: bitter, unclean, dizzying.

When she stopped going, he was disappointed. "Come on,
Ruth. Roberta Sherwood's at the Copa. A nice clean act."

"It turned out he had as good a time without me. Better,
because he knew what I felt. It was no big shock when he got
himself a friend. Actually, it was a big shock. It was no
surprise but it was a shock."

She had known almost immediately. "Harry was a terrible
liar." Presents, unexplainable, began appearing. Suddenly
there was a portable bar in the back of the Cadillac with Mark
Cross's imprint on its bottom. Then there was the slow
emergence of the two official nights a week he'd spend in
Manhattan "playing pinochle." "Yes, I minded. I minded
terribly. But I was also relieved. No more boy singers."

She read. She worked for Hadassah, sitting in front of the
supermarket with a bridge table and blue-and-white can. She
took a course, casually, at Keen College. "Art Appreciation
with April Pollack," was the way she described it to Nicky.
But April dropped out after the second class. "If I want to look
at a fat woman's private parts, I'll go to Forty-second Street,
thank you very much." Discounting her language, April was
very much a prude at heart.

Ruth completed the course. In her late fifties she learned a
new language she immediately understood. She discovered the
solace that paintings, that art, could give.

Ruth began to have her own "days." Not that Harry had
minded, objected, or was even aware that she was having
them. She would dress carefully, leaving the mink and the
charm-laden gold bracelet at home (the diamonds were in

the vault, awaiting the next *bar mitzvah* or wedding), and take
the train into New York. She would spend her day wandering
through a chosen museum. It took time but she began to know
them intimately, like old, quiet friends. The Metropolitan,
the Guggenheim, the Whitney, the Frick, the Modern. With
their calm, even lighting, their large, open rooms, they were
the antithesis of Harry's nightclubs.

She wouldn't share her days with anyone. She understood,
she thought, what the paintings were trying to communicate.
She found she could look at a Velázquez or even a Rubens (she
liked his fat, drowsy women, not a *balabuster* in the lot) and
come away, if not happy, certainly more content.

In the beginning she was catholic in her tastes. She enjoyed
all but the most modern. Mary Cassatt and her dappled
women. Giotto and Bellini and Eakins and Hopper. Then, one
day in the Museum of Modern Art, she fell in love.

She had attached herself to a guided tour, led by a young
man who wore glasses and multipleated trousers. He began his
lecture in the first room on the second floor with Gauguin,
"the father of modern painting. *The Moon and the Earth,* the
painting you see here, like so many great works of art, is filled
with symbolic meaning," he said in his high, pleasing voice.
"The woman, with her solid feet planted firmly on the ground,
is reaching up toward the massive, rich brown man. He is the
moon, the provider, the father, lover, husband. She is
the child-woman, the fertile earth." He went on to say that
the painting was obviously a masterpiece, that it had been
painted on burlap, that it had once been owned by Degas, and
that it revealed the artist's "great awe of nature's simple
formula for life and creation."

She let the group go on to Rousseau's *Dream* while she
stayed with *The Moon and the Earth.* There was something
about the painting—certainly not the guide's textbook

analysis—that thrilled her. It was the sense of place, she decided. "It looks like the Garden of Eden," she thought. She had always fantasized living in a place so lush, so tropical. She had always, in her own unpoetical way, longed for the moon.

She began to read about Gauguin. His "right to dare anything" had cost him a great deal, but still he had chosen to exercise it. She began to have new fantasies of traveling to Tahiti, of daring anything, something.

Meanwhile, Harry was doing the traveling. To Venezuela, the Dominican Republic, El Salvador. The trips were taken ostensibly to investigate cigar manufacturers . . . and night-clubs. Of course, he took his friend.

Once, when emptying his pockets before sending a suit to the cleaners, she found a carbon of two airline tickets. One was made out to a person named Amanda Frazer. It was the name—so classy, so un-Jewish—that made her angry. She knew it wasn't reasonable but there it was. Harry didn't notice her furious silences. She thought, for the first time, of divorce. "I'll take my alimony and run to Tahiti."

But divorce was as foreign to her as the South Seas. She hardly knew any divorced people except for one cousin, Lenny Hertzberg, who had always been considered beyond the Pale. Still, she thought about Tahiti and she thought about divorce.

Then came the first sign that Harry's years of overeating, of underexercising, had damaged what had always seemed an invincible machine: the early stroke. "Nothing to get excited about," Leona's little husband had said. "But maybe you'd better go into New York, Harry. See a specialist. Get good advice." It was while he was in the hospital in New York, seeing the specialist (the Bastard), that he had had the second, and major, stroke.

Ruth's role changed again. From the quietly discarded wife, she became the very necessary nurse.

Only once did she reproach him. Early on, after Nick had helped to bring him home from the hospital. She had finished feeding him and was wiping his face with the cloth napkin he insisted upon. "Where," she asked, "is your Miss Frazer now? Do you want her now?" He had looked up at her, tears filling his eyes. "No, Ruthie," he said. "Only you." She had been bitterly ashamed of herself.

Now, as she sat in the living room of the house they had shared, at the end of the week of mourning, she wondered how much of that devotion she had shown him during those three long years of sickness had been based on love and how much on guilt.

She knew it was she—not Harry—who had not played fairly. He had contracted for a housekeeper to make a home for him and a bunny to make whoopee with. "I made the home. I couldn't make the whoopee. I was the poor sport. *I* broke the agreement."

Nick appeared above her, a glass of steaming tea in his hand. "You crying?" he asked.

"I'm not allowed?" she asked, wiping her eyes.

"Don't get cranky with me, madam," he said, sounding exactly like Harry. "Drink your tea."

"In a glass yet."

"All the cups were dirty."

"They're going to think I'm some awful *balabuster,*" she said, smiling, sipping the tea.

Five

It was Saturday morning. Selma was in the kitchen, surveying "her" floor with anguish, one hand on her hip, the other grasping a mop. "What they done to you, baby, shouldn't have been done to a dog."

Nicky's and Linda's bags, packed and strapped, were sitting in the middle of the living room like neglected children. Linda was in New York, seeing her publisher. Nicky was lying on the brown velvet couch, noshing on an apple, looking sixteen years old.

"If Selma comes in here and catches you with your feet on the arm of that couch, I won't be responsible for her actions," Ruth said.

She was sitting in Harry's wing chair, her fingers drumming on its arm, wishing, despite herself, that everyone would leave, that she could start the business of living again. She touched her hair, wondering when Gina would be able to squeeze her in.

Audrey came halfway down the stairs at that moment, spotted her brother, and said, "There you are. I wonder if you could step upstairs for a minute, into my bedroom?"

"Little late for incest," Nick said, finishing the apple, putting the core in Ruth's good ashtray.

"Would you please come up here, Nicky?"

He sat up, looked at his mother, shrugged, and went up the stairs, saying, "Let me know when Linda arrives, okay? I don't want to miss that plane."

"No one wants you to miss that plane," his sister said.

Ruth sat on in the wing chair, thinking about her beautiful, talented, non-Jewish daughter-in-law, when suddenly, for no reason at all—as she later told April—she "smelled" trouble. She got out of the wing chair and went up the steps, standing on the landing, listening to the voices coming from the room that had once belonged to Audrey.

Audrey was making one of her announcements. "We Have to Talk about Mother," she said, one arm supported by the maple chest of drawers in which she had once kept sweaters and numerous diaries. Ronald, her husband, sat behind her on the old rocking chair, his round, balding head wearing its customary smile of peace at any price.

"So talk," Nick said, assuming his favorite position, horizontal, on the sofa bed, hands behind head.

"I can see this is not going to be pleasant." She looked up, presumably at God, and sighed. "Ronald and I," she said, still with her eyes directed at the blue ceiling, "have decided that the best place for Mother is Autumnal View. It's only twenty minutes from the office . . ."

"What office?"

"Ronald's office. What other office is there? And it has a very nice group of senior citizens . . ."

"What exactly is Autumnal View, Audrey?" Nick asked, sitting up, looking at his sister.

"A perfectly lovely retirement community managed by several business associates of Ronald's. There's a waiting list six miles long but since we know the managing director, Mr. Kidder, personally, we can get Mother in now, *and* at a very good price, I might add."

"And there's a large turnover at Autumnal View," Ronald volunteered.

"Anyway," Audrey went on, pursuing her thoughts,

"there's no real problem about money. Father left Mother everything. Though one would have thought . . ."

"How do you know?" Nick asked.

"What do you mean, how do I know?"

"How do you know Father left Mother everything?"

"How do you think I know, Nicky? I read the will." She held up a sheaf of thick papers.

"Where was the will?"

"In the chest of drawers, where else and what difference does it make? I had some time finding it, I can tell you. I had to turn the drawers upside down . . ."

"Are you out of your ass?" Nick asked, standing up.

"I'm not going to stand here and take abuse from you . . ."

"Where the fuck do you come off going through Father's chest of drawers? Where the hell do you get the nerve to go messing into things that don't belong to you? You're the one who should be installed in Autumnal View. Not Mother. That lady can take care of herself, believe me. She's got all of her faculties and then some. A few more than you and Wonald do."

"I've asked you, Nick, a hundred times not to call me Wonald, and this time . . ."

"This time what? Shut up, Wonald, before I put my foot in your mouth. You two sitting up here going through the family papers—Jesus H. Christ."

"I don't want that man's name mentioned in my presence," Audrey said.

"You know something? You're disgusting. Just because our mother is sixty-six years old doesn't mean she has to retire from the human race, my dear, sweet, benevolent sister. She can still walk, talk, and blow her nose."

Audrey slammed the papers down on the maple chest of drawers. "Why," she asked the superior authority hovering above her, "does he have to get so angry about everything? Why does he have to overreact to every single little thing I say? Here we are, having a perfectly reasonable discussion about—"

"—about how to dispose of our mother now that we've buried Father. Let me tell you something, you middle-class, low-brow suburban bitch: our mother is capable of making her own decisions about how she lives and where she lives and if she ever, God forbid, chose to live twenty minutes from Wonald's office, in any kind of proximity to you and your neurotic, parasitic children with their stunted psyches and their New Jersey morals, then I'd know goddamn well she wasn't—"

"May I say something?"

They all turned. They hadn't seen her standing in the doorway. "Audrey, I want to tell you something and I want to make it crystal clear: I have no intention of becoming another leaf at Autumnal View."

"It'd be a fine investment, Ma," Ronald said from the rocking chair.

"I might not live to see it pay off."

"Mother," Audrey said, flashing a little hate at her husband, "you're in perfect health . . ."

"Exactly. And I intend to remain that way, making all decisions about my own future, myself."

"Fine," Audrey said, retreating, smoothing the sheaf of papers. "What I propose then is that for the next six months Nick and I chip in and give you an allowance. Enough to tide you over till the will is executed . . ."

"What the hell are you talking about?" Nick asked her. "It doesn't take six months to execute a will."

"If I have anything to say about it, it will," Audrey said, smiling her careful smile. "And I have a good deal to say, according to this." She waved the will in the air. "You and I, brother dear, are co-executors."

"Why should we wait six months? The bank accounts will be frozen until the lawyer—"

"There is a Jewish tradition (something I shouldn't expect you to know anything about) that says one is supposed to wait at least half a year before—"

"You're crazy," Nick shouted, jumping up again. "We're going to keep Mother on an allowance because you have some *facoctah* idea about waiting six months . . ."

"There is such a thing," Audrey said, folding the will, tucking it into her purse, "as respect for the dead, Nichlaus."

"Fuck you," he shouted at the top of his voice. "Fuck you. The time to respect the dead was the three years he was lying here dying. Where were you? At a dental convention? You think those quarterly white-gloved visits helped? It's too goddamned late for you to show respect. You missed your chance, you manipulating, castrating, pious-mouthed bitch. You . . ." He walked across the room and raised his hand, the years of hate and rivalry pushing him over the edge of his control.

"Nicky, that's enough," Ruth said, grabbing his hand, getting between him and his sister. "That's enough. May I see the will, Audrey?" She held out her hand and Audrey placed the papers in it. Ruth looked at the first page and then looked up. "I have to tell you, Audrey, that you've been looking at a will your father made fifteen years ago. The most recent one, which is in the vault, states quite clearly that I am the sole executor. And Monday morning I plan to go straight to Bobby Fiebach and have him execute it so there's no need, thank you, for an allowance or a six months' wait. That religious I'm not."

"You know, you don't need a lawyer," Ronald said, getting

out of the rocker, acting as if the preceding twenty minutes had been one more interlude in a calm, unruffled day. "When my folks died, my brother and I went right down to City Hall and executed it ourselves. Saved a ton of money."

"For an estate of one hundred and fifty-three dollars," Audrey said acidly, "you don't need a lawyer."

After Audrey and Ronald left, the three of them—Ruth, Nick, Linda—sat around the dinette table, drinking more tea.

Linda looked at the tired face of her mother-in-law and put her hand on her arm. "Come to California, Mother. The house we've rented has a dozen bedrooms. You'll have your own entrance, your own bath . . ."

Ruth put her hand over Linda's. "Such a *shanah madella*. Such a face. But tell me, what would I do in California? That good a driver I'm not."

"Come to California, Ma," Nick said. "We like you. You like us. It will be warm, healthy, and you'll be three thousand miles away from Audrey, Wonald, and Autumnal View."

"I don't want you to talk about your sister like that."

"I swear I'll never mention her again."

"Anyway, I have another plan."

"And that is?" Linda asked.

"And that is I'm thinking of selling the house."

"What?"

"Eventually. Not right this second. Eventually."

"And then?"

"And then I'm thinking—just thinking—of moving to Miami Beach."

"Miami Beach?" Nick said. "You hate Miami Beach."

"I do not. I hated Miami Beach with your father. The races! Horses, dogs, rabbits. If he won, we had a good time. If he lost, everyone was miserable. And you know your father when he's miserable." She realized her mistake immediately. "When he was miserable."

Nick took her free hand. "And besides," Ruth went on, "they even have an Elizabeth, New Jersey, Club."

"Some incentive," Nick said.

"And Meyer is there. And Frieda and Saul . . ."

"You sure you don't want to come to California?"

"Nothing's definite. I'm merely thinking."

"Look, Ma. Linda and I don't have to be in L.A. for another month or so. I can write the film in Miami as well as I can write it in Hollywood. Better. We'll come down with you and find you a place."

"Not necessary. Nothing's definite but it's all been arranged. *If* I should happen to decide."

"Who arranged it, if I may ask?"

"You may. April and I."

"You're going with April Pollack?"

"I should go alone."

"Vay es meehr."

"Nothing's definite."

The taxi came and they left, Nick giving her a rueful last glance. "You call me if you want me," he said. "For anything."

"And vice versa," she had told him, kissing them both.

"Ma . . ."

"Nick, you're as bad as your sister. I'm sixty-six years old. It's time already I started taking care of myself."

She told April, who called, that she definitely did not want company, that she would go to bed early, which she did. She didn't sleep. Instead, she thought of Harry again, of their life together, of his death, of the week of mourning that had finally passed, of the heart-wrenching anger her two children felt for each other.

She cried a little and turned over on her side. "Here comes another sleepless night," she said to herself, a moment before she fell asleep, just about the time that the word came flashing into her mind, all lit up like a "Welcome to Vegas" sign.

"FREEDOM!" the neon bulbs sang out. "FREEDOM!"

"Just what I need at my time of life," she thought, as the vision dimmed and she fell asleep.

"FREEDOM!"

 Six

The young couple "adored" the house.

("Did you ever see anyone wear a dress like that, an unironed *schmata,* to go looking at houses?" Ruth asked herself.)

It was, they said, their "dream house."

("They must be Italian.")

She thought the price was "very reasonable, honey."

("He's going to kill her when they get home.")

He "dug" the neighborhood.

("Hippies, yet.")

Ruth found herself telling them about the willful downstairs half bath, the basement floods, the peculiar odor in the attic. Nothing Ruth said daunted them. "A crumbling wall, an army of termites marching across the dining room wouldn't stop them." She was already planning where the gold sofa would sit. He was thinking of converting the garage into a workroom. "Or maybe we could just add on to it."

"That's a great idea, honey."

After they finally left, taking their oohs and aahs with them, Jan Weiss (who, with her husband, Scott, ran the Weiss Real Estate and Insurance Agency on Elmora Avenue) agreed to a cup of tea. She drank it sitting at the dinette table, her strong hazel eyes trying to make contact with Ruth's wavering blue-gray ones. She was a young woman, in her forties, who had a frightening amount of patience.

"Look, Mrs. Meyer," she said, "are you genuinely serious about selling this house?"

"Would I waste your time if I weren't?" Ruth poured more tea into Jan Weiss's barely touched cup from the everyday set.

"That little performance in the attic. All that sniffing. Somehow it gave me the idea . . ."

"Jan, I am very serious. I also happen to be very honest. I wouldn't want them to buy the house and then have them tell everybody in Elizabeth that I didn't mention the smell in the attic."

"Very commendable of you, Mrs. Meyer."

"Cookie?" Ruth held out a plate of tinned Danish imports.

"No, thank you. I'm dieting. Now, if you are serious . . ."

"They're only fifty calories apiece."

Defeated, Jan Weiss took a cookie. "Then if you are serious, Mrs. Meyer, I am happy to tell you that the Lipsteins have met your price."

"Lipsteins? That's not an Italian name."

"I believe they're of the Jewish faith."

"Suppose—and this is merely a suppose—I decide I don't want to sell after all?" She could feel her heart beating uncomfortably.

"Legally, you offered the house, the Lipsteins met your offer, a contract has been entered into. Legally, you are obliged to sell. However, the Lipsteins have not put down a binder."

"Thank God."

"Also, they are not, in my opinion, the type of people who would sue." Jan stood up. "If you don't mind, I'll just call them and tell them you've changed your mind."

"They'll be disappointed?"

"Very. But I'm sure they'll understand. After all, there are other houses."

"I haven't said I've changed my mind. I only said 'suppose' "

Jan Weiss put on her gloves carefully, making certain each finger was in its allotted space. "Mrs. Meyer," she said, "why don't you think about it over the weekend and then, on Monday morning, give me a call at the office? I'll put the Lipsteins off. Though I'm very much afraid they believe they virtually own their dream house."

Ruth was also very much afraid. Each time she looked out of a window on that gloomy Friday afternoon ("Who could buy a house on a day like this?") and the following, gloomy Saturday morning, she saw the Lipsteins' homely gray car circling around the block, their plain oval faces peering out anxiously, the wife's mouth opening and closing continually, like a fast fading goldfish.

Ruth inventoried the house, walking from room to room, looking, examining, remembering. The floors needed new carpeting badly.

"How can I leave and where am I going to?" she asked herself several times. "Maybe I should call Nicky? No, I have to do this on my own. What's he going to tell me that I don't already know?" She let out a ladylike belch. "I shouldn't have eaten that stuffed cabbage at the Deborah luncheon. I knew I would suffer. Imagine, a person can't eat stuffed cabbage. I'm old. Too old to eat cabbage, too old to change. Who do I think I am, selling houses, gallivanting off to Florida?" She had to take half a Valium ("junkie," she told herself as she swallowed the sliver of yellow pill) to go to sleep and still she hadn't come to a decision.

April's phone call woke her at seven on Sunday morning. "So how's the house-selling?"

"Not bad. Not good. So-so."

"You sound very positive and cheery this morning. I told you not to eat that cabbage, Draisal."

"It wasn't the cabbage."

"No, it was the waiter with the salami stuffed in his crotch. He got you so excited, you immediately came down with indigestion."

"I'm hanging up."

"Such a charming woman, Ruth Meyer. That's what they say. If they only knew what I know. Listen, *yenta:* would you like to grace my table with your sylphlike presence this afternoon? I'm doing my masterpiece, Steak Diane Varsi. Or you going to the wedding?"

"It's not a wedding. It's a re-wedding. If you don't know the difference . . ."

"Oh, God. Help her, God. Please, God, you shouldn't let her be so miserable. Give her a little happiness, a little light, a little love. Make that sour nature sweet. Take away the indigestion you gave her when she indulged herself like a pig, taking two helpings of stuffed cabbage when at her age and with her disposition, she should only eat a little white bread and skim milk . . ."

"April, enough already."

"So you're going to the re-wedding, dear Ruth?"

"I don't know. Harry's only been gone a month. . . ."

"Listen: you go, you hear me?"

"I could hear you, April, if I were in the South Bronx."

"If you were in the South Bronx, Draisal, you wouldn't be alive to hear me. You'd be tied to a kitchen table, being *schtupped* by a twelve-year-old *schwartza* with a fourteen-inch *schwong* . . ."

"I don't want to hear that kind of prejudiced talk on my telephone."

"I beg your pardon. For a second I forgot I was talking to Eleanor Roosevelt. What's the matter with you today?"

"I shouldn't have eaten that cabbage."

"I told you . . ."

"So I forgot. So lock me up and throw away the key."

"You're a very difficult person, Ruth Meyer."

"And you're easy, April Pollack?"

"You want to hear what came in the mail yesterday or not?"

"Not."

"The confirmation came in the mail yesterday. We are both assured, now, of—and I'm quoting—'two ultra deluxe apartmentettes in Miami Beach, Florida's, luxury-class Monte Excelsior Hotel and Country Club on the ocean at First in the center of all that's alive and exciting in the playground capital of the world. Your hosts, Morris and Belle Fleischman.'

"In less than a month, my dear Draisal, we shall be sunning ourselves on the beach, ordering the boy to remove the pits from our prunes, asking the masseuse to massage with a lighter touch. Excited? Happy? Orgasmic?"

"What should happen if I decided, just because of happenstance, not to go?"

"You'd lose your one-hundred-dollar deposit and your best friend. So why don't you want to go?"

"Who could sell a house in a month, I'd like to know?"

"Don't give me any of your famous Ruth Meyer White Lies, I beg you. It so happens Jan Weiss was coming out of the bakery on Westfield Avenue yesterday afternoon as I was going in. She told me about the house."

"Oh."

"Listen," April said, "you let me know by Monday what you're doing. For once in your life you could think of me for a second."

"What does it have to do with you?"

"Jesus, the insensitivity of the woman. Do you think I want to go by myself? I'm counting on you, Ruthie."

So were the Lipsteins. She spent the better part of her morning at her bedroom window, watching the gray car circle the block. Jan Weiss called at noon to say, "The Lipsteins want all of the furniture, too. They love the house exactly as it stands."

"How can I," she asked herself, drinking her fifth cup of Lipton's, "sell the house, move to a new place, a new climate, a new environment at my age? How can I give up what I've known for the past forty years? And, to the bargain, go *schlepping* off with foul-mouthed April Pollack to some hotel I never heard of?

"At my age?"

She went down to the living room and sat down on the brown sofa Audrey coveted (and which she would get, *if*). She felt guilty about April. She felt alone, afraid, and sorry for herself. She crossed her legs, folded her arms. "I want Harry back," she thought. "I want him to tell me what to do."

She tried to call Nick but the answering service told her he was away for the weekend. "Nothing serious," was the message she left. "Nothing serious," she said aloud when she had replaced the receiver. "Your mother is having a very late midlife crisis and you're hitting tennis balls around Palm Springs."

She began to walk around the house once more, summoning memories. Harry had bought it without her even seeing it. She had felt trapped when they had first moved in. Overwhelmed. "Who knew from houses? Even when I was a kid, we rented.

Overnight, I had nine rooms to furnish and a boiler to worry about."

"Get a decorator," Harry had told her.

"For the boiler?"

The fat, fastidious man from Sloan's had done it all. Though she had insisted on keeping the bedroom set. "But how I suffered for that bedroom set. Every time that *fagala* strolled into this house, putting his hurricane lamps on the mantel, matching the gray of the wallpaper in the dining room to the gray of the carpet in the foyer, he would make some little mention of the 'furniture upstairs.' I wanted to kick him in his double-breasted behind."

She went upstairs, lay down on the bed (the hospital bed had long been gone, donated to the Elizabeth General Hospital), turning on the television. She watched Bette Davis catch diphtheria and grow old while the thought came to her that she was still trapped by the house. It was Harry's house. Harry's and the fat man from Sloan's. Harry had bought it. The fat man had wallpapered it.

"I'm the custodian. I supervise the least likely cleaning woman in the world (only Selma can break unbreakable objects like stoves and dining-room tables). I tell the boy from the supermarket where to put the groceries. I'm like an ex-prisoner who has spent his adult life in jail. I don't know what to do or where to go now that I'm free."

She sighed. She burped. She damned the stuffed cabbage.

The phone, her lifeline to the world, rang. She picked it up, lowering the volume on the television, expecting Nicky, getting Audrey.

"We'll pick you up at twelve-thirty sharp," Audrey said.

"I'm not so sure I'm going."

"Why not?"

"It's been such a short time since Daddy . . ."

"Please. It's too late to start being a traditional Jew. That's not the reason."

"Then what is?"

"I don't know and I'm not sure I care but don't use Daddy. Anyway, it's all been arranged. We'll pick you up at twelve-thirty."

"What does one wear to a re-wedding?" she asked herself, getting off the bed and heading for her closet. She left the television on for company.

Seven

Her son-in-law was driving. Ever since Nicky had started in with the Wonald business, it was all she could do to keep from calling him that. "I am not fond of Wonald," she found herself admitting. He was a cowardly driver, a brake-and-pedal man, afraid of bridges and any road that demanded a toll.

"Would you please get on the Parkway?"

"I'm driving, Audrey."

"Is that what you call it?"

Not a very spirited exchange. Ruth added fuel to the fire. "What time were we supposed to be there?" she asked, knowing very well.

"Forty-five minutes ago."

There was a short silence broken by Audrey tapping her red nails on the padded dashboard. "How's Nick?" Ronald asked, hoping to distract both of his passengers with an issue larger than his driving.

"Working hard," Ruth answered from the backseat.

Audrey snorted.

"If he's working so hard," Ronald asked, attempting to divide the unlikely alliance of mother and daughter, "how come he's not a success?" Though thin, Audrey had a fat woman's smile. She displayed it.

A number of answers occurred to Ruth, her favorite being: "And you, you think you're a success, you *schnook,* drilling cavities in that plywood paneled office of yours, setting yourself up to be knocked down by my daughter and other strangers? At the very least, Nicky is willing to take risks."

Instead, she decided on an oblique attack. "Ronald, maybe you should take the Parkway?"

Ronald continued to wend his way through the side streets of Linden, Roselle, Roselle Park ("Where's the park?" Ruth wondered, as they crawled past acres of grim split-levels), Rahway, Metuchen.

"We'll soon be there, Ma," Ronald said, attempting a conciliatory note.

"Do me a favor, Ronald," Ruth said.

"Yes, Ma?"

"Don't call me Ma."

The relentless November landscape, filled with ugly buildings—factories, two-family houses, yellow brick schools—did nothing to lighten Ruth's mood. "I live in a very ugly world," she thought. "I've lived in it all my life. Who knows if I could change now?

"And Miami Beach is so beautiful? Tahiti would be one thing. Miami Beach is another. The Jewish Graveyard. Where old Jewish ladies go to die. I can die right here, thank you very much. So it happens to be gray and cold and ugly. I've lived with it this long, I could live with it a few years longer."

The Oldsmobile pulled into the circular driveway that led to Plantation Casino Caterers, Inc. Audrey snapped the visor

down with such force that the vinyl around it gave. A jagged
rip appeared around the mirror where she was examining her
lipstick.

"Goddamn it," Ronald said, almost vindicated. "That's
going to cost us . . ."

"Still under warranty," Audrey said indistinctly, using her
lipstick to outline her lips.

"I doubt it very much," Ronald began but Audrey was out
of the car, pulling the not quite first-rate mink around her,
climbing the Tara-esque steps of the Plantation.

In the lobby, Audrey was blotting her lips. Ruth stood
behind her, looking at the both of them in the fake antique
mirror, struck by the sad expression in her own eyes. "Am I
feeling sad?" she wondered. "Or just old?" She didn't like the
way she looked. The in-fighting in the car had left an
unpleasant taste in her mouth, as if she had eaten one of April's
famous sardine health salads.

Harry's nephew, Ira Meyer—the re-groom—came out of a
room to her right, looking annoyed and nervous. "Hello, Aunt
Ruth, how are you?" he asked, bending down to give her a
kiss. With Meyer retired and Harry gone, Ira was now the
head of the cigar company. He reeked of Aramis cologne and
insincerity. "Ronald," he said, catching sight of his cousin-
in-law, "would you mind taking the ladies down right now?
The ceremony is about to begin." Typical of Ira, Ruth
thought, that he would assume she and Audrey needed to be
"taken down."

The chapel, filled to capacity, was aglow in dim lights that
had been artistically placed above and below Corinthian
columns which supported an elaborately carved plasterboard
dais. Audrey, plunging into the near darkness, led the way to
three seats in the last row.

Her eyes growing accustomed to the light (or lack of it),
Ruth counted the house. "Everyone's here," she decided.

"Three hundred relatives and two hundred business associates." The associates were easily identifiable by the telltale bulge of the cigars they wore in the breast pockets of their sharkskin suits.

"You comfortable, Mother?" Audrey asked audibly, making a bow to the tradition that daughters, after a certain age, were responsible for their mother's well-being.

"In a tent," Ruth said, staring up at the billowing striped material of the ceiling, "I thought you were supposed to sit on pillows."

"If you're making believe this is a tent, you could make believe that folding chair is a pillow," Rose Slotkin, sitting directly in front of Ruth, said. She turned her head with its tiny banana nose. "So sorry to hear about Harry, may he rest in peace." She was from Norma's (Ira's wife) side of the guests. Her husband, an extraordinarily obese man of seventy-three buttoned into a gray flannel suit, sat next to her. He once had the reputation of being a ladies' man. "Now he's a food man," Ruth thought as she tapped Rose on the shoulder and asked, "How's your blood pressure, Rose?"

"Rising."

Tiny pink spotlights on overhead tracks were turned on, picking out Norma, standing on a slowly rotating drum, several feet above the audience. The ceremony had begun. Music from speakers throughout the chapel/tent played the couple's favorite song, "I'm Just a Prisoner of Love."

As the drum turned and the music played, many members of the audience—mostly though not exclusively women— made oohing and aahing noises. "Just like their first wedding," Rose Slotkin said. "Remember, Ruth?"

"I remember," Ruth said as the drum came to a halt and Norma stopped rotating. The lights came up so that the audience now had a perfect view of Norma's body, clearly revealed despite the expensive dress she was wearing.

"Who knew it was transparent?" she asked later, in a way that made it obvious she did. Cousins and aunts and uncles and cigar wholesalers stopped talking, mesmerized by the skin-colored sashlike affair supporting Norma's French-bread breasts. A similar-hued panty girdle embraced her stomach and bound her thighs.

"She looks," Rose Slotkin whispered at the top of her not inconsiderable voice, "like a supermarket chicken in a plastic bag."

Norma, no longer virtually nude (the lights dimmed as she stepped off the drum), descended a ramp and met her husband where it joined the center aisle. As they marched toward the Greek-columned Middle Eastern tented dais, the taped music became vocal as well as instrumental.

At the top of the dais, Rabbi Bernard Shapiro was waiting, Bible in hand. He stared at the couple who stood towering over him as if he weren't quite sure who they were (and where he was) and then transferred his cloudy gaze to the five hundred people staring up at him. He cleared his throat and began to speak. He spoke for forty-five minutes, in Hebrew, a language that neither Norma nor Ira nor any member of the assemblage (with the exception of the young man taking hand-held movies) understood.

Ruth spent her time looking at her hands, which she felt were relatively unlined for a woman of her age; wondering if Rose Slotkin was wearing a hat to cover a bald spot; thinking she would get Harry's niece, Summer, and her husband, Pete, to drive her home. Then, as the ceremony continued, she tried to guess at which table Norma had placed her, and hoped it would be with the cousins.

It was to be some time until she found out. As the rabbi ended his celebration of Norma and Ira's twenty-five years of

marriage in Hebraic chant and verse, all of the lights went out
and a great whooshing sound followed, as if the tent had
collapsed. There was momentary hysteria, calmed only when
the lights came on again.

The tent had disappeared along with the wedding party,
and the guests found themselves in a replica of the Colosseum,
the Corinthian columns suddenly appropriate. Ruth joined the
orderly line of guests which led to the central columns where
Norma and Ira were "receiving." On the far side, the hors
d'oeuvres and drinks were being served under a canopy.

Ruth kissed Ira, Norma, their two children, and various
assorted relatives before making her way to the hot-and-cold
table. It featured a variety of such miniature specialties as little
hot dogs; little meatballs bobbing around in a sauce that had
separated, tomato to the right, oil to the left; little potato
pancakes with little flecks of green representing parsley in
their center; little gefilte fish balls; little watermelon balls;
little quiche Lorraines; little Chinese egg rolls.

"It looks," Ruth said to Bessie Wallowitz from Philadelphia, "like a feast for Jewish gremlins."

Waitresses with tough, bland, decidedly un-Jewish faces
carried trays of the assorted delicacies around the area for those
who couldn't make their way to the hot-and-cold table, now
surrounded by dedicated *fressers*. Ruth speared herself a little
stuffed cabbage, figuring, "What's the worst that can happen?
I already have indigestion," holding a little napkin under it so
the grease wouldn't stain her dress.

"Where's the chopped liver, Ma?" Ronald asked, handing
her a plastic glass greasy from his pastrami-coated fingers. It
was filled with a greenish liquid that might have been flat
ginger ale.

"There isn't any," a bland waitress handing out glasses of
tepid champagne told him.

As a three-piece ensemble (live) struck up "Peg of My Heart," Ruth made her way back through the columns to the ladies' room where two teenaged girls were redoing their already extensively done faces. They said hello tentatively. One of them, got up to look like Farrah Fawcett-Majors, belonged to Norma and Ira.

Ruth went about her business, thinking, "There's too few members of my generation at this re-wedding. I almost miss Meyer, Frieda, and Saul." They were all in Miami Beach and had decided not to travel north for the affair.

"For a regular wedding, maybe," Frieda had said. "For a re-wedding, nothing doing."

She left the ladies' room, which had been designed, she learned from a plaque affixed to the wall, to replicate a French boudoir, circa eighteen fifty. At the foot of the stairs leading up to the main dining room, she picked up the pink folded card with her name carefully written on it from the linen-covered table. She learned that she was to be seated at Table Number Twenty-four.

She went up the stairs and entered the Plantation's Scarlett O'Hara Room, an enormous space filled with round tables surrounding an oval dance floor. Audrey and Ronald were sitting to the right of the entrance at the cousins' table.

"Where were you, Mother?" Audrey asked accusingly.

"Urinating."

"We were worried."

"She's a big girl now," Shirley said. "She can take care of herself."

"Exactly," Ruth agreed, sitting next to Shirley, always billed as the prettiest of the cousins.

"Are you at this table?" Bea asked.

"Where else should I be?" She surrendered her card to Bea's husband, Mel, a tall, thin, protective man who said, "No, Aunt Ruth. You're at Table Twenty-four."

Ruth looked in the direction Mel was pointing. Her heart sank. Rose and Sam Slotkin were the two youngest members of Table Twenty-four. Next to Sam, a woman in a wheelchair was being spoon-fed by the nurse who sat at her side.

"My mistake," Ruth said, standing up, trying to smile, allowing Mel to accompany her to Table Twenty-four. She sat in the only vacant chair. Rose Slotkin was on her left. Sam was on her right. He promptly put one of his pudgy hands on her thigh.

"So hel-lo, Ruthie. Nice to see you. Sorry to hear about Harry. My heartfelt condolences, you understand?" He gave her thigh a little squeeze.

"Perfectly." She took Sam's hand and placed it on the table as Henny Sheck and His Scintillating Syncopators launched into "Love Me or Leave Me." This was the signal for Norma and Ira to march into the Scarlett O'Hara Room accompanied by their two children, for the guests to applaud their hosts. The girl was the one Ruth had seen in the ladies' room. The boy, Howard, was nineteen. He wore a fitted black suit, high-heeled shoes, a pink shirt opened to reveal a thin, dangerous neck. A gold-plated cocaine spoon was hanging on a chain around it.

Ira made a humorous speech about how happy he was to have survived twenty-five years with Norma. Norma kissed and hugged him and made a serious speech about how gratified she and Ira were that their children were giving this party for their parents.

The girl, Meryl, looked startled at this announcement and the boy said audibly, "News to me." Norma kissed Ira and the band went into their one rock song for the event, "Proud Mary."

"Is that Farrah?" Sam shouted into Ruth's ear as she raised a spoonful of thin Consommé Supremo to her lips. The Syncopators were directly behind them.

"No," Rose shouted through Ruth, "that's Norma's daughter, Meryl."

"You watch TV?" Sam asked Ruth, who had decided to do without the soup.

"No," she said, lying.

"Looks just like Farrah to me," Sam said, finishing his soup with a satisfied slurp, placing his hand back on Ruth's thigh. She took her salad fork and placed the dull edges of its tines into Sam's puffy hand, not firm enough to draw blood but with enough pressure to give pain.

"What're you trying to do, kill me?" Sam asked, putting his hand to his lips, kissing it. "You crazy?"

Ruth excused herself and performed the Ritual of the Tables, moving around the room, talking to relatives she hadn't seen since the week of mourning, not returning to her table until the moment Henny Sheck announced that the main course was being served.

The slab of roast beef on her plate—thick, red, and lined with fat—made her feel definitely ill.

"Is that Farrah?" Sam asked, apparently recovered from his salad-fork wound. Meryl, who was also "doing" the tables, was approaching Table Twenty-four. Her hair, blond tipped, flipped, and dipped, bounced aggressively with a life all its own as she walked.

"Sam," Rose shouted, "what's the matter with you today? That's Meryl, Norma's daughter."

"You Farrah?" Sam asked as Meryl came up to the table, smiling as she thought her idol might smile in similar circumstances.

"No, Uncle Sam," Meryl said, bending down, giving him a theatrical kiss. "I'm Meryl."

"Oh," Sam said as he watched Meryl kiss her way around the table before going on to Number Twenty-five. He remained quiet while his wife cut his roast beef into tiny pieces for him, while Ruth passed his plate back and forth during this operation. The plate returned, he forked a piece of roast beef into his mouth, and chewed it slowly and loudly. Then he put his fork down and turned to Ruth. "Didn't I tell you it was Farrah?"

Luckily, Summer and Pete announced they were leaving after the first dessert but before the cake and the Viennese table. "I'm not feeling so hot, Aunt Ruthie," Summer said.

"What's the matter?"

"Unspecified illness," her niece answered. "You want us to give you a lift?"

"Please."

They said good-bye to a great many people, Pete got the boy to bring the car around, and Summer described her unspecified illness in graphic detail ("the blood!") to her aunt.

Summer continued her account of what the doctors had missed ("Come on, Summer," her husband pleaded, "I just ate") as Ruth sat in the backseat, not listening. She was thinking. The process was made easy by the fact that Pete used the Parkway, traffic was light, and Summer's voice, while not as melodious as it might have been, was soothingly unhostile and totally self-involved.

They let her off in front of the house and waited until she had gotten in and flashed the light over the front door three times. "A lot of robberies in Elizabeth," Pete, who worked out that ingenious system, had said.

Ruth watched them drive off as she stood by the living-room window, still thinking. Just before she closed the curtains, she caught sight of the Lipsteins' small gray car circling the block.

Despite the robberies, she ran to the door, threw it open, and shouted at the car's retreating back, "It's all yours. Lock, stock, and barrel. Take it. I give it to you. It's all yours."

Feeling better, she slammed the door and went up the stairs to soak in a hot bath. The November chill had gone right through her. While she soaked, she made a mental note to tell Jan Weiss that the Lipsteins could have all of the furniture with the exception of the brown sofa. "That goes to Audrey," she said aloud. "It's shot anyway."

After her bath, comfortably wrapped in her terry robe, she called her friend April. "The answer is yes," Ruth said.

"You think I didn't know that? Now go to sleep, *mamala*, and get your beauty rest. We want to be gorgeous when we hit the Monte Excelsior Hotel and Country Club, right? Fasten your girdles, Miami Beach: two hot mamas are coming to town."

Ruth wore her flannel nightgown to bed and turned up the electric blanket. She laughed out loud as she thought of April and herself going to Miami Beach. She couldn't think of two mamas who were less hot.

 Eight

Miami Beach is a long island off the east coast of Florida, connected to the mainland and the city of Miami by a series of causeways stretching across Biscayne Bay. The rich live in Spanish-style houses on the small islands that dot the bay. The well-to-do live or vacation in the northern section of Miami Beach at hotels and condominiums that strive for elegance and virtually always achieve a kind of comfortable cleanliness. The well-off stay in hotels just above Lincoln Road which are, at this point in time, making efforts to "keep their heads above water" while at the same time attempting to attract a new kind of tourist to Miami Beach. The old clientele is dying off, their children snorkeling in the Virgin Islands.

Men and women who are making do, who are over sixty and not expected to increase their incomes or their life expectancy in any appreciable way, live below Fifteenth Street, a section of Miami Beach alternately known as South Beach or the Jewish Graveyard.

The place to live in South Beach is Ocean Road, the long street which features the Atlantic Ocean on the east and fifteen blocks of fading pink and white hotels, apartment houses, and efficiency units on its west. Ocean Road begins with a patriotic grouping of such establishments at Fifteenth Street: the Jefferson, the White House Hotel and Apartments (Dietary Laws Strictly Observed, dining room open to public), and the Betsy Ross Hotel and Apts. The White House features a mock facade designed to resembly its namesake in Washington, D.C., and the Betsy Ross is often called the Bessy Ross but, still, patriotism is in the air.

A little ways past the White House, Lummus Park begins. It is a very green stretch of parkland extending some ten blocks to the south, a pleasant barrier between sidewalk and beach. A stone wall and benches, facing the ocean, provide places to rest. There is a building, run by the city of Miami Beach, which houses an auditorium and several offices, all devoted to helping South Beach senior citizens have a better life.

In the afternoons these senior citizens come to Lummus Park, eschewing the benches and the wall, *schlepping* their own metal and plastic folding chairs. They form groups to play cards, to talk, to sing, to dance, to practice for the annual folk dance contest. Even on the warmest days the shade under the palm trees is cooling and the breeze from the ocean refreshing. Lummus Park would seem to be a picnic that never ends.

The picnickers are people who range in age from their late sixties to their mid-nineties. Women, with rolled stockings and bright, pinched faces, are in the vast majority. The men, in cotton caps and green visors, are more quiet, less demanding. Having worked for most of their lives, it's difficult for many of them to sit back and relax.

The hotels and apartment houses facing Lummus Park nearly all feature fabulously inappropriate names: the East Atlantic Gardens, the Waldorf Towers, the Netherland, the Cavalier, the Cardoza, the Colony, the Majestic, the Savoy Plaza, the Barbizon Apartment Hotel. They are, for the most part, clean but slightly seedy, like a group of respectable women secretly on welfare. The more prosperous ones have constantly operating public address systems: "Calling Mrs. Gittle. Calling Mrs. Murray Gittle. Phone call for Mrs. Murray Gittle." Most of them have tiny lobbies filled with men playing pinochle and afterthought porches where the women sit, knitting and gossiping, bragging about children, complaining about neglect.

If you close your eyes as you walk along Ocean Road, you might think you were in Brooklyn or the Bronx. Or perhaps in a cosmopolitan Middle European ghetto before World War II. The rhythm of the voices, the sentences punctuated by heartfelt sighs, the minor key underlying the most mundane statements ("So how's by you, darling?") all bespeak persecution, chronic and uncurable unhappiness.

Yet, once your eyes were open, you would see that most everyone is smiling, busy, intent on pursuing his or her own interest. These are the people who traveled from obscure villages in Poland and Russia in the early part of this century, escaping indescribable living conditions, to spend their adult lives in New York, their final days in Miami Beach, Florida.

No matter how cramped their rooms or how tasteless their

food, it is far better than the rooms and food of their youth. And the strength and resiliency that served to help them escape their early deprivation help them to cope with whatever deprivation they are now experiencing. The braver ones often, in conversation, count their blessings: they are alive, living in the sunshine, having—if not a wonderful time—at least one of their own choosing.

The Monte Excelsior Hotel and Country Club, on the ocean at First Street, does not cater to the usual residents of South Beach. The Monte has pretensions. Built in the Spanish rococo style so beloved of Floridian architects, it is a square, pink, concrete structure built around a tiled courtyard. It features arched windows, scrolled concrete columns, and elaborate wrought-iron staircases and gates. It boasts three floors, seventy-five apartmentettes, each with tiled and private bathrooms and "kitchenellas" (a phrase conceived by its management) hidden by folding laminated screens.

"I think it's terrific," April said, surveying her new home, looking at Ruth, waiting for her to say something. "So what do you think?"

"Me?"

"No, I'm talking to the wall." There were another few seconds of silence. "So?"

"I imagine we'll be spending a lot of time outdoors," Ruth said, going to her own apartmentette, studying the brochure she found there, finally quieting April by agreeing, "It's not so bad. Not so good. But not so terribly bad."

When the Monte Excelsior first opened in the spring of nineteen thirty-one, it was considered private, chic, expensive, and ill-fated. However, people who valued discretion (millionaires from the mainland with mistresses to hide from the prying eyes of Presbyterian wives) kept it solvent.

A kidney-shaped swimming pool had been installed in the center of the courtyard in time for the winter season of nineteen fifty-one but much too late to hold on to the Monte's former clientele. New patrons, less interested in privacy than in cheaper rates, took their place.

In nineteen fifty-three, after eighty years of overeating, the resident owner of the Monte, Stanley Fleischman, died, leaving the hotel and its mortgage to his forty-five-year-old son, Morris, a person he had often and widely described as "Life's Biggest Disappointment."

Despite the fact that the Monte was on the last block but one of Miami Beach, in an area that was increasingly given to Spanish-language signs *("Limpios"; "Bajos preciosos")* and teenaged surfer dope peddlers, Morris had big plans for the Monte which he put into effect immediately following his father's demise.

The first step in his master plan was to court and win Belle Wenk, the fortyish spinster daughter of a deceased Philadelphia clothing manufacturer who was at the Monte recovering from the shock of her own father's death.

"We are both recently bereaved," Morris told her in his most continental manner. "But we must go on. Fortunately, you are a woman with several gorgeous options. You can choose to recline all day in our suite on the second floor, watching television, reading French novels, eating imported bonbons, leading a leisured, unstructured life, free to indulge yourself in all that I, your willing love slave, can provide, dear little Belle.

"Or you may choose to be my helpmate, my partner, and work side by side with me in the field of endeavor I have designated as my life's work. We can, dear Ding Dong Belle, be innkeepers together in the rich Old World sense of the phrase, leading a life healthy in material and spiritual rewards, helping weary travelers regain their sense of proportion and repose."

Belle, with her long nose and short torso, was quick to realize that if she chose the former, no marriage contract would be in the offing; not one ratified by a rabbi, at any rate. "I'd love to help you with your business, Morris," she had said, letting that relentless lover into her room for the third night in a row.

She had been left a certain amount of money by her father, half of which was poured into the Monte's concrete during their first year of marriage. The other half was kept in a credit union in Philadelphia.

"I'm saving it," Belle answered when questioned by her husband, "for the day when you drop dead, Morris, and this pile of shit falls down."

Belle's postmarital disposition was not all that Morris could have wished, but her dowry had allowed him to turn the downstairs lobby into a restaurant known as La Salle à Manger. Morris had spent the Second World War as an assistant cook in a PX near Paris.

In addition to the new dining room, Morris upped the rates, hired a modest public relations firm, and took advertisements in the *New York Times* Sunday travel section in which he offered in tiny type "a full program of social and intellectual activities geared for the young at heart." He patched the pink concrete where it persistently cracked and, to everyone's surprise, managed to keep the Monte in the black.

" 'Tis the ambience," Morris liked to say.

His guests were mostly women, not in their first youth, but a generation younger than the other residents of South Beach. They were women who either didn't mind where the Monte was located or who were too unsophisticated to know that First Street was now, in Belle's estimation, "the pits."

 Nine

It was an early December morning and all should have been right with Morris Fleischman's world. The Monte was three-quarters full and the thermometer was hovering around seventy, two unexpected but well-appreciated dividends at this off-season date. Belle, however, was being unreasonable.

"Dear Ding Dong," Morris was saying to that woman as they stood in the abbreviated and much carpeted lobby of the Monte, "Mrs. Solomander and I are mere *bon amis,* nothing more."

"You can take your dear Ding Dong, Morris, and stuff it. Or better yet, you can pay me back the money you owe me and I can split."

"But, *mon vie,*" Morris said, "my relationship with Mrs. Solomander is purely an aesthetic one, a question of kindred spirits meeting on an astral plane of pristine innocence . . ." But Belle was already off to the third floor to give the maid Monday morning hell.

Morris reflected that it was perhaps a good thing that Rosalie Solomander was returning home to Manhattan Beach on the morrow. That tiny mass of contradiction who was his wife (how could she hate him so and, at the same time, be so spectacularly jealous?) had often threatened to "split" but never had gotten very far. The idea of alimony made his stomach, never his strongest organ, shaky.

On the other hand, Rosalie's departure would leave him, for the moment, without a "sex kitten," and that was a state that would be insupportable.

Morris's sex drive—which had caused him much trouble and concern in his early life and which he had confidently believed would abate in later years—constantly surprised him: the older he got, the stronger and more urgent it became. Sex continued to take up a great deal of his waking and sleeping time.

"Still obsessed," he noted often and with sadness, wondering where all the men and women were who had advised him, "One day, Morris, you'll pray to God to help you get it up." His manhood, he prayed to God, should please lie down. It evinced itself each morning when he arose and each evening before he put himself to bed next to the sonorous Belle. It was like some electronic flag, triggered by tricks of light.

What was most embarrassing, it would sometimes rise all by itself at inappropriate moments, as if the mechanism were broken. As when he was lying on the chaise by the pool, charming his guests. Or worse, when he was conducting his popular exercise classes.

It also seemed to be getting larger with age. His doctor said he did not have an exotic form of cancer, as Belle, who regarded it as a malevolent but harmless snake, suggested.

Luckily, he came into contact with many lonely women who were willing to experiment, who needed just that tiny soupçon of encouragement to show how much sexual courage they had been repressing. It was true, many of the ladies were not physically prepossessing. But Morris had come to realize that though beauty was a plus, it was not necessary (and sometimes not even desirable) in a sex partner. Willingness and an ability to experiment more often than not compensated for varicose veins and a roll or two of unjustifiable fat. Most difficult of all to find was a certain suppleness, elasticity, that many of the women who came to the Monte simply did not possess and could not manufacture without severely injuring themselves or him.

But the immediate problem was finding a replacement for Rosalie. The very thought forced him to walk behind the desk, a maneuver that made the switchboard operator, Armando (who was also the bellhop and, on occasion, the waiter), nervous.

"I can't work this switchboard with you standing over me, Mr. Fleischman."

"Pretend I'm not here, dear boy. Pretend I'm a figment of your somewhat overripe tropical imagination." He stared through the plate-glass window into the Monte's understaffed, underutilized dining room at the two women breakfasting there, sizing them up.

April Pollack, he thought, was probably the better bet. She was tall and lean and looked as if she might bend rather than break. Her hair had recently been dyed red (recently, he decided, because it was so bright), always a good sign, and her face—under its makeup and sunglasses (bifocals?)—had clearly seen a certain amount of living. She cursed, he knew, like a sailor, a trait he found charming in women of a certain age, and she did not look as if she were used to a great deal of pampering.

But though she was the better bet, Morris knew himself well enough to realize that he was going to make a move in Ruth Meyer's direction first. To begin with, she was clearly a Lady Used to Finer Things and Ladies Used to Finer Things often made surprisingly dextrous partners once they let their manners down. Also, she was a remarkably good-looking woman and though good looks, it was true, were only a plus, he preferred to be as much on the plus side of events as possible.

She was slim and her hair was an attractive blue white which emphasized her unusual gray-blue eyes. She did not wear glasses, so there would be no midnight fumbling with those annoying aids to vision. Her skin was relatively unlined and

her legs were thin and shapely. Really, she might have been in
her fifties. And she was recently bereaved, a good omen. New
widows were always a bit frantic about their sex life, even if
they hadn't had one in years.

She was also extravagant, treating her friend to breakfast in
La Salle à Manger, while all other residents of the Monte were
ingesting their prunes and Sanka in the privacy of their
kitchenellas.

Morris began to have a fantasy in which Belle "split
permanently" (he'd give her a tasteful going out) and Ruth
Meyer became his regent. He wondered how much money her
husband had left her and whether or not she would want to
invest it in an expansion plan he had for the Monte.

Morris checked to see if his manhood was dormant or awake
behind his houndstooth trousers and, finding it quiescent,
prepared to join the ladies from New Jersey in the Dining
Room.

"Where you going?" Ruth asked April. "You haven't
finished your Sanka."

"If you look behind you, Draisal, you'll notice that your late
husband's sister is converging upon us." Ruth turn and looked
through the glass windows that looked out on the Monte's
courtyard. Her sister-in-law was headed in their direction.
"What did she do, God," April asked, "that she should
deserve this punishment? By what terrible stroke of fate did
this have to happen to her and to me?"

By a coincidence Ruth felt too awful to contemplate, Frieda
and Saul had moved into the Monte Excelsior Annex (a small,
arid building attached to the main structure) the day after
Ruth and April had checked in. "If you really know how to
hotel-hop," Frieda had confided to April, "you can save a lot of
gelt in this town."

"She's parked Saul by the pool," April told Ruth as she

stood up, "so she must have something serious to say because
normally he's not allowed out of her sight for a minute."

"Don't leave me, April."

"If I don't get to a bathroom in the next sixty seconds, we'll
all be swimming and I don't mean in the pool."

"*Bonjour,* Mrs. Pollack," Morris Fleischman said as he
entered La Salle à Manager from the lobby. "I hope and trust
all is satisfactory?"

"My shower drips," April said, going through the door that
led to the ladies' room.

"*Charmant,*" Morris said, walking across the indoor/outdoor
carpeting to the Formica table where Ruth sat, sipping her
Sanka. "Such *je ne sais quoi.* I can't remember meeting a
woman with so much sparkle and zest as your dear friend,
Madame Meyer. Perhaps I might join you for my midmorning
demitasse? So kind of you. Armando," Morris shouted, "a
black American, *por favor, tout de suite.*"

The coffee was duly brought to Morris in a tiny cup.
"*Gracias,*" Morris said. "It helps when one speaks their
language," Morris whispered to Ruth. "And may I say '*gracias*'
to you, dear lady, for allowing me to share your table. It's very
lonely for me here, plying my humble trade. 'People
come / people go / it's all the same in Grand Hotel.' One longs
for genuine conversation, for intellectual stimulation, for the
sort of conversation one had in Paris during one's youth, *n'est-ce
pas?* But alas, here we are, two *simpático* strangers, stranded
together on a culturally deserted island— Ah, dear Mrs.
Glaser. I fear I didn't see you standing there behind the palm.
Won't you join us, *chère madame?*"

"I'm sure you didn't, Mr. Morris Fleischman," Frieda said,
moving out from behind the palms that blocked the door
leading to the pool and the courtyard. She sat in the chair
April had vacated, putting her two thick elbows on the table,

grasping her hands, and leaning forward. Behind her, Ruth could see April leaving the ladies' room and climbing the stairs, which led to their apartmentettes, especially quietly. "I'm going to lay it on the line, Mr. Morris Fleischman," Frieda continued. "Keep away from this woman. She's my sister-in-law, for openers. For enders, she's already spoken for. And in the middle, if you need a middle, you already got a perfectly good wife, if a shade *cvetchy,* upstairs. Go tell her about the kind of French stimulation you're looking for, Mr. Morris Fleischman. *Capiche?* Or don't you speak Italian?"

Morris stood up and took a step backward. "I have the feeling I speak Italian at least as well as you speak English, dear Mrs. Glaser. The last time we had a conversation in your adopted language, yesterday morning, I believe, it was about your bill, which is payable in advance. Your reputation, you see, has preceded you."

"Saul's taking care of it," Frieda said, removing a piece of dry and cold toast from Ruth's plate, buttering it with Ruth's knife, placing it into her own mouth.

"Ah, and I see the gentleman in question with his feet in the pool. I shall go and help him dispatch his fiscal duties. *À bientôt,* dear ladies."

"Skunk," Frieda said without passion, snaring herself another slice of toast.

"What did you mean, Frieda," Ruth asked, taking her butter knife and laying it down on the far side of her plate, out of Frieda's range, "when you said I was already 'spoken for'?"

"A figure of speech. You going to finish that orange juice?"

"Yes, I am."

"Orange juice never agrees with me first thing in the morning."

"That's a peculiar figure of speech, Frieda. Do me a favor, Frieda: don't use it again when referring to me."

"So I beg your pardon, your royal highness. I shouldn't breathe. I shouldn't speak. I shouldn't try to protect my baby brother's wife from that lady-gayer's hands. I should let him seduce you and worse, right?"

"What could be worse?"

"A little four-letter word known as R-A-P-E."

"Somehow I'm not worried, Frieda."

"What about that coffee?"

"It's Sanka and it's all yours."

"Maybe this time it won't give me such heartburn."

Ruth watched her sister-in-law draining the last drop of beverage from the cup. She wondered, aloud, if Frieda intended to remain at the Monte Excelsior indefinitely.

"For the time being. We'll stay here until the rates go down uptown, on April fifteenth, and then we'll move into the Sutton-Grand until June first. Anyway, darling, I wanted to ask you something."

"Shoot."

"Are you planning to attend the T.G.I.S. tonight?"

"What exactly is a T.G.I.S.?"

"A Morris Fleischman concoction. Thank God It's Saturday. He gives a dance on the pier every Saturday night, weather permitting, for—you should excuse the expression—senior citizens. The city pays him to do it or he wouldn't, believe me."

"Doesn't sound like my cup of tea."

"Meyer is planning on attending."

"I still doubt if I'll go."

"Ruthie, cookie, you been here over a week already and you never even called him, you never even said boo to him on the phone. When he comes to see me you're always off with that *yenta* friend of yours. Ruthie, a man can only wait so long."

"Frieda, let me put your blood pressure at rest. Do not

attempt to play matchmaker between me and your brother Meyer."

"He's your brother-in-law. Don't forget that."

"It's not only that I'm not interested in Meyer, Frieda, I'm not interested in men. I'm still mourning the death of my husband. I'm also liking not being married. I'm free."

"You can't fool me, kid. I've known you since the day Harry brought you around for all of us to meet. Remember?"

"Too well." Their mother had asked to see her teeth.

"Now tell the truth: you're miserable, aren't you? It shows all over you. You need someone to lay down the law for you . . ."

"I have you for that, Frieda."

". . . and you need a man around the house. Meyer will take good care of you."

"Meyer should learn to take care of himself." She stood up, brushing toast crumbs from her pink skirt. "And if Meyer wants to see me, all he has to do is pick up the telephone. I would very happily spend time with him. He's my brother-in-law. But you should let him know, Frieda, that I am not interested in marriage."

"For the time being," Frieda amended.

"For ever and a day," Ruth said, going toward the door.

"Where you going so fast, Ruthie? You want to play a little Hollywood rummy, eighth of a cent a point, by the pool?"

"I'm going to get my watercolors."

"*Oy vey*. Watercolors, yet. Morris Fleischman's going to come in his pants from so much intellectual stimulation."

Ten

"So what're you wearing?" April asked, sponging the laminated blond wood table on which they had eaten dinner.

"So who says I'm going?"

"They're all wearing slacks." April took the dishes from her friend and piled them in the inconvenient sink.

"Who's all wearing slacks?"

"Every single *yenta* at this not-so-deluxe hotel. They were talking at the pool while you were painting palm trees. Muriel Resnick is wearing a new pair of beige pleated trousers with cuffs and a real button fly she bought on sale on Lincoln Road. Probably in a men's store. If you can imagine Muriel Resnick's two-hundred-pound *tuchas* in trousers, pleated, cuffed, and buttoned, you have a better imagination than I." She turned on the tap and waited for hot water to appear. "Pauline Cohen is wearing her pink cotton slacks, she announced, which is no big surprise since she's been wearing her pink cotton slacks since the day we arrived here in Paradise. Mae Weissman is wearing the sequined blue jeans her granddaughter sent her for Chanukah last year, gold glitter heels, and a fisherman's vest. She also intimated that she's leaving her hearing aid at home, just in case. 'Just in case what?' I asked. 'Just in case,' Mae answered. How I loathe and despise that Mae Weissman. Miriam Siegal is wearing culottes and Esther Weiner is wearing what she calls her 'slinky blacks,' which happen to be a pair of ordinary black polyester trousers with bell bottoms." The hot water having arrived, April began to wash the dishes. "So what are you wearing, Draisal?"

"My white dress with my low white heels. *If* I go."

"You'll be sorry."

"I'm already sorry."

"You hate this place, Ruth?"

"Hate's too strong a word. After the winter, we'll go back to Elizabeth and take a two-bedroom apartment in Chilton Towers."

"Try and get one."

"We'll get one, believe me. Betty Levy's son-in-law owns Chilton Towers and Betty Levy and I are just like this."

"With Betty Levy's body odor, I'd rather be just like that."

"April, do you ever have a kind word to say about anyone?"

"You, for one. The girls around the pool were implying, in not so heavily veiled allusions, that you were a snob. I sat up in my chaise lounge and said: 'Ruth Meyer is not a snob, ladies. She simply happens to have a little more money and culture than most of the guests at this hotel and thus she finds that she has little of common interest upon which to base idle discussions. When her husband, Harry (may he rest in peace), was alive, every winter like clockwork they would come down and stayed, if not exactly in the Fontainebleau, at least next door. Ruth Meyer is used to the finer things of life, ladies, and you should not make judgments on a person simply because she feels deep down in her heart that she is better than you.'"

"If I ever need a defense lawyer, April, remind me you don't have a license."

"In some states you don't need one."

"I'll try not to commit a crime in them. So what're you wearing to the T.G.I.S.?"

"I'm betwixt and between," April said, going to the mirror, tucking stray strands of her fisherman's wife's hairdo back into the hairpins they had escaped. "Either my orange go-go trousers or my midnight-blue silk look-alikes. Which would you wear?"

"My white dress with my low white heels."

"You're starting off on a bad foot with those low white heels, alienating every woman at this hotel."

"Because I'm wearing a dress?"

"Exactly. You have nice legs. The rest of them have enough varicose veins to make up and fill in a detailed road map of the continental United States and Canada."

"What difference will it make? There are exactly two men at this hotel: Saul, who's married to my sister-in-law, God help him; and Morris Fleischman, who is nominally married to Belle. Who's going to look?"

"For your information, dear Ruth, any man over sixty, residing in the city of Miami Beach, is invited to attend the T.G.I.S. gratis."

"And women?"

"Naturally all residents of the Monte and its annex are invited guests. Everyone else, female and over fifty, has to pay a sixty-cent service charge during the season, thirty-five cents thereafter. You didn't read your brochure."

"I got bogged down in the middle of Morris Fleischman's biography." Ruth stood up. "You want me to dry those dishes?"

"You kidding? Two little Melmac plates. They self-destruct after ten minutes."

"Thanks for dinner, April," Ruth said, kissing her on the cheek. "I'm going to get dressed."

"What're you wearing?"

"My white dress with my low white heels. You want me to knock when I'm ready?"

"No, you go on. The word is it's not such good public relations when two women come in together. The men don't like it when a woman has a friend."

Sighing, Ruth let herself into Apartmentette Number One

Two Three, a mirror image of April's Apartmentette Number One Two Four. A door fitted with paint-cemented louvers led from the balcony into a ten-by-fourteen-foot room, carpeted in what the brochure described as sea-green plush. The room was lit by forty-watt bulbs placed in one modernistic floor lamp and in a crystal chandelier made of one hundred percent plastic. There was a davenport on one wall which became a bed at night, several pieces of laminated blond wood furniture, the kitchenella, and an enormous blond wood television console. A narrow door at the far end of the room led into a tiny bathroom tiled in chartreuse and black. There was one window in the room, half of which was taken up by a noisy, overeffective air conditioner. The other half, the top, looked out on Ocean Road. If one took the trouble to lift the dirty Venetian blinds, one could see a small beach with seven skinny palm trees, a concession that sold suntan oil and kosher chicken hot dogs, several trash cans fairly well filled. A squat cream-colored concrete structure to the rear of the beach featured two doors, one labeled "Girls," the other, "Boys."

Depressed, Ruth turned on the television and sat down on the davenport. An intricate game show was being aired but she was too indolent to get up and switch the channel. She reached over to the end table and pulled over one of the few books she had brought with her.

It was a volume of Georgia O'Keeffe's paintings. Nicky and Linda had given it to her. She thumbed through the book, picking out her favorite paintings and began to feel better. The colors seemed so much more real than the colors around her. She remembered Georgia O'Keeffe saying, during a television program, that she had always lived life as if she were walking on the edge of a razor.

Ruth closed the book. "My life has been a walk along a soft, mushy mattress. Here I am, free for the first time in my life, free to do whatever I so choose, and what am I so choosing?

"Just what my husband and my father would have wanted me to choose. I've been well trained. A little hotel off the beaten track in Miami Beach, Florida, filled with lovely widowed Jewish ladies whose main concern is what they're going to wear to a dance attended by other lovely Jewish ladies.

"The others—my father, Harry, even Frieda—were allowed to walk along the razor's edge, at least once in their life. They pulled up their roots, moved to a country they knew nothing about. They were the pioneers. I'm the retired housewife.

"I have twenty-one thousand dollars a year on which to live. I am not dumb or afflicted with any severe illness. Yet. There must be some better way to live, some better way to make use of my life. What am I doing here?

"I'll tell you what I'm doing here. I'm being scared. I'm choosing the second easiest way out. The first would have been to have stayed put in Elizabeth, going to Hadassah meetings and Deborah fund raisers until I couldn't hold another can in my hand, until I couldn't prop myself up in front of another supermarket.

"Here I can tell myself: Look, Ruth, you took a chance. You sold the house. You moved to Miami Beach, Florida.

"Why didn't I take a bigger chance? Why didn't I pick myself up and go to Tahiti or New Mexico or Paris, France. You know why? Because you don't have the guts, Ruth Meyer. You're a frightened old lady getting older, making your statement in Miami Beach by wearing dresses instead of slacks.

"Oh, Harry," she said, aloud, "why didn't you take me with you?"

There was a triple knock on the door. "You in there, Draisal?"

She wiped her eyes and called out for April to come in. "So

nu? Where's the famous white dress and the low white heels?"

"I'm not going, April. I'm not in the mood."

"Suddenly her highness has to be in the mood. And you think I'm in the mood? But what's the alternative? We should go play bingo on Washington Avenue? Now, get up and put a cold washcloth over that pretty face. . . ."

"April . . ."

"Get dressed. I'm sitting here waiting for you. So what if two ladies walk in together? Maybe they'll think we like kinky sex."

"April, I don't—"

"Move it, lady. And stop feeling so goddamned sorry for yourself and your lost opportunities. We all have our regrets, Ruth. What you need is some lights, action, and excitement. You got the blues? So does everyone whose last name isn't Rockefeller. And speaking of blues, perhaps your powder-blue trousers . . ."

"The white dress," Ruth said, getting up, allowing her friend to hug her.

"You okay, *mamala?*" April asked.

"A touch sad."

"What have you got to be so sad about, anyway?" April asked, zipping Ruth into the white dress. "Count your blessings."

"I'm a senior citizen going to a dance given for and by senior citizens, April. I don't have what to be sad about?" She turned around. "How do I look?"

"Stunning and exquisite. For a senior citizen."

 Eleven

"Never let the same dog bite you twice. Never let the same guy two-time you . . ." Piccolo Pete (né Sid Baumgarten) was singing one of his risqué songs as Ruth and April made their appearance. He stood on the stage of the shallow bandstand halfway down the pier, holding a microphone to his mouth with one hand, keeping the cord from soiling his powder-blue dinner jacket with the other. Only one of the five members of the rumba band—the piano player—was awake. He played accompaniment to Piccolo's somewhat raspy rendition of the Sophie Tucker favorite.

There were one hundred women and half a dozen men on the pier, most in trousers. Though the temperature was a balmy seventy-five degrees, warm for a Miami Beach December night, the women sported stoles of wool, fur, and unidentifiable fabrics.

The pier is a concrete structure some twenty-five feet wide and perhaps a tenth of a mile long. A plaque in its entrance portico dedicates it to Colonel Mitchell Wolfson, "a true champion of the people." The portico is supported by twelve concrete columns. On its roof is a balcony where marijuana is sold and graffiti ("Anita Bryant Sucks Oranges") are written. Every few feet along the pier are English and Spanish signs alerting the reader that "it shall be unlawful to dive, leap, or jump from the municipal pier. Police order."

The pier is an extension of the first street in Miami Beach, Biscayne Street. To the south is the First Street Beach, used by surfers from the city of Miami. To the north is the small beach that faces the Monte Excelsior and beyond that, a postcard view of Miami Beach's palm trees and sand-colored hotels.

With its green macadam floor and its gray concrete walls, the pier is an ugly intrusion during the day. At night, with its lamplights shining—and especially when the bandstand is in use—the pier becomes a genuine promenade, as Colonel Wolfson might well have wanted it.

Toward its far end, the pier becomes wider. A high chain-link fence which doesn't extend from wall to wall stands in its center like a makeshift room divider. Behind it is a wooden table with four faucets, used for cleaning fish and equipment. Propped up against the pier's most easterly wall, looking out at the Atlantic Ocean, are the fishermen, twenty-four-hours-a-day habitués, ignoring the bandstand and the music, concentrating on the darkness and their sport.

At the bandstand, Piccolo Pete, his forehead shining, swung the entire band into "Apple Blossom Time" as Morris Fleischman, in a black tuxedo, greeted Ruth and April. "*Buenas noches, señoras.* One is overwhelmed that you could make your lovely presences known at my *petite soirée ce soir.* I confess," he said, taking both their arms, leading them past his wife, who was collecting admission fees from non–Monte Excelsior guests, "that I had despaired of your condescending to attend this modest entertainment, *n'est-ce pas?* But now that you are here, I do wonder, Madame Meyer, if you would do me the inestimable honor of accepting my offer of a dance with me?"

He dropped their elbows and held out his arms. Mistaking her silence for acquiescence, Morris took Ruth's hand, tucked it under his arm, kissed her fingers, and prepared to lead her to the dance floor.

Ruth retrieved her hand but before she could disabuse
Morris, a squat and familiar figure, wearing trousers a size too
small, came between them. "So look who's arrived? We
thought you were never coming," Frieda said. "Hello, April.
We have the same pants on. Everyone will think we're sisters.
Anyhow," she said, turning her attention back to Ruth,
"you'll never in a million years guess who's here tonight.
Don't even try. Just come with me." Parroting Morris's
gesture, she tucked Ruth's hand under her arm and led her to
one of the benches that ran along the north side of the pier.
Looking back, Ruth saw April's hand being kissed by Morris
Fleischman's mouth.

Saul and Meyer, sitting on the bench, looked like pigeons,
nesting. A trio of ladies stood watching them as if it were
breakfast time and the men were not pigeons but especially
delectable cheese danish. Meyer made a move to rise as he
spotted Ruth but Saul held him down.

"If they stand up," Frieda explained, "they lose their seats
and then we'd have to stand for the rest of the evening which
would be a fine how-do-you-do, considering the state of my
feet. Meyer, you're not saying hello to Ruthie?"

Meyer, in a gray silk suit, crossed his leg to reveal black
rayon anklet socks. He smiled his tentative smile, the one he
always wore when Ruth was in the neighborhood. "How are
you, Ruthie?" he asked, not leaving his seat.

"Fine, Meyer," Ruth said, bending down to kiss him on his
cheek, feeling a quick rush of affection for her husband's
brother. "How are you, Meyer?"

"Not so good. Not so bad. At our age, you know,
everything starts to go wrong, right?"

"Not everything, Meyer."

"What could go right in a capitalist state like America?"
Saul said. "Our body is a machine and when it begins to wear

out, when it needs new parts, it's thrown on the junk
heap . . ."

"Why don't you get up and take Ruthie for a little
schpitzeer?" Frieda asked.

"What about my seat?"

"I'll save it." Frieda sat on the arm of the bench and, as
Meyer stood up, she slid into the seat, next to her husband.

"No fair," the woman standing closest to the bench said.
"That's not fair play. I been waiting for that seat all evening."

"I have a bad heart," Frieda lied.

"And I have crippling arthritis."

"If you have arthritis, you shouldn't be at a dance in the first
place."

"I'm going to complain to the management. I paid sixty
cents . . ."

"Sixty cents," Frieda said, "doesn't entitle you to a seat.
Sixty cents only entitles you to that dirty dishwater Morris
Fleischman has the gall to call lemonade and to the music, if
you call those filthy songs music."

"Davie in his dinghy / Took out his little thingy / And said to
sweet Marie," Piccolo was singing as the woman and her
companions marched to the spot where Morris Fleischman
stood, listening to something apparently distasteful his wife,
Belle, was saying.

"You want to take that walk, Ruthie?" Meyer asked.

"Sure, Meyer."

They walked past the bandstand and the "Boys" and "Girls"
rooms to a bench that faced away from Miami Beach. It looked
south, at the surfers' beach and, past that, at Fisher Island and
Virginia Key. Ships and tankers moved across the Government
Cut, heading out to sea.

"We could be in some genuinely romantic spot," Ruth
thought. "Some faraway place." Visions of half-caste women

and feverish painters came to mind as Meyer said, "Not what you'd call a very high-class clientele," referring to the people dancing.

They sat quietly for a moment, the music and the crowd off in the background, like part of a film being shown in an outdoor theater. They looked at the black sea and the tiny lights coming from the ships and pleasure boats and airplanes. "I feel very comfortable with Meyer," Ruth thought. "It's nice to be here with him."

As if he were thinking the same thought, he took her hand. "Ruthie, I have something to say to you."

"Don't say it, Meyer." She tried to retrieve her hand but his grip was firm.

"Why not?"

"Because I can't hear it now, Meyer."

"Ruthie, we're two people all alone in this world. At my age I'm not looking for magic. I'm looking for companionship. Someone to eat with, to watch the television, to go to the movies on a Sunday night. I'm not like Harry, may he rest in peace. I never was one for high living. I'm content to stay put in one place, to be quiet, to be peaceful. Since Fanny's gone I've been very lonesome.

"Look, I have a comfortable income, too much for one person. I don't know what to do with all that money. I know you're a different kind of person than me. You were born in this country. You're smart. You're interested in cultural affairs. . . ."

"Meyer . . ."

"Ruthie, please. Listen to me." He put his arm around her and tried to bring her close to him. "I want you to come and mar—"

She disengaged herself and stood up. "Stop. Don't say another word, I beg you. It's too soon. I don't want to hear it now, Meyer. Please, I'm asking you, let's not have this conversation now."

He left the bench and went to her. "Then when, Ruthie? Time's not standing still for either of us."

"In six weeks, Meyer. Talk to me in six weeks."

She put her hand on his arm. He petted it. "Okay. Six weeks. Give or take. Now come. Let's go back and have a lemonade."

"You go back, Meyer. I'm going to sit for a while and think."

"A good sign. The lemonade and I will be waiting for you."

She sat down on the bench again, watching him walk back to the crowd. He had a distinctive walk, exactly like Harry. His toes pointed out and he shifted his weight from leg to leg. "So maybe I should marry him. I'd have a nice home, a pleasant, undemanding companion. The kids wouldn't have to worry. I wouldn't have to worry. Nobody would have to worry. There'd be no guessing, no chances, no nothing.

"That's the trouble with Meyer. Always has been. I know what he's going to say before he opens his mouth. Harry may have been a *bullvon,* but he was exciting. Meyer's sweet, but he's so boring."

She sighed as she watched him disappear into the crowd around the bandstand. She put her hands over her head and stretched. "It's nice to be alone for a moment." She breathed in the warm night air, allowing herself to enjoy being away from the depressing hotel room with its air-conditioner hum, its smells of age and mildew and the inexpensive perfumes that had been spilled by who-knew-how-many women who had ended up in the Monte Excelsior, pursuing the Jewish widow's dream of love among the elderly.

She looked back, guiltily, at the crowd. She could see April in her orange pants dancing a cha-cha with Morris Fleischman.

"Oy vey." And, off to the right, she could just make out Meyer's silhouette as he stood talking to Frieda and Saul.

Once again she was reminded of Harry. She looked out to sea and thought of the day they had first met.

In the winter of nineteen thirty-three, she was the only working member of what was left of her family. Somehow she had gotten herself a job as a bookkeeper at the A&B Poultry Company on Fourteenth Street. It paid thirty dollars a week. "Thirty dollars is nothing to sneeze at," she remembered her father saying. "Thirty dollars a week is a lot of money."

She had felt so proud. But that trip back and forth! The BMT. Bums, Murderers, and Tramps. Though she loved the job. She sat in a small, glassed-in office above the area where the girls plucked the chickens. Allen Rabinowitz, the owner's son, sat at a desk next to her. He had either been thrown out of Harvard or forced to leave because "business wasn't so hot." She'd work the adding machine and do the books while he sat at his rolltop desk, his moon-shaped face tilted to one side, singing college songs, accompanying himself on the ukulele. Until his father would come in. Then Allen would put the uke away and pretend to get down to business.

"He never could," she thought, smiling. "I wonder what happened to Allen." She could almost hear him singing, in his thin, high voice, "Oh, we ain't got a barrel of money . . ."

It was Allen who had introduced her to Harry. They were walking across Fourteenth Street. It was December, it was snowing, and, at five-thirty, it was already dark. "Say, Ruth," Allen had said. "There's a fellow I have to talk to. He lives in Brooklyn and has a car. Maybe he'll give you a lift." The way he said it made her suspect the fellow was one Allen didn't want to talk to alone.

"That'd be great, Allen," she had said, putting her arm through his. She had felt motherly toward him.

He led her into a warehouse that looked like the New York headquarters for Al Capone, the sort of place where mobsters were killed. They went up a flight of stairs into a small, overheated office filled with a large table. Four men, all wearing hats, all smoking cigars, were playing serious pinochle.

"Hello, Harry," Allen said to the back of one of them.

"How you doing, kid?" Harry had asked, not looking around, playing a card. "You got the do-re-mi?"

"That's what I wanted to talk to you about, Harry . . ."

"Goddamn it to hell," one of the other card players said as Harry made a meld.

Allen looked at Ruth and then at the players. "There's a lady present, gentlemen," he said in a voice that threatened to break.

"Oh, yeah?" Harry had said, turning around, looking Ruth up and down from head to toe. "Oh. Sorry. I didn't see you, miss." He stood up and took off his hat. "I'm Harry Meyer."

Allen introduced her. "She lives in Brooklyn, Harry, and I thought if you were driving there . . ."

"How else would I be going, kid?" He looked at Ruth. "Whereabouts you live?"

"Avenue L off Ocean Parkway," she said in a tiny voice. He was big and tough and good-looking. A regular gangster. Nothing like the men—boys—she went out with who were too thin and going to night school to become CPAs. He looked dangerous. But nice dangerous. Like Cagney.

"It's right on my way. Meyer"—he turned and Ruth saw the resemblance between him and one of the players—"do me a favor and collect my winnings. I'll see you later."

"Sure, Harry." And Meyer had looked her up and down, from head to toe. But she wasn't looking at Meyer. She was watching Harry put on a navy-blue coat, adjust his slouch hat. He placed one big hand on each of their arms and escorted

them down the stairs, out of the warehouse, and into the
street. A black Studebaker was parked in front of the
warehouse.

"About the money, Harry . . ."

"Pay me when you get it, kid."

"But, Harry . . ."

"Listen, Allen, we don't want to talk business in front of the
lady. I said—now listen carefully—'Pay me when you get it.'
You never get it, you never pay me. I ain't losing sleep over
fifty bucks."

"Gee, thanks, Harry. Harry, thanks . . ."

"And I'm going to give you something else, too, kid: a
word of advice. Next time you borrow money from someone
you don't know so hot, be careful, huh? These loan sharks
down here, they put you in cement for twenty-five cents. You
understand?"

"I understand. I'm going to get you the money, too,
Harry."

"I'll never see it if I live to be a thousand," Harry had said,
starting the Studebaker, heading west across Fourteenth
Street. "You sweet on that *schlemiel?*"

"Allen? No. He's the boss's son."

"Who are you sweet on?"

"No one. At the moment."

He kept glancing at her as he drove. It made her nervous
but she liked it. He told her about the cigar business and how
he and his brother were thinking of moving over to New Jersey
with it. "Less competition in Jersey. It's too tough in New
York. In Jersey, I figure we can be ninety percent legit."

A block from her house, he stopped the car. "It's on the
next block," she told him.

"I know." He turned to her and looked at her. "You're some
classy dame, sister," he said. And though it was a line straight

from a George Raft film, it thrilled her right through. Being close to him thrilled her. "What're you doing tomorrow night?"

"I have a date," she said, frightened to admit it.

"Break it."

"My father has to approve all my dates in advance." Implicit was the belief that her father would never, ever approve of Harry.

"What time's this guy picking you up?"

"Seven-thirty."

"You like this guy?"

His name was Irwin Dermer and every time his long, skinny fingers touched hers, she felt queasy.

"He's a very nice person."

"I get it." He turned to start up the car but suddenly he pulled her to him and his mouth was on hers and she struggled, but not for very long. She found that her arms were around him. She had never felt sexual desire before, and long after she was in the house, her face burned with shame.

"You getting a fever, Ruthie?" her father wanted to know.

"No, Papa. I'm fine."

The next night, Saturday night, she and Irwin Dermer had just reached the corner when Harry drove up in the Studebaker, stepped out, and took Irwin's arm. "I'm going to give it to you straight, kid," he said in a soft voice that was hardly menacing. "I like this lady. She likes me. We want to be together tonight but I haven't passed her old man's inspection, see? So what I'm asking you is to do all of us a favor: go on home or to the movies or wherever you want to go and let us spend the evening together. What do you say?"

To give Irwin credit, he had turned his face, now a pale shade of gray, in her direction. "Is this what you want, Ruth?"

"I'm afraid it is, Irwin."

"Then why not? Sure." He reminded her, in that moment, of his own father, Simon Dermer, the tailor.

Harry removed his hand from Irwin's arm, asked him if they could drop him off anywhere ("No, thanks, no, that's okay") and had taken her to an upstairs Chinese restaurant on King's Highway where they ate chop suey and talked and talked and talked.

And later, in the car, they had kissed and kissed and kissed and his hands went over her body in places where they had no right to go and finally she pushed him away, saying, "I'm not that kind of girl." Even though she was certain, at that moment, that she was very definitely that kind of girl.

"I know. When can I pass Papa's inspection?"

He never did. Her father had become sick that week (well, he had been sick since the day Mama had died) and had died within the month.

Three months later, still a virgin (but just), she married Harry. They spent their honeymoon making love in their new apartment on Prospect Street in Elizabeth, New Jersey.

"And that," Ruth thought to herself, "was that."

She stood up, putting her memories away, thinking that she had better get back. She turned and the crowd around the bandstand separated for a moment. She had a glimpse of April and Morris doing a tango. At that distance, they looked quite good together, tall and slim and professional. She had no wish for a close-up. She walked in the opposite direction, to the end of the pier, where the fishermen were leaning against the concrete wall, looking out to the Atlantic, as silent as the darkness around them.

"Catch anything?" she asked one man because she was nervous and lonesome and a little scared.

He looked at her and smiled. The moonlight struck his face. He had thick, white-blond hair with a mustache and beard to

match. The moonlight picked out the laugh wrinkles around
his green eyes.

"Not a doggone nibble," he said. "Maybe you can bring me
luck, ma'am." He had a soft, southern accent which made him
seem especially polite.

He made room for her along the wall. After only a
moment's hesitation, she leaned up against the concrete. "To
hell with this white cotton dress," she thought. "I never liked
it from the day I bought it."

"You ever fish, ma'am?" the man next to her asked.

"You two want to talk, why don't you go back there?" one
of the other men said. "You're scaring all the fish away."

"Shoot, Abel," Ruth's fisherman (as she thought of him)
said.

"There ain't hardly no fish tonight anyway," another man
said. "The goddamn music drives them away."

"There's a lady present, Smitty," her fisherman said,
reminding her again of her first meeting with Harry.

"Quiet!" the little man called Abel shouted.

"Here, you go on and hold the rod," her fisherman
whispered. "I'm all tuckered out from holding on to the
bastard. Excuse me. The pole."

She took the fishing rod, feeling as if she had just been let in
on some kindly, conspiratorial group. It felt good in her
hands. Almost at the moment she took it, the string at the end
gave a sharp jerk and began to move up and down.

"You did it, honey," her fisherman shouted. "You got
yourself a bite. Reel the bastard in."

"I don't know how."

"You learn, by God." He put his arms around her.
Together they brought the fish up.

"It's not terribly large," she said, watching him carefully
remove the hook from its mouth.

"Large enough," he said, tossing it back. Then he looked at

her with those green eyes and explained, "I only fish for the sport. I can't stand the taste of them."

"Tell you the truth, I'm not too fond of fish, either."

"You did a fine job, ma'am, in reeling him in."

"I couldn't have done it without your help."

"Will you two stop that jabberwalling and allow me to get a little fishing done in peace now that they stopped that dangblasted music for a second?" Abel said.

The music. Ruth turned from the contemplation of her ruined (well, maybe it would wash) dress and looked at the opposite end of the pier. The crowd had split in two. Someone was lying on the dance floor. A woman. In orange trousers.

"Oh, my God in heaven," Ruth said, starting to run as fast as she could in her low white heels. "That's my friend April . . ."

 Twelve

Dr. Abraham Bellskie's office is on the fourth floor of the Financial National Federal Building, a green edifice at the corner where Washington Avenue meets Lincoln Mall in downtown Miami Beach. The waiting room, painted a cool lime green, has no windows. Its furniture is Danish and comfortable. There is a series of Utrillo prints on the wall, which, under almost any other circumstances, Ruth would have found interesting.

She tried to appreciate them but the effort that entailed was too much for her. Two women, of her age and station, were seated at the far end of the room under the sliding glass window through which could be seen a nurse, stiff and blond and efficient.

Ruth put her forefinger in the issue of the *Ladies' Home Journal* she had been attempting to read, then removed her finger and replaced the magazine on the table in front of her. She gave up. Neither the Utrillos nor the magazines could take the edge off the nervous fear she was feeling. "I hate this office," she told herself. "I hate the lime green walls and the prints and the magazines and the lack of windows. More than the waiting room, I hate the waiting."

The office reminded her of the waiting she had had to endure in the New York doctor's office way up on Fifth Avenue. "Your husband should be in a hospital," the doctor, the Bastard, Joseph Albender, had come out and said, abruptly, in front of a roomful of people. He had made it an accusation, as if she had kept her husband out of a hospital. "I'm getting someone to have him admitted."

"But what's the matter with him?" she had managed to ask.

"What's the matter with him?" Dr. Joseph Albender had repeated, looking down at her. "What's the matter with him? He's been suffering from arteriosclerosis for the past five years and the small-town quack you've been taking him to has told him to lay off the salt. The disease could have been arrested had your husband been put on a proper diet and exercise program. It could even have been reversed. Now he's suffered Jesus-knows-how-many strokes and I'm putting him into the Clinginstein Pavilion in a last-ditch effort to save what's left of him. But I'm not promising anything."

He had strode out of the room leaving one of his assistants to deal with her. "That bastard," she had said later, after Harry had been put into a room in the Clinginstein, after Nick had driven her to Elizabeth for Harry's pajamas and toiletries, and then made her move into the spare room in that terrible, filthy apartment he and Linda were subletting on West Seventy-eighth Street.

During the weeks that followed, as she walked helplessly around the Clinginstein's cavernous rooms, *yenta*-ing with the other patients and their families, waiting for Harry to be brought upstairs from the tests they were making him take, she was told that Albender was a famous bastard. "Maybe a great doctor," the night nurse had told her. "But that man has no heart, Mrs. Meyer. No heart."

And Harry lay on the high bed in the middle of the too large room, watching the rented television, not saying anything.

"There's nothing I can do for him," Albender had said on the day Harry was discharged. "He may live six months. He may live six years. The best place for him would be a nursing home but I can't see you doing the best thing. Talk to my assistant about medication and diet."

"You're a bastard," she had said to him in front of all his assistants and the nurses.

He hadn't responded, the almighty Dr. Albender. He turned and left the room, his coterie of white-coated guppies swimming after him. The nice assistant detached himself and gave her the printed diet, the prescriptions, the pat on the shoulder.

Later, in the Cadillac, the last of the Cadillacs, Nicky had driven and she had sat in the back. She was so frightened she had trouble speaking. But she knew she had to try. She had to try to pretend he was going to recover his memory, his sense of balance, his knowledge of who he was and where he was.

"I told you I was a little bit nuts," Harry had said, apropos of nothing, as they drove over the George Washington Bridge on that glorious sunlit day. She was glad he was sitting in the front seat, next to Nicky, so he wouldn't see her crying.

The nightmare had begun. Day by day, over the next few

years, his mind seemed to go like sand through the kitchen timer. "One day he couldn't remember his name. The next he couldn't remember mine."

The fear she was experiencing now, sitting in Dr. Bellskie's lime green office, was worse than the fear she had felt in the Bastard's. Then she didn't know what to expect. Now she did.

She stood up, sighing, and asked the nurse where the ladies' room was. She followed the girl's directions, went in, locked the door, picked up her dress, and pulled down her pants. She was very careful not to let any part of her body touch any part of the toilet seat. She was very careful not to think of April, not to question why it was taking her so long to be examined. She didn't want to cry.

She finished urinating, stood up, wiped herself, washed her hands, and leaned her head against the cool of the bathroom mirror. "That poor man," she said, Harry back in her thoughts again. "Did anyone ever suffer like that? He was so strong. So vital. Like a god out of a Rubens painting. To be reduced to that suffering, quivering child. Harry. My poor, poor Harry." She blotted the tears around her eyes with a tissue from the pack she always carried in her purse, reapplied lipstick, and went back into the waiting room, all the time praying, "Don't let it happen to April. Dear God, I beg you, don't let it happen to her."

April had always been there for her, through it all. Every day she came, like clockwork. "Go. Go," she'd shout.

"He's calling me. How can I go?"

"You put on your little coat and your little boots and you go."

"Would you go?"

"Draisal, if you don't get the fuck out of here, I'm going to have two patients on my hands. Now move it."

She had forced herself to leave the house, to drive to Elmora Avenue, to sit in the plastic-walled room while Gina cut her

hair, washed it, set it, sprayed it, and sent her on her way,
feeling better for the weekly ritual.

"How is he?" she would ask, before she had gotten out of
her coat. "Did he behave himself?"

"He was terrific. I took off all my clothes and I got into the
bed . . ."

"April!"

"You should get out more, Draisal. We watched 'Midday
Live,' I fed him his chopped liver, and now he's sleeping."

"He'll be calling me any minute."

"Only because you let him. You have to get out more,
Ruth."

"How can I get out more?"

"By putting on your little coat and your little boots . . ."

She had allowed April to convince her to start going to the
museums again. Once a month.

"That April!"

The fear that something was really wrong, that April hadn't
passed out on the pier's dance floor because she suddenly
realized she was "falling madly in love with Morris
Fleischman," cut through the chill of the over-air-conditioned
waiting room and made her shiver. "Please, God. Don't let
there be anything wrong. Nothing serious. Please."

The office door finally opened and April came out, a little
more color in her ravaged skin. "So?" Ruth asked, getting up,
feeling weak. "So?"

"We'll discuss it when we get outside," April said, looking
at the two women at the end of the room as if they were enemy
agents, taking her friend's arm, steering her out of the waiting
room.

"It couldn't be such good news," one of the women said in a
loud voice, "if they have to wait to get outside to talk about
it."

Ruth looked up at April in the elevator. "Well?"

"Wait until we're out on the street. This isn't a topic for public discussion."

They stepped out of the building onto Lincoln Mall, Ruth looking anxiously up into her friend's face every few seconds. "Are you going to let me know what the doctor said or do I have to wring it out of you?"

"I'm too weak, Draisal. I need a pastrami sandwich before I can summon up the strength to tell you."

"I'm going to kill her," Ruth said, feeling better because surely April wouldn't joke if it were anything serious. They crossed the mall and walked down Washington Avenue to the slightly kosher delicatessen they both enjoyed. It was a relief to get away from the mall with its shoppers' train, its stores filled with *chatchkas* and clothing. She remembered and preferred the old Lincoln Road with its four-door convertibles and higher reality.

Not that Washington Avenue had changed. If anything, it looked older, more like Pitkin Avenue than ever. The fish stores, Irving's Meat & Poultry Market, the Shopper's Paradise with everyone talking at top gusto in either Yiddish or accented English, haggling over oranges and plastic sandals and loaves of challah. If she closed her eyes, she was back in the Brooklyn of her youth.

In the dark, cool, and not particularly clean delicatessen dining room, they ordered pastrami sandwiches and Dr. Brown's Cel-Ray Tonics.

"If you don't tell me what Dr. Bellskie told you, April, I'm going to beat you up like you've never been beat up before."

"You and what army?"

"Me and this army," Ruth said, making a fist with her left hand.

"Pass the mustard."

"April!"

"Be quiet, Draisal. People are looking. He didn't say anything." She spread a lavish amount of mustard on her sandwich.

"He didn't say anything? You were with him for a little over two hours and he didn't say anything?"

"He asked a lot of questions."

"And you gave a lot of answers?"

"When I felt like it."

"April, so help me God, if you don't tell me . . ."

"I'm telling you, *yenta*. Listen: he said nothing was the matter."

Ruth examined her friend's face. There were deep wrinkles under her sad brown eyes. Her hair, with its red tips and brown roots, seemed especially forlorn, hanging limply across her too wide forehead. Her lips, needing lipstick, were set in a frown, as if she wanted to cry.

"You look like something's the matter."

"This pastrami is too fatty."

"April, a woman doesn't pass out because of nothing. She passes out because of something. Right or wrong?"

"I'm looking down at the mouth, my dear Draisal, because the good doctor laid a few home truths on me, as they say. One, I am a woman no longer in her first, second, or even third youth, I am an officially designated senior citizen, sixty-seven years of age . . ."

"Sixty-eight, going on sixty-nine, but who's counting?"

". . . who is in the midst of making a major emotional adjustment (moving to Miami) as well as a major physical adjustment (moving to Miami). I am not used to strenuous exercise. Dancing is strenuous exercise. I have to work up to it. In the beginning, one cha-cha a night. Later on two, and so on. It's like Anita Sarno and her contact lenses. I, too, have to establish wearing time.

"In short, darling Ruth, you can take that concerned look off your *punim* because, after two hours, that *fahstukenah* doctor told me, and I'm quoting, 'You're not a kid anymore, Mrs. Pollack.' "

"That was it? You're not lying to me, April?"

"That and I have to take B-twelve shots a couple of times a week for a while. Maybe I have a little anemia."

"Ah. Pernicious anemia."

"Right away it's pernicious. I think you're only comfortable when you have someone really sick around you."

Ruth put her sandwich down. An instant lump had developed in her throat. "April. April! Is that nice? Or even true?"

"No. I'm sorry. I take that back. I deny I even said it." She put her hand on Ruth's. "I was upset."

"You know I'm only concerned because I care about you, don't you?"

"I do, Ruth. I do. The whole episode made me crazy. Forgive me. It was a terrible thing to say."

"Forgiven. Now, let's go back to the Monte and rest." They had emerged into the sunlight and the crowds of Washington Avenue. Men stood along the curbs between the parking meters, looking lost and stoic, as their wives bargained with the merchants.

"I'm going shopping."

"Now you're shopping? What're you buying, April?"

"A new bathing suit."

"You just got a new bathing suit."

"There's a Miami Beach law that I'm not allowed two?"

"You know something, April? You're impossible when you're in this mood. Come back to the Monte and I'll make you a cup of tea."

"I'll meet you there later, darling. Okay?"

The two women kissed. "April?"

"What?"

"I'm so glad it was nothing."

"*You're* glad? I'll see you later, *mamala.*"

Ruth watched as April made her way through the crowd toward Lincoln Mall. She walked so tall and straight. Once she turned and waved. A reassuring wave. "I don't like it," Ruth thought as she joined the line waiting for the bus. "I don't like it one little iota."

The thought of Frieda and the girls waiting for her at the pool wasn't what she would call "an appetizing proposition." When the bus came, she didn't get on it. Instead, she hailed a taxi.

The city of Miami Beach's Bass Museum of Art is located behind the public library and indeed was once the library before the city planners decided, in nineteen sixty-three, that what Miami Beach needed was a rectangular glass and steel building for its books rather then a multiniched, multi-columned extravaganza. The old museum building hides behind the new library as if it were ashamed of its age. A statue of Dr. Luis Henry Debayle, given to the city of Miami Beach by Nicaragua, faces the museum and looks uncomprehending, as if it can't decide what either it or the museum is doing in such a location.

Directly inside the doorway is a pamphlet describing the foundation of the museum in a short paragraph and going on to give a fairly well-detailed biography of Mr. Bass. Ruth was not surprised, after looking at the pamphlet, to find several works by Mr. Bass hanging in the museum's central gallery. She thought they had nice colors.

She wondered why there were two Steinway grand pianos in the gallery as she looked at Rubens's *St. Anne and the Holy Family,* the reputed gem of the collection. She didn't usually respond to religious art—even Rubens's—and passed on to inspect "a pair of priceless handwoven Belgian tapestries," each forty by sixteen feet, in what was called the Tapestry Room. She wondered how long they had taken to weave, but again was not moved by the artistry involved.

She climbed to the second floor, where Daumier and Picasso prints were on display along with more religious art— madonnas and baby-faced Jesuses.

She had turned to leave when she noticed a wrought-iron staircase leading to an unpublicized third floor. She stepped up it and emerged on a small landing. There had been a few people on the lower floor, but here she was by herself. She went through an arch into an oblong room where two men had just hung a painting that took her breath away, though she couldn't say why.

It was a large painting, some five feet high, depicting a pink teakettle, steam pouring out of its spout. It seemed as if the kettle was moving, as if the boiling water it held were forcing it to rock back and forth on the old-fashioned stove on which it sat. It was an amusing painting, almost a cartoon. At the same time, it was especially appealing in a way that the Rubens in the main gallery never would be. The kettle was not an inanimate object but had a life and a personality of its own.

She was distracted by the voices of the two men coming from the opposite side of the gallery, where they had hung one of Mr. Bass's still lifes, as different from the kettle as could be.

The shorter man, wearing a pin-striped northern suit, placed his hand on the shoulder of the taller, blond man. The blond man flinched and stepped back.

"Did I hurt you, Max?" the shorter man said.

"No, sir. Not at all. It's just that I'm peculiar about being touched. I never like to touch anyone unless I really like them. And vice versa."

"Does that mean you don't like me?" the shorter man said lightly.

"It simply means that I don't know you very well."

They turned to find Ruth staring at them. "I'm sorry, madam," the shorter man said. "This is a private gallery . . ."

"I know the lady, Carter. It's all right."

The bearded blond fisherman came toward her, his green eyes smiling. "Last night I didn't have an opportunity to introduce myself, ma'am. My name is Max Rhoads."

She wondered what it was before it was changed (Rodzinski?) as she told him her name. She noticed that he didn't shake her hand and wondered if he was allergic to her touch, too.

Feeling awkward, she turned to reexamine the teakettle.

"Do you like it?" he asked in his soft southern voice.

"I think so," she said. "I think I like it very much." She looked up to find him looking down at her. "Do you work here?" she asked, flustered.

"On rare occasions. Once in a great while I help them to hang paintings for exhibits. I'm what you might call their gentleman picture hanger." He smiled his private smile. "Is your friend all right?"

"Yes, thank God. Case of too much cha-cha-cha."

"I come down with a touch of that myself every now and then." As with April, she had to look up to talk to him. She hadn't realized, on the pier, how tall and broad he was. Like Harry. He had touched her on the pier, she remembered, when they reeled in the fish together.

"Do you paint?" he was asking her.

"No. No. I'm just an appreciator."

"I have a feeling, ma'am, that you are very fine appreciator."

At that moment, the other man, Carter, called to him from an inner room. "It's been nice seeing you again, Miss Ruth," he said. "Perhaps we will meet on the pier again? Soon?"

"Perhaps," she said, leaving the oblong room, descending the wrought-iron staircase, annoyed that she had neglected to find out who had painted the teakettle, stepping out into the afternoon sunshine.

All the way downtown on the bus she found herself thinking of Max Rhoads, of his green eyes, of the two silver rings he wore on his right hand (Harry had worn a diamond on his pinky; Meyer, a star sapphire), of the white-blond hair that came down over the collar of his shirt.

She wondered if she would have time, after going to Meyer's for dinner, to take a little stroll along the pier.

 Thirteen

"For a few dollars more, I could have had the ocean. But I said to myself, 'Meyer, what do you need the ocean for? All you have to do is go down to the pool and you see the ocean.' This way, I look out the window and I got the Indian River."

Ruth looked through the picture window at the still waters and split-level houseboats of Miami Beach's Indian River and thought she'd have spent the few dollars more.

Meyer excused himself to see "how the kitchen is doing" and Frieda led her through the high-rise apartment Meyer had bought in Turretsky's Alpine Palace and Spa, a condominium at Fiftieth and Collins, in the heart of the lush apartment strip.

"You can imagine what it cost," Frieda said, as she opened the closets in the master bedroom to reveal Meyer's collection of silk suits and polyester leisure clothes. "And not everyone

can get into TAPS. You have to go before a board, yet." Frieda
switched on the exhaust fan feature in the master bath.

"TAPS?" Ruth asked.

"Turretsky's Alpine Palace and Spa," Frieda explained,
guiding Ruth down the long, carpeted hall to the guest
bedroom with the half bath. "It's what they play when you go
to bed in the army."

"Perhaps they should have called it Reveille."

Frieda led her through the small kitchen, where a short
Cuban woman was sweating, despite the central air condition-
ing. They passed Saul, seated next to a lazy Susan filled with
meatballs and chopped liver, and entered the living room,
which featured a motel-like glass door on its far wall.

"Step out onto the terrace, Ruthie," Frieda said, sliding the
door open with some difficulty. "It's like another room."

"I'm not fond of heights," Ruth said, allowing Frieda to
propel her onto the small square of poured concrete. Frieda,
also not fond of heights, followed cautiously, sliding the
glass door back into its closed position ("We don't want to
let the air conditioner out"), keeping her back to the building's wall.

"You know," Frieda said, trying not to look down at
Collins Avenue, sixteen floors below, with its six o'clock traffic
and joggers, "this could all be yours. Every square parqueted
foot of it. All you have to do is say one little word."

Ruth moved a step forward and managed to sit in one of the
molded plastic lounge chairs Meyer had bought with the
apartment.

"So, Ruthie," Frieda said, having followed her example,
"let's quit all the kidding around. What do you say? Do you or
do you not want to marry Meyer and live like a queen in this
palace which is, even I have to admit, as clean as gold? Did
you see the sculpted carpet on the living-room floor? Not a

drop. Not a stain. Looks brand new. Admit it, Ruthie.
Doesn't it look like it came right out of the showroom?"

"As if it were woven this morning."

"One hundred percent nylon."

"I thought for one terrible moment it was wool."

"So, Ruthie, tell me, will you or won't you . . . ?"

"Why don't you let Meyer speak for himself, Frieda? And
speaking of that gentleman, I think we'd better go in now
because he's snapping his fingers at us."

Inside, the heavy cherrywood furniture, souvenirs of
Meyer's northern household, looked as if they were temporary,
on loan. The Cuban woman announced that "dinner is now
being served" and they took their seats around the mahogany
dining table.

"She's a wonderful cleaner," Frieda whispered, as she tucked
the cloth napkin into the bodice of her dress.

"It's how she is as a cook that we're concerned about," Saul
said, tucking his own napkin into the elastic waistband of his
trousers. "If this were a perfect world, we would all be cooking
for ourselves."

"And you would starve, *yonkle*. Be quiet and eat your soup.
If you stain that shirt, God help you."

"You're some advertisement for marriage," Saul said,
poising his spoon like a conductor positioning his baton,
moving his head down to the bowl, examining the liquid in it,
and then proceeding to slosh the soup into his open mouth.

"You understand," Meyer was saying, "I don't eat this way
every night. I want to be on the up-and-up with you, Ruthie.
Mirabelle is here only because it's an extra-special occasion. I
mean, if we were to . . . I mean, if I were to marry again, I
should expect my wife to cook, no?" He cut through the
enormous slab of brisket Mirabelle had slid onto the plate in
front of him and looked at her. Ruth put her hand on his. The

brisket, Mirabelle, the heavy furniture, his disingenuousness made her feel tender toward him.

"I do think," she said, "that if you were to marry again, Meyer, you should definitely expect your wife to cook."

Later, after the iceberg salad and the cherry torte, he asked Ruth if she had seen the terrace. "I wouldn't mind seeing it again," she said. She felt she couldn't deny him the terrace.

"Ruthie," he said, once they were safely seated above Collins Avenue, "have you given any more thought to the possibilty of marrying me? I wouldn't expect to share your bed, Ruthie. It would be, what they say, a convenient marriage. You'd have a nice home, a free life. What could be so terrible?"

"No one said it would be terrible, Meyer."

"So say yes, Ruthie."

"It's too soon, Meyer."

"At least say you won't stop me from asking every now and then."

"All right, Meyer, I won't stop you from asking . . . every now and then."

He smiled a smile that was almost too reminiscent of Harry. "I wouldn't want to wrap you up in any boxes, Ruthie. You know that, don't you?"

"I know it, Meyer," she said, kissing him on his solid, unblemished cheek.

Meyer drove them down to the Monte in his Coupe de Ville, received yet another kiss from Ruthie with embarrassed gratification, waited for the three of them to get safely inside the Monte's courtyard, pushed the button that locked the car doors, and drove back uptown whistling, "I'm getting married in the morning. / Ding dong the bells are going to chime . . ."

In the meantime, Ruth was saying good night to Frieda and Saul, who were arguing about how much brisket he had eaten. ("I'm going to regurgitate, Saul, if you say brisket one more time." "Brisket.") They disappeared down the walkway that led to the Monte's annex and Ruth climbed the stairs, wondering if she was going to get acid indigestion, resolving to take a Tums "just in case."

"It's only ten o'clock," she said to herself as she took off her good navy, hung it carefully in the closet which still smelled of mildew though she sprayed it religiously every morning with Lysol. She put on her comfortable girdle and her tan trousers and went outside. There was a dim, unusual light coming from under April's door. There was also the sound of romantic music, Mantovani and his strings.

Ruth knocked and called out softly, "Yoo-hoo." It took several moments for April to open the door and then she flung it open and said, before she realized Ruth was standing there, "Come in, my darling."

"Certainly." Ruth stepped into the room, which no longer looked like any part of the Monte Excelsior. Every possible surface—the davenport, the tables, even the television set—had been covered with tie-dyed Indian bedspreads. Candles flickered around the room in blue glass holders. Incense burned in the lap of a brass Buddha. A portable stereo system, hidden under the dining table, was responsible for the Mantovani. "My God," Ruth said.

"Ruth, dear," April said, taking her friend by the arm, "if you don't mind, I'm going to bed early . . ."

"April . . ."

"I decided today that if I'm going to live in this joint, I'm going to make it as attractive as possible. Now, darling Draisal," April said in what she thought was an upper-class accent, "I must get my beauty sleep, *n'est-ce pas?*"

Before she knew it Ruth was on the landing, April was kissing her and returning to her transformed room, shutting the door firmly after her.

Slightly dazed by the heavy and new and presumably expensive perfume April had been wearing, by the new decor and the new makeup and the new chenille robe April had been sporting, Ruth went down the stairs, wondering if her friend were having her much heralded nervous breakdown.

She went through the lobby, where Armando was dozing at the switchboard and Morris Fleischman, wearing the sort of quilted smoking jacket Ronald Coleman once wore, was staring at a gold pocket watch he was holding in one hand, gently tapping it with the other. The gesture was meant to indicate, Ruth supposed, that Morris was waiting for someone. She almost asked who the lucky lady was but decided she didn't want to know.

"Good evening, Madame Meyer," Morris said, looking up as if he were being called back from a deep hypnosis. "May I help you in any way?"

"No, thank you. Just going to get a little fresh air, on the pier."

"They say," he said in a voice of imminent doom, "that one shouldn't walk out on the pier late at night. One could be attacked." He put the watch to his ear and shook it. "Or worse."

Ruth escaped into the night and out onto the pier, which did have an ominous quality. A light fog enveloped it, dimming the lamplights. "Still," she thought, feeling a momentary qualm, "who'd want to rape me besides Morris Fleischman and it looks like he has other fish to fry tonight."

It was lonely on the pier but she was feeling lonely ("What's got into April to make her get up her room like a house of ill repute? Those terrible *schmatas* everywhere!") and it seemed an appropriate place to be. She liked the smell of the salt air, the sound of the waves slapping against the pylons. She suddenly felt an anticipatory happiness which evaporated as she reached the end of the pier and it didn't look as if anyone were there. She was ridiculously disappointed.

"He didn't say definitely. He only said perhaps," she told herself, continuing to walk to the very end. The thought that she might marry Meyer after all came to her. "I'm not enjoying being a widow. And as Frieda so delicately pointed out, I'm lucky. Someone wants me. Look at all the women around no one wants."

She reached the end of the pier. She saw a flash of yellow beside her and gave a little gasp. She hadn't seen the fisherman in the yellow slicker kneeling behind the washbasins, packing his equipment.

"Hello, Miss Ruth," he said, smiling, standing up. "I was ready to give up on you."

"We didn't make it definite."

"No, that's true. Would you like to fish some? I could reassemble the—"

"No, thank you. I only wanted to say hello and good-bye. It's so late." She smiled up at him. In the moonlight he seemed especially blond and tall, like a drawing of Paul Bunyan in a child's book.

"You look like a pioneer," she said after a moment, surprised that she had said it.

"And you look like a good woman."

"Not so good. Not so bad. How were the fish tonight?" she asked, changing the subject. She felt as inept at conversation as a twelve-year-old girl with new braces on her teeth.

"Sleeping."

"That's just what I should be doing."

They walked back along the pier together, not speaking.

The silence was companionable. She felt, for no reason she could think of, comfortable walking alongside the big blond man. She almost took his arm.

When they reached the Monte, she told him it was the place where she lived.

"I know that, Miss Ruth. I followed you the other night when you took your friend home. Just wanted to make absolutely certain you were all right." He looked down at her, smiling with his green eyes.

"You like that beard?" she asked, again surprised at herself.

"I sure enough do. You like it?"

"You know something? I think I do."

He was about to say good night, to turn away, when he thought better of it. "Ruth," he said, "you know, I lied to you back there on the pier and I think I had better set the record straight. No use starting off on a lie, is there?"

"What was the lie?"

"I wasn't thinking you looked like a good woman. I was thinking you looked like a damned attractive one. You got a sparkle in those eyes that makes me just know you're full of piss and vinegar under that ladylike exterior. You're just holding it all in because that's what you Yankee women have been taught. I'd like to see you sometime when you let it all out."

"You've got a lot of nerve, Mr. Rhoads. A lot of nerve."

"Max, Ruth. I know. People been telling me that since I can remember. I've been trying to curb my mouth ever since I realized how much trouble it could get me into. I haven't had too much success. I sincerely do apologize if I gave offense, ma'am."

"Apology accepted and I'm not even sure, big shot, if I'm offended. I have to think it over."

"Would you like to think it over over dinner one night?"

"Yes, I think so."

"Then I will call you very soon. Good night, Ruth."

"Good night, Max."

She watched him walk back toward the pier where presumably he had parked his car. "He moves nicely," she thought. "With purpose."

She tiptoed through the lobby, not wishing to awaken Armando, and went up the stairs, thinking of the funny conversation she had had, of the odd feelings she experienced whenever she was near "that Max," of the fact that she had wanted to touch him even though she was aware he didn't like being touched.

She sighed and realized a door farther along the landing was being opened. "Who could be strolling around at this hour?" No one at the Monte stayed up much past ten-thirty. She stopped, supporting herself against one of the wrought-iron posts. Whoever it was, was being especially quiet. Then she saw a familiar, too thin shadow step out of a room, tasseled loafers held high. Even after the moon revealed it to be Morris Fleischman, an enormous but melancholy grin spreading across his face, she still found herself not wanting to believe what she had seen.

"But facts are facts," she said, letting herself into her room. Morris Fleischman had been waiting in the lobby for a late rendezvous. April had spent one hundred dollars on Indian bedspreads, candles, and incense. The apartmentette Morris had been slinking out of belonged to April.

Morris Fleischman had made another conquest. "And I had to be an eyewitness," Ruth thought, folding her trousers, giving the closet a spritz of Lysol, feeling lonely again. April had always told her everything.

 Fourteen

It was to be two days after Chanukah before Ruth and April were to meet again. The witnessing by Ruth of Morris Fleischman slipping out of April's apartmentette had estranged the two friends in a way nothing else ever could. "I never thought she would go that far," Ruth told herself. The truth was that she felt betrayed. "She didn't even discuss it with me."

Ruth refused Frieda's invitation to accompany her to the Washington Avenue bingo parlors and spent her time revisiting Mr. Bass's museum (where the entrance to the third floor was disappointingly locked) and sitting in Lummus Park watching the men and women who might have been her parents play cards and practice square dances for the upcoming folk dance festival.

On Christmas Day, a holiday observed only by Armando, who had left Belle in his place at the switchboard, she woke up feeling she had overslept, groping for her watch, which had unaccountably stopped. She picked up the telephone and asked for the time.

"A quarter past," Belle answered, switching off. It wasn't until Ruth had jiggled the buttons several times and got Belle back on the wire that she learned it was a quarter past nine.

"I'll go down to the coffee shop," Ruth said to herself, getting dressed. "If I have another bowl of Special K, I'll be ill." She wondered if the stores on Lincoln Mall would be open. "Maybe I'll do a little shopping." She had always disliked Christmas and its *Saturday Evening Post* promise of family happiness.

There was but one occupied table in the Monte's La Salle à Manger. April was eating an English muffin, discussing life with Mae Weissman and Miriam Siegal. "Her new pals," Ruth thought.

"Hello, Draisal," April said impudently. Ruth sat at a table set for one, next to the plate-glass window that looked out on the pool.

"Your friend," the elephantine Mae Weissman said, in what for her was a whisper, "isn't so friendly."

"She's suffering," April said, *sotto voce.*

"From what, may I ask?" Miriam Siegal said, touching the back of her bright red hair, which had been arranged to resemble a kaiser roll.

"Jealousy. Pure and simple." April lifted her orange-juice glass, draining it as if it were whiskey and she were John Wayne.

That did it. Ruth got out of her chair and quickly left the coffee shop.

"Well, you certainly told her where to get off," Mae Weissman said as the door swung to and fro.

"I certainly did," April said, not looking happy.

It was not until New Year's Eve day, the day of Morris Fleischman's Gala New Year's Eve Party, that Ruth and April were to come face-to-face again.

Ruth, determined not to be driven to Lummus Park, knowing that the library and the museum had given her all they could, had left her apartmentette early in the morning, wearing her dark blue bathing suit and her white terry-cloth robe. "I'm here to get sun," she told herself, "I'm going to get sun." She hesitated on the landing, looking down at the courtyard.

The girls had already staked out their seats. The boys— Saul, Morris Fleischman, and two brothers-in-law with hearing aids from Cincinnati who fought incessantly—were playing pinochle. It was a scene she had been part of at resorts up and down the eastern seaboard throughout her life. When she was a child, at Far Rockaway, on the beach in front of the house her father, at great expense, had rented for a month. In the Catskills hotels Harry had enjoyed, early in their married life. Later, as a mother, in Bradley Beach, New Jersey. And still later, when they were richer and less happy, here in Miami Beach.

It was a scene—the girls in their chaises longues, the boys at the card tables—that never failed to depress her. "There must be a better way," she thought, "to kill time."

As she walked down the stairs she saw Miriam Siegal waving to her from her place by the pool, pointing to a chaise next to hers. "I've been holding it for you, Ruth," Miriam, the redheaded diminutive *yenta* from Jamaica Estates, Long Island, declared. She had been quick to see the possibilities inherent in the well-publicized estrangement of the two friends. Ruth would be an honorable catch as her own best friend while April's discomfort would add piquancy to a season that already promised to be amply rewarding to those residents of the Monte interested in social interaction.

"I'm not taking any pleasure out of this," Mae Weissman announced. "It breaks my heart to see two such pals suddenly enemies. However, as an observer of human nature, I certainly will keep my eyes open for future developments and report them as they occur."

The other girls, while not precisely echoing Mae's words, shared her sentiments. "What's going to happen?" was the question. Would the split escalate, like the famous war between Harriet Kartzman and Minnie Marcus? That one resulted in the two ladies moving, at first to opposite ends of the pool, and later (the pool was barely big enough for Mae Weissman, let alone for those healthy eaters), checking out of the Monte on the same day and, oh, wonderful coincidence, checking into the Ponce de León some fifteen minutes later where they fell into one another's arms and instantly became best friends all over again.

No one liked to choose sides, but it was true that both April and Ruth, in their short tenure at the Monte, had won their allies.

Frieda, by virtue of kinship, was expected to lead Ruth's campaign and did so, taking the offensive by announcing at poolside that "Ruth comes from a much finer background than April and, of course, as you know, ladies, background will out. Ruth's father was a manufacturer of children's clothing, while April's father, well, least said, soonest mended, and far be it from me to spread scandal, but when the police raided his office on Nineteenth Street in New York City, I wouldn't want to tell you what they found there. Every single one of those girls was under sixteen.

"And," she went on, putting her hand on Muriel Resnick's shoulder, signaling her that she was not through yet, not by a long shot, "do you know what that woman had the *chutzpah,* the colossal gall to do at my nephew Nicky's *bar mitzvah?* Just before the Viennese table was wheeled out, she put her arm around the sweet *boichek* and said, right into the microphone so that everyone could hear: 'Now that you're a man, Nick, what're you going to do about it?'

"She's always been man crazy even while her poor *schlemazel* of a husband, may he rest in peace, was alive. And I wouldn't put it past her to be after the men right now." Frieda laid down her knitting needles, took a deep breath and a long, slow look at Belle Fleischman, who was working the *TV Guide* crossword puzzle. When Belle looked up to meet her gaze, Frieda found new breath and resumed. "And now, when Ruth is on the verge of becoming engaged to my eldest brother, Meyer,

which is fitting and well and as it should be, April has gotten
on her high horse and caused this argument."

"What argument?" Belle, pencil poised, wanted to know.

"The argument between Ruth and April."

"Yes, I hear you, Frieda. But what *is* the argument?"

Frieda had to admit that she didn't know the details.

"That's not all you don't know," Belle said, putting on her
bifocals, giving up her chaise, going to the third floor to have a
word or two with Maria Carmen.

"Ruth gives herself airs," Mae Weissman, a more succinct
speaker than Frieda, said. "And she's a snob. Furthermore, she
also happens to be insincere." With some effort, Mae turned
herself over on her back, resembling a beached whale in a
plum-colored bathing suit.

"As if she would know sincerity if sincerity came over and
knocked on her head," Miriam Siegal said, taking an apricot
from the brown paper bag at her side, popping it into her
mouth, sucking noisily on the pit.

At that moment, Ruth forced a smile onto her face and,
sitting down on the chaise Miriam had been patting, said good
morning to everyone. Everyone, supporter and nonsupporter
alike, felt it their duty to return the greeting.

Ruth closed her eyes, saying: She didn't feel like a little
canasta; no, she was feeling fine and only wanted a short nap in
the sun.

"You're sure you have enough sunscreen?" Miriam wanted
to know. "Sun can do terrible things to your skin. Look at
poor Mae."

After a while they left her alone, going on to talk of sales
and grandchildren and other feuds, other adulteries.

"The girls," she thought, as she allowed herself to drowse.
"The girls." Throughout her life they had been there, a
continuous-play tape of aphorisms, bon mots, sage and pithy

advice. "Maybe if they had had to work, they'd have something better to talk about."

A bitter memory came to her. She had been in her forties. Nicky and Audrey were both in school. She had had absolutely nothing to do. So, as a kind of surprise, without Harry knowing, she had applied to be an Avon lady. She had had enough of being a Temple B'nai Israel sister-girl.

The interview, to be held at the Elizabeth Carteret Hotel on North Broad Street, made her nervous. Until she found herself in the Jefferson Room with all the others. She had realized that though they were gentile and came from less affluent households, the other women were after the same thing as she. Not money. Though for most of them there was that. But self-esteem.

Mrs. White, the interviewer, was pleased. "I don't believe we've ever had an Avon lady based in your neighborhood before, Mrs. Meyer. And do you know something? I have a feeling you're going to do extremely well."

She had been given a green-and-white Avon bag, hers to keep no matter what happened, a kit that went inside it, and a one-hour selling lesson.

Harry had forced her to return the kit. "I ain't working fourteen hours a day so my wife can go out and be a traveling saleswoman. And what about your feet?" he had asked, when he saw the expression on her face. "You never want to go anywhere because you're always squawking about your feet being tired and now you want to *schlep* all over Elizabeth? Nothing doing."

"I'll use my car."

"Forget it. You need a bigger allowance? I'll give you a bigger allowance. You return that kit. Harry Meyer's wife is not going to be the Avon lady."

She had returned the kit. With apologies. Mrs. White had

been sympathetic. She understood. Ruth had, too. It was her last chance, she felt, to be someone other than Harry Meyer's wife.

She had kept the free Avon bag. She still had it, storing her own cosmetics in it.

"If only I had been stronger. But I was a Draisal, as April would say." April. She opened her eyes and saw April sitting next to her, on Miriam Siegal's chaise longue.

"You sleeping, *yenta?*" April asked, and Ruth knew that the worst was over.

"A little snooze. Where you been?" They were going to pretend—at least for the girls—that nothing had happened.

"At the doctor's for a shot of B-twelve."

"I knew a woman who died from a shot of B-twelve," Mae Weissman said, not pleased to see the adversaries having a peaceful talk.

"I knew a woman who died from a big mouth," April said. "Not to mention advanced obesity and a loose pussy."

"You calling me a 'loose pussy,' April Pollack, is like Nixon calling Agnew a thief." Mae Weissman gathered her mammoth robe and beach towel around her and made her way to her room. "Such a low class of clientele at this dump, I never saw before."

Ruth put her hand over her mouth and laughed. April didn't bother putting her hand over her mouth. "I'm a mean old bitch, ain't I?" April said.

"No one ever said that just because you get older, you get nicer."

"More words of wisdom from the Yiddish philosophy major."

"You missed them, didn't you?" Ruth asked.

April looked at her friend and put her hand on Ruth's. "You bet I did, *mamala*. You bet I did." There were tears in her eyes. "We buddies again?"

"Yes, April, we are buddies again."

"About Morris . . ."

"That's a subject we don't have to discuss."

"I just want to say one thing: it's more than sex, Ruthie. That man is giving me something I've always wanted and never had: romance with a capital *R*." She leaned over, kissed Ruth, and sat back, taking a deck of cards from her TWA bag. "Now that that's settled, what about a little gin rummy, kid? Tenth of a cent a point."

 Fifteen

"Ten days ago he said he'd call me and I haven't heard a peep out of him." The green eyes were haunting her. She had been to the pier half a dozen times, at all hours of the evening, and found several fishermen, none of them six feet two with white-blond hair growing over the collars of their shirts. In one way, she hadn't minded the feud with April: it had taken her mind off Max.

When the telephone gave its startled ring that New Year's Eve day afternoon, she grabbed the receiver.

"Hello, Ruthie? Meyer. How are you?"

"Fine. How are you, Meyer?"

"Fine. What's new?"

"Nothing, Meyer. What's new with you?"

"Nothing, Ruthie."

There was a long pause as they both listened to the sounds of the Miami Beach telephone system in operation and tried to think of something to say. Meyer was first. "I'm calling, Ruthie, because we have a date tonight, right?"

"Right."

"I thought we could have a bite to eat and then go on to the dance."

"Maybe we could eliminate the dance, Meyer."

"The Monte's Twenty-sixth Annual New Year's Eve Dance? I promised Morris Fleischman I would come. I couldn't go back on my word, Ruthie."

"What time are you picking me up?"

"Say about five-thirty?"

"Say about seven."

"We'll compromise: six-fifteen."

She felt tired as she took the good black out of the closet and inspected the jet beads. "I want to go to a dance with Meyer like I want to go to Perth Amboy." She laid the dress carefully on the davenport and sat down next to it. "What I feel like doing is taking a long walk up Madison Avenue. A nice, slow walk." She wanted to look at the rich Italians in the expensive Italian shops. She wanted to be shocked at the prices of the shoes. She wanted to walk over to Fifth and the Frick Museum, to sit on a bench and enjoy Rembrandt's *Polish Rider*. It was one of the few Rembrandts she genuinely enjoyed, mostly because the rider was so beautiful and the horse was so obviously a fake.

Sighing, Ruth stood up, put on the good black, and went to April's apartmentette—still covered with the tie-dyed fabrics—to have it zipped up. "You don't look so hot, April," Ruth said, after the zipping was completed, trying not to let the odor of the incense overcome her. "You're as pale as a piece of gefilte fish."

"My new makeup. It's supposed to give me a bloodless vampire look. Why are you dressed at this hour?"

"I'm going to Wolfie's with Meyer for a bite before the dance."

"I don't envy you. Your brother-in-law is a very dear man, Ruthie, but table manners he hasn't got."

Ruth acknowledged the truth of April's observation some forty-five minutes later as Meyer chomped and chewed his way through the imported skinless and boneless sardine salad topped with raw onion he had ordered at Wolfie's.

"You got everything you need, Ruthie?" She was eating a pastrami sandwich with a side of potato salad and a cup of weak tea.

"Yes, thanks, Meyer."

They were sitting in the Celebrity Room under a blown-up photograph of Katharine Hepburn taken when she was a young woman. Ruth wondered what Hepburn, young or old, would make of the Celebrity Room's plywood paneled walls, red banquettes, and curvaceous hostess.

"You seem a little quiet, Ruthie."

"I'm sorry, Meyer." She put her hand on his. He was, in so many ways, a child. A great big child concerned for her well-being. "I was thinking."

"Tell you the truth, Ruthie, so was I. Remember when we used to come here in the old days, when Harry was alive, may he rest in peace? How that boy could eat. Remember how he could eat?"

Ruth remembered with what gusto her late husband had eaten and what he had eaten and that both had contributed heavily to the way in which he died.

"You eat sensibly, Meyer."

"I do what the doctor tells me. No eggs, not too much meat, easy on the pastry. No salt whatsoever. That's why, knock on wood"—he rapped the Formica tabletop with his knuckles—"I'm in good health." He looked at her. "You wouldn't have to take care of a sick man, Ruthie."

"That's a comforting thought, Meyer."

"By the by," he said, spearing a sardine, cramming it intact into his mouth, "how's your health?"

"A drop of high blood pressure but nothing to worry about. You wouldn't have to take care of a sick woman, Meyer."

"But I would, Ruthie," he said putting down his fork, "I would. You know that, don't you?"

"Yes, I do know that, Meyer."

"Even if you were confined to a wheelchair, I would still go through with it, Ruthie."

"I know, Meyer."

"So what do you say, Ruthie?"

"I say I'd like another cup of tea, Sweet 'n' Low on the side."

"And I say a baked apple, no cream."

Ruth and Meyer arrived at the pier as the New Year's Eve Twenty-sixth Anniversary Dance was just getting under way. Pink balloons and yellow streamers had been tied to the benches, the lampposts, and the door handles of the girls' and boys' rooms. Gold glitter letters, six feet high, stood atop the bandstand, spelling out HAPPY NEW YEAR.

Attired in matching gold glitter tuxedos, Piccolo Pete and his band were swinging and swaying with their version of "Rum and Coca-Cola." Belle, in a satin ball gown with an old sweater on her shoulders, was collecting invitations and selling tickets, announcing over and over again, like a damaged record, "No discounts tonight. Absolutely no discounts tonight."

Morris, who looked as if he had applied a full bottle of Vaseline to his thinning black hair, wore a navy-blue dinner jacket with a frilled, powder-blue dress shirt. As Ruth and Meyer entered the pier, Morris stepped up to the podium and Piccolo Pete brought "Rum and Coca-Cola" to a close, the band members standing up and singing, "Working for the Yankee dollar, cha-cha-cha."

Morris waited until the crowd had achieved a relative silence before he picked up the bullhorn through which he made poolside announcements ("Happy Birthday, Sharon Lee Shuster. Happy Birthday, Sharon Lee"). By arrangement, a spotlight was turned on, momentarily blinding him.

"Dear and exquisite shipmates," he said in his announcer's voice when he recovered his sight, "I should like to take this occasion, the twenty-sixth anniversary of my assumption of command of that good and noble ship, the U.S.S. Monte Excelsior, to thank those amongst you who have faithfully piled aboard over the years. And, on this eve of a great and bountiful New Year in which there shall be peace in the homeland, please God, I should like to welcome those new travelers who may wish to join us on our sumptuous pleasure cruise.

"I would be the first to admit that the ride has not always been smooth. Both I and my first mate—where's Belle? Put the spotlight on Belle."

"No, Morris, please."

The spotlight was put on Belle, who stood at the entrance to the pier, hand raised to protect her eyes from the glare.

"Both I and my first mate," Morris resumed when the spotlight had been redirected, "have weathered many a storm since we set sail that becalmed New Year's Eve twenty-six years ago. Troubled waters we have seen, but I am proud to say that we're still all aboard. Our flag is flying higher than ever. And tonight we're here to celebrate, to ring in the new, to ring out the old. Let the corks pop. Let us raise our glasses high: here's to that great Miami Beach flagship, Morris and Belle Fleischman's Monte Excelsior Hotel and Country Club."

Almost everyone raised a paper cup filled with the orange soda Morris was dispensing free of charge and drank. Morris Fleischman had a great many faults, it was generally admitted; but he was not the worst hotel proprietor in South Beach, not by a long shot.

After the toast, Piccolo Pete launched into the mambo

version of "Moon over Miami" and the crowd readjusted itself, centering on the table where the hors d'oeuvres—pretzels, popcorn, potato chips, Fritos—were displayed.

Ruth, searching for April, led Meyer to an empty bench. "I wonder where my sister Frieda is?" Meyer said, assuming the lost look he wore in crowds.

"Eating," Ruth said.

Meyer belched. "I think I'd better go home, Ruthie, if you don't mind," he said, after a moment.

"What's the matter?" Ruth asked, concerned.

"Acid indigestion. I should never have had that raw onion." He belched again. "When you get to be our age, Ruthie, you can't eat everything like we did when we were kids." He let out a series of tiny belches.

"I'll come with you, Meyer."

"No. No. You stay here and enjoy yourself, Ruthie. Believe me, I know the cure for this: two Alka-Seltzers and a Tums. Does it every time." He stood, emitting three quick burps.

"You certain you don't want me to come with you, Meyer?"

"Positive. But it's nice of you to ask, Ruthie. This is the time when a man like me needs a woman like you." He patted her shoulder and made his way through the crowd.

Ruth stood as Piccolo Pete took up his microphone and announced, "An exhibition cha-cha-cha, ladies and gentlemen, brought to you courtesy of Morris Fleischman and his world-famous Monte Excelsior." Ruth looked around, trying to find April as the band went into "The Saint Louis Blues Cha-Cha-Cha." A blue spotlight was focused onto a small oval in front of the bandstand. Morris stepped into it as the opening chord was played, his hand held out into the darkness outside the oval. He brought it in like a conjuring magician. Holding it was April, her red slip dress and her good rhinestone earrings making her look like a lesser known talk-show star.

"Cha-cha-cha," April said, snapping her fingers and facing Morris, who was slightly shorter than she, thanks to her new Cuban heels. Morris stared into April's breasts, looked at the crowd, said, "Cha-cha-cha," and they began to dance. Their dancing, with its butterflies and other intricate steps, seemed extraordinarily professional. It was evident that they had done a certain amount of rehearsing.

Ruth closed her eyes. "I mustn't make judgments," she said to herself, opening her eyes, catching a glimpse of Morris and April cha-cha-ing in a most suggestive manner. "They're happy, they should live and be well." Still, she turned and walked away from the dance, toward the end of the pier. Only Abel, the tiny, gnarled fisherman, was there.

"Howdy," he said.

"Happy New Year," Ruth said.

Abel went back to his fishing and Ruth looked out to sea, wondering why she felt so melancholy. "It's New Year's Eve," she said to herself, as if that were an explanation. "He wouldn't be fishing on New Year's Eve."

The music from the other end of the pier told her that the exhibition cha-cha had been concluded and "The Mexican Hat Dance" was under way. She said good night to Abel, who grunted, and started to walk back when she realized someone was coming toward her. It was a man, a tall, broad man, wearing a white dinner jacket.

"Ruth," he said.

"Max," she said.

They stood looking at each other, not touching, as, in the near distance, the band concluded "The Mexican Hat Dance" and segued into "The Miami Beach Rumba."

"What're you doing here?" she asked, after a moment, avoiding his eyes. "All fancy-shmancy."

"I just got back today," he said. "My daughter forced me to spend the holidays with her and her husband and kids up in a place called Larchmont. I meant to call you, Miss Ruth. Somehow I didn't. I guess I'd better admit it: I'm afraid."

"Afraid?" she asked, looking up at him. "Afraid? What could you be afraid of?"

"You, Miss Ruth. I swore off the ladies a long time ago and for a good while I've been successful. Suddenly I find I'm being haunted by a pair of blue-gray eyes of the deepest intensity all the way up in Larchmont and I'm scared." He held out his hand and put it against her cheek. After a moment, he took it away. "Tonight, I went to a party at the Bath and Tennis Club and I was sitting at a table with a great many proper ladies and gentlemen and I got to thinking about you and asking myself what the hell I was doing there and before I knew it, I was here."

She didn't know how to respond, to his touch, to his sincerity. She fell back, as she so often did, on social convention. "Was it fun? The party?"

"You ever try to digest Chicken Mornay, ma'am, while listening to an overgrown boy play Beethoven on a white baby grand?"

"You ever try to drink orange soda while listening to 'You and the Night and the Music, Cha-Cha-Cha'?"

He laughed. "I sure am glad I came down here tonight, Miss Ruth."

"You want to know something, Mr. Max? So am I."

They had walked back to the edge of the crowd while they were talking. "I wonder if you would do me the honor of accompanying me to a romantic little coffee shop I know . . ." Max started to say.

"That Alka-Seltzer did the trick. What did I tell you?" Meyer said, coming up to them. "That and the Tums. Never fails. I'm as good as brand new. Waiter, you want to bring me a diet black cherry, one cube of ice?"

"Meyer, he's not . . ."

"Yes, sir," Max said, about-facing, going toward the "bar."

"I want to make you a present, Ruthie," Meyer said, handing her two packets of Alka-Seltzer. "Keep these in your purse at all times. You should never be without them. I learned my lesson." She took them as Max returned with the soda and Frieda and Saul approached.

"I want you should all know," Frieda said, "that I won the raffle prize."

"Which is?" Meyer asked.

"A round-trip ticket up the Indian River and back, by boat."

"Congratulations," Meyer said, taking the cup Max was handing him, drinking from it, turning his attention to Frieda, who was talking at top voice about her luck, about her chronic seasickness, about her fear of canoes and crocodiles.

"I couldn't win a round-trip ticket to Paris, France, and back?"

("Tomorrow?" Max asked Ruth.)

"The last time I got on a boat was when I came to this country and I was sick as a dog, believe me."

("Yes," Ruth answered.)

"If I saw a crocodile, I'd have a heart attack right on the spot. When I walk into a store and see a stuffed one, I get palpitations."

("I'll call you," Max said, turning and leaving. "Happy New Year, Miss Ruth.")

"I'll give the prize to Saul. Let him go on a boat up a river filled with crocodiles."

"Who was that?" Meyer asked Ruth.

"Who was who?"

"That guy who brought me the soda?"

"How should I know? A waiter."

 Sixteen

There was no one at the pool the following morning. The girls were at the Ponce de León, playing bingo in that establishment's annual New Year's Day Bingo Tournament.

Ruth, relieved, lay in a chaise and tried to read a paperback thriller about transplants April had pressed upon her ("It will scare the underpants off you"). She couldn't concentrate. A pair of green eyes kept coming between her and the pages. She closed her eyes, remembering the touch of his hand on her cheek.

"Mother," a refined, unpleasant voice said from the direction of the lobby. Ruth opened her eyes to see her daughter, Audrey, striding across the court, her blue-and-yellow traveling dress, with the epaulettes and the ammo belt, looking as if it had just come out of the cleaners. Her son-in-law, Ronald, in a polyester leisure suit of an appalling muddy brown, followed.

"Mother, what are you doing, sitting here all alone? I knew this would happen," Audrey turned to say to Ronald. "Didn't I tell you she would come down here and end up lonely and miserable, not knowing a soul? Didn't I?" She bent over, gave her mother a perfunctory peck, and sat on the neighboring chaise longue while she inspected her. "She looks in good health but you know how deceptive looks can be."

"Look, Ma," Ronald began, kneeling at the foot of Ruth's chaise, taking her hands, and putting them between his, "I want you to listen very carefully: Audrey and I are on our way to a mini-convention in Key West. We only decided, at the very last moment, to go when we realized we would have a couple of hours before our connection to drop in on you, to see how you're doing.

"Ma, it's clear you're not doing so well. Sitting here in this deserted dump, all by yourself. Ma, I know it's hard to admit you were wrong and I'm not even asking you to do that. All Audrey and I want is the best for you. Now, say the word and we'll skip the convention and turn right around and take you back to New Jersey where you belong. I can still swing a very good deal for you at Autumnal View. Charlie Kidder would give the shirt off his back for me. So what do you say, Ma?"

Ruth removed her hands from his, sat up in the chaise with some effort, and said to her daughter, "What're you going to do all day in Key West while Ronald's learning about the latest methods of drilling?"

"I don't drill, Ma. I'm not that kind of dentist."

"There's plenty to do there. They have a new Jewish Center and I'll visit Rabbi Kauffman . . ."

"Rabbi Kauffman is in Key West?"

"Her memory's going," Audrey said to Ronald. "I wrote to you, Mother, and told you he retired from the Murray Street *shul* and went to Key West to head up the Jewish Center there. His daughter lives there, with . . ."

Audrey went on while Ruth thought about Rabbi Kauffman. He was the closest to a religious leader she had ever known, a neat little man with a million wrinkles and a good heart. "I'd love to see him again."

"Who? (Dear God, she's wandering.)"

"Rabbi Kauffman."

"Ma," Ronald said, "check out of this dump. Come to Key West with us. You'll see the rabbi and then you'll shoot right back to Jersey with us."

"What time's your connection, Audrey?" Ruth asked.

"I'd like to see your room, Mother, before we leave, if you don't mind?"

She was about to tell Audrey she minded very much but Ronald had looked at the computer he wore strapped around his milk-white wrist and found that it was later than he had thought, that they had to rush back to the airport.

"We would stop in on our return trip but the association has chartered a plane to take us all to West Palm Beach to see an exhibition of the latest orthodonture equipment. However, I want you to remember, Mother, that if ever . . ."

"Audrey, we have two hours to return the car, to check in with our luggage . . ."

"Say hello to Rabbi Kauffman for me," Ruth said, wishing them a safe trip, blessing the association for its ability to charter planes and West Palm Beach for its dental exhibits and direct flights to Newark.

Ten minutes after Audrey and Ronald had ended their blitzkrieg visit, when she had begun to doze and fantasize again, Morris Fleischman came bounding out of the lobby, his hair slicked back, a liquid gleam lighting up his dry eyes.

"*Bonjour,* beautiful lady," he boomed. "Beautiful, beautiful lady. What a wonderful day on which to start the New Year. The sun is shining, all is right with the world. You know, Madame Meyer, I rose this morning from my conjugal bed, looked at my wife and said, 'Dear Ding Dong Belle, are we not fortunate to be living and thriving in this land of milk and honey?' "

"And what did dear Ding Dong reply?" Ruth asked.

" 'Tis a pity but Belle is not of the poetic nature. Her reply is not quotable. Ah, but you, *madonna mío,* you understand, *n'est-ce pas?* You, who know the value of the sunshine as opposed to the pallor of the gaming rooms, you, ravishing lady, who remain loyal to your old Monte despite the blandishments of less scrupulous innkeepers who wouldst turn this enchanted isle into a Las Vegas. You, *chère madame*, are *au courant* and *déshabille* and I shan't forget you for this, believe me."

"*Buon giorno, mi amigo,*" April called out from the top of the staircase. "*Feliz Navidad, mi amore,*" she shouted as she descended the stairs.

"Ah, am I mistaken or is that the femme fatale who stole my heart at our naughty *soirée* last *noir? Mon ange.* You look *ravishment.*"

April descended the stairs in new high-heeled sandals, a luminous purple robe, and a light blond wig.

"April!" Ruth called out.

"Ruth," April called back, removing the purple robe as she walked, revealing a one-piece matching bathing suit.

"April," Ruth said. "A one-piece bathing suit?"

"I have the figure for it."

And she did. She had lost weight in the right place. The bathing suit seemed very right on her. Even the wig wasn't so awful, her thin, red-brown hair never being her best feature.

"Are you out of your mind, April?" Ruth felt compelled to ask, even, at the same time, admiring the renovation.

"Out of my mind with love." She inserted a cigarette into an imitation jade holder and looked at Morris through lowered, inch-long eyelashes. "Darling, a light, *s'il vous plaît.*" She lifted her cigarette to Morris's shaking hand and the quivering match he held in it.

"April, you're smoking?"

April inhaled, exhaled, and blew a smoke ring at Morris.

" 'I'm going to live till I die,' " she said. " 'I'm going to fill my cup until my number's up, I'm going to live, live, live until I die.' "

"Adorable, reckless lady," Morris said, taking her free hand, its nails thickly coated with Real Ritz Red, "allow me to escort you to my office *privé* where we may toast in the New Year with a tequila sunrise."

"The only time I ever said no to an offer like that, I was under ether." April draped the robe over her shoulders and followed Morris into the dim room behind the lobby he called his office.

"You think perhaps she should see someone?" Armando asked, having witnessed the scene from the equipment room.

"Herself," Ruth answered.

"I meant a doctor, *señora*. When my aunt was going through her change of life . . ." Armando went on about his aunt's change of life for a few minutes and then left quickly in response to a call from Belle.

Ruth had the pool to herself for the remainder of the morning, images of the new April Pollack, the old Rabbi Kauffman, and leaf-green eyes keeping her from reading her book. It was a shock to wake up to find Meyer standing over her, his hands behind her back.

"Sleeping, Ruthie?"

"Dozing."

"You should have been at bingo," Frieda said, pulling up two chaises, sitting Saul in one, Meyer in the other. She herself sat on the bottom half of the chaise Ruth was in. "Saul won seven dollars."

"Little by little," Saul said, "I'm paying the capitalist state back for its years of oppression."

"We're trying to decide what to do with it," Frieda said.

Ruth thought she could tell her but instead looked at Meyer, who was acting strangely, clutching a brown paper bag. It looked as if it might be his lunch. He started to say something, held up the bag, and closed his mouth.

"You want to tell me what's in the bag, Meyer?"

"Go ahead, Meyer," Frieda said.

"I want you should do me a favor, Ruthie." He paused.

"Would you like to tell me what it is?"

He couldn't. He handed her the bag. Ruth opened it and looked in. It was filled with odd socks. She pulled one out. It had a hole where the big toe should have been.

"You want me to mend your socks? Is that what you want, Meyer?"

He found his voice. "First I asked Frieda but she said you, as my intended, might not like the idea."

"I wouldn't want to be a *buttinsky* sister-in-law, Ruthie," Frieda said.

"And after all," Meyer went on, "we are engaged to be engaged, unofficially."

Ruth stood up, took the paper bag, and walked the few feet to the edge of the pool. Looking at Meyer and Frieda, she very purposely upended the bag. The socks, mostly ankle-length black rayon adorned with clocks reading midnight, dropped gracefully into the pool, as if in a slow-motion ballet sequence.

As the last one hit the chlorinated water, Ruth carefully folded the bag, handed it to Frieda, and turned to go to her apartmentette. She felt, she decided, surprisingly calm.

Before she could reach the stairway, the tentative crackle of the Monte's PA system made itself heard, Belle's staccato voice boomeranging around the courtyard. "Mrs. Ruth Meyer. Mrs. Ruth Meyer. You have a phone call in the lobby. Mrs. Ruth Meyer." Ruth changed directions and went into the lobby, picking up the dusty receiver of the lone house phone.

"Miss Ruth? Max Rhoads. I'm calling to wish you a Happy New Year and to ask if you'd like to dine with me tonight."

"Well," Ruth said. ("What do I know about him?" she thought. "He's a perfect stranger. Who knows what he wants

from me?'') She turned and looked through the lobby window.
Meyer, Saul, and Frieda were attempting to fish the socks out
of the pool. "I'd love to, Max."

"Wonderful. I'll pick you up at seven."

She rarely ate dinner later than six but she'd have a little
nosh late in the afternoon to tide her over. She used the lobby
phone to find out if the beauty parlor on Washington and
Third was open on New Year's Day.

"Of course we're open. This isn't a Jewish holiday, last I
heard," the fat voice who answered the phone said. "Enrique
can just manage to squeeze you in."

 Seventeen

"Israel? Don't talk to me about Israel. My poor, suffering
Israel. Don't even whisper her name. *Oy vey,* Israel. I could tell
you stories about the early days in Israel, my darling Goldie,
that would make what little hair you have left curl. You're
saying 'Israel' to me, me, Pearl Goldstein, a woman who has
been to Israel and back four times, and once not on charter?
You've never been, Goldie? You should be ashamed. You
should hide your head. A Jewish woman who has never been to
Israel is like a goldfish who has never been in a tank. What
pleasures you are missing. What glory you will never know.
When your plane touches down on that runway and suddenly
you feel in every bone of your body (even your body, Goldie)
that you are home, at last. Home. Where you belong. Goldie,
I can't believe you've never been. Tell me you're fooling."

Enrique Lizzardi's mother was having what she liked to call

a political discussion in the front of his salon with an old customer who had to lift the heavy and ancient dryer she was sitting under each time she wanted to reply. Early on, Mrs. Goldstein had recognized the need for her son to change his name for "business purposes." "Whoever heard of a Jewish hairdresser?" She had seen no reason to change her own even if she was his cashier and receptionist.

Chez Chez Enrique had been recommended by Mae Weissman, who, with her son in the business, would have seemed to be as good an authority as any. Ruth didn't like it. She didn't like the window display with its pastel wigs and photographs of women sporting hairstyles of the beehive persuasion. She didn't like the not particularly clean tile floor. Most of all, she didn't like the way the cashier was talking to the customer.

She missed her Gina's Golden Jewel Salon, where the cashier never talked to anyone (her English wasn't conversational) and everything was spotless. At Gina's, only doctors' wives and other ladies of prominence were given appointments. So the talk was on a very high level, focusing on best-sellers, Broadway plays, and only very occasionally on divorce or a child gone wrong.

And at Gina's, there was no Enrique Lizzardi wearing black pants so tight you could see his whats-it, wearing a shirt open to his belly button, revealing a shaved chest and a twenty-dollar gold piece dangling on a thick, plaited chain.

"Call me Ricky," he said as he washed her abundant hair. "You want a scalp massage?"

"Magic fingers, that boy," his mother found time to say, interrupting her conversation with Goldie. "Magic fingers."

"Just a wash with a very, very light-blue rinse. And a set," she thought wise to add.

Enrique leaned over her, his mouth next to her ear. The

abusive cologne he wore fought with the other odors of the salon (permanent fluid, hair spray, sweat) and won. The glint of a gold earring pierced through Enrique's right lobe was something Ruth convinced herself, later, that she had imagined. Obsidian lids closed over Dean Martin eyes as he whispered, "What about an entire new you, *señora?* What about letting Enrique go wild in your hair? What about letting Enrique turn you into something so *scin*-tillating, so far out, your friends won't know it's you?"

"That boy has magic scissors," his mother called out. "Let him go all the way with you. You'll never regret it."

"I'll take ten years off your face, *señora.*"

"Who knows?" Pearl, a mountain of flesh in a pink acrylic jump suit, shouted. "Maybe twenty. You should've seen Goldie when she marched in here this morning."

Ruth managed to escape with a wash, a rinse—slightly more turquoise than she had expected—and a set.

"Come in for a comb-out in a few days," Enrique said. "And we can talk about getting into something really outrageous."

She took a taxi back to the Monte and immediately began to comb out the tight curls Enrique had put in when there was a rat-a-tat-tat on her door. It was April in her blond wig and purple robe.

"I want to know two things, Draisal: what time's your date and what's your fiancé, Meyer, going to say when Frieda tells him you've taken a lover?" She sat down on the davenport and fitted a cigarette into her holder.

"Who told you?"

"You think Belle Fleischman sits at the switchboard because she enjoys it?"

"Anyway, Meyer's not my fiancé and I haven't taken a lover. Also, could you blow the smoke toward the air conditioner? I thought you gave cigarettes up years ago."

"Only until age eighty. So I've decided to take them up again, only a few years earlier. I have a suggestion about your hair."

"And I have a suggestion about yours: go get your money back."

"Are you being a bitch, Draisal, because that's your natural nature or because you're a nervous wreck about going out with the fisherman?"

Ruth sat down on the davenport and took April's hand. "I'm a nervous wreck. What do I know about him? I met him on a pier and suddenly I'm going to dinner with him. This is a man who wears two rings on one hand, has hair coming down over his collar, and speaks with a southern accent. To top it off, he has a beard. What do I think I'm doing? I'm going to call him up and tell him I can't make it. Only I don't know his number."

April put out her cigarette and put her arm around her friend. "How old do you feel, *mamala?*"

"Seventeen."

"Darling, you're not seventeen. You're a mature woman going out with a mature man. You like each other, right? So what's the worst that could happen? You could have a good time. You could let yourself enjoy the evening."

"April, this is the first time I've ever been out with a stranger. A southern, bearded stranger."

"Would you do me a favor, Draisal? Go wash the turquoise out of your hair and relax a little. He's not a murderer/rapist. He's a nice *mench* of a man."

"Come with us."

"Are you crazy?"

"Max will love you. Go take off your wig and get dressed. Hurry up."

"Ruth, go wash your hair, I'll help you dry it, and then I'll hold your hand until he comes. If you want, I'll tell him you have to be home by midnight or you'll turn into a *knisha*."

"Why am I being so foolish, April? I never feel like this when I'm going out with Meyer."

"With Meyer, you're not taking any chances. With this guy, who knows? You might even get kissed."

"Not on the first date," Ruth said, going into the bathroom, running the shower. "No funny stuff on the first date."

The wrought-iron confection known as the Second Floor Balcony by seasoned Monte Excelsior guests was a narrow, insubstantial place, rarely used. Occasionally, however, it had its advantages, overlooking Ocean Road and the main entrance to the Monte. On that early and mild January night, two women of like bulk were sitting on it, side by side. They were discussing Ruth Meyer's date, word of which had spread like wildfire (courtesy of Belle Fleischman) around the hotel.

"Personally," Mae Weissman said, "I'm expecting if not a hunchback, at the very least, something missing. His hearing. His teeth. When a man wants to make a move in Miami Beach—be it toward bed or marriage—he doesn't start in with a dinner. There's got to be something missing."

To Mae's disappointment, Max Rhoads was missing nothing visible. He was tall, broad of shoulder, lean enough of waist, and, with his dark tan and white-blond beard, he seemed much too good to be true. "Take it from me," Mae whispered, "something's missing somewhere."

Frieda was not sent away disappointed. "Ruth looked like a princess," she was later to tell Miriam Siegal as they clicked the tiles of her Mah-Jongg set in the Monte's game room. "I personally love the way she wore her hair, hanging straight down as if she had washed it and forgot to set it. But him.

That *schlub*. Khaki shorts, a shirt without a collar, and sandals, the kind you buy in the drugstore. My poor sister-in-law. If she gets to McDonald's, she can count herself lucky."

"In that truck," Mae Weissman said, "she can count herself lucky if he drives around the block and lets her off."

The truck was a Jeep, red and topless. Aware of her audience on the Second Floor Balcony, Ruth had studied her date's outfit and vehicle, looked up at Mae and Frieda and back at Max. One of his husky forearms was resting on the door of the Jeep. He had a wide grin on his face, showing through his white-blond beard. If Ruth looked like Ingrid Bergman (as Frieda would have it), Max looked like Ernest Hemingway.

"To appear dressed like that." Frieda's whisper could be heard wafting down to them. "Such a nerve I never saw before."

Ruth smiled her gracious smile—the one she once wore when dealing with Nicky's teachers on PTA nights—held out her hand and shook Max's. "How nice to see you," she said.

"It's a great pleasure to see you, ma'am." He held open the door of the Jeep and pointed to the passenger bar. "Now, you hold on to that, good and tight." Ruth grabbed it, soiling her good white gloves as Max gunned the engine, U-turned illegally, and managed to go from zero to thirty miles per hour in as many seconds.

It wasn't until they were speeding across the MacArthur Causeway, headed for the city of Miami, that Ruth managed to say, "You can take me right home, Mr. Rhoads."

"This old heap too fast for you?"

"When a gentleman takes me out to dinner," she said, looking down at her soft, pink dress, "I am used to his wearing at the least long pants."

"You didn't think I would take you out looking like this? I was fishing all afternoon and only just got off this fellow's boat. I thought it would behoove me to pick you up first and then go home and put on my gentlemanly attire." He looked at her and smiled, his green eyes lighting up. "I didn't want to be late for our first date, Miss Ruth."

She moved her hair out of her eyes, saying, "Where, may I ask, is this change supposed to take place?"

"At my cottage in Coconut Grove."

"You expect me to sit around your 'cottage' while you change? That's a hot one."

He laughed. "You can lock me in the bedroom until I'm presentable."

She allowed herself a smile. "That won't be necessary." She wondered if it was his southern accent that made him so attractive. "I've met Jewish people from the South before," she thought. "None of them were anything like him."

The cottage was at the end of a narrow road. A sign read PINDER LANE, PRIVATE. Huge palm trees, surrounded by thick foliage, lined the way. A chorus of insect sounds came up from the junglelike plants and flowers, drowning out the engine of the Jeep. There were no houses, or at least none that she could see. As they bumped along the unpaved lane, the dense and colorful foliage making it seem warm but not uncomfortably so, Ruth thought that "this must be what Tahiti is like. I've never seen such big red flowers in my life. Red flowers! I'm thinking about red flowers when I should be asking myself what I'm doing, riding with a stranger in a Jeep, at my age, on a deserted road in the middle of nowhere."

But she wasn't genuinely nervous. With the sun setting behind the palm trees and Max giving her reassuring smiles as the Jeep bounced along, she felt ridiculously happy. Even the jangling ride didn't upset her. "It's good for the *kischkas*," she told herself.

At the end of the lane, Max drove the Jeep around a circle of grass and entered a driveway. A stucco house with arched windows and a red tile roof stood in the center of an acre of the greenest grass she had ever seen. Behind the house were two royal palms, guarding what looked from that distance like a tropical pond. The first floor of the building was a series of stucco arches in which were set french doors. The second floor rested on twirled stucco columns.

"Some cottage," she said.

"A long time ago it was a gatehouse," Max told her as they walked toward it. "The big house it belonged to burned down some twenty years ago. Rumor has it that the family who owned it needed the insurance money. This is all that's left."

"You rent it?"

"Not exactly," he said, taking her arm, leading her up the pebbled path her heels weren't meant to walk on. "I have what is known as a 'lifetime lease.' It was my daddy who supposedly burned down the house."

"You miss it?"

"Not for a second. It sure was ugly. What my brother called Spanish Protestant architecture. The cottage used to house the servants. It's ugly, too, but it has a kind of old Floridian charm."

"So you were brought up rich?"

"I come from what the social workers down here politely call a privileged background." He took her inside.

"You make a habit of leaving your doors open?" she asked, shocked.

"I don't have much anyone would want to steal. Now, would you like a drink before I go and change into my courting suit?"

She told him she wasn't thirsty and watched as he went up the stairs, two at a time, that led to a balcony overlooking the

room she was in. Off the balcony, she guessed, was a bedroom
and a bath. Under it was the kitchen.

She looked in. "Not even a dishwasher." The rest of the
house seemed to be the living room. It had a thirty-foot-high
ceiling, covered with yellow and blue ceramic tiles. The
balcony, which ran the length of one wall, was supported by
more twirled columns, these carved of wood. A six-foot-high
fireplace mantel dominated the opposite wall. The two
remaining walls were taken up by french doors and pale pink
stucco.

Ruth sat in one of the oversized leather sofas flanking the
fireplace. "I have such a funny feeling," she thought. "Such a
peculiar feeling. Like indigestion, only pleasant. This room is
so strange, but wonderful. Douglas Fairbanks, Sr., could've
lived in a place like this. Romantic. A little frightening. It's
so quiet, I can hear my heart beating. What's making me feel
so odd? The quiet? The man upstairs getting (one hopes)
dressed?

"Or is it because this is the first time in my life that I'm in a
house not surrounded by other houses? That I'm on a street
that has no sidewalk, no pavement, no people?"

She stood up and walked to the far corner of the room,
switching on the lights, floor lamps standing on sisal rugs. She
was about to return to the sofa when she noticed a small door
on the fireplace wall.

She opened it and entered a room that had two stucco and
two glass-paned greenhouse walls. It had evidently been added
after the original structure was built. The stucco walls were
covered with paintings. Large canvases, for the most part
unframed. A giant rose filled one canvas, threatening to spill
over onto the wall and take over the room. There were other
hypnotic flowers and more mundane subjects, vegetables and a
portrait of a Hoover vacuum cleaner.

"It's not that they look so much like what they're supposed to be," she thought. "But I can smell the flowers, almost taste the vegetables." A cauliflower, small and precise and curiously moving, stood on a tray, ready to be steamed. There were horses, finely but not realistically drawn, that seemed to be speeding off the canvas. "The genius behind these paintings," she thought—and she was certain there was genius— "is that the artist has been able to give everything both movement and personality."

The exhibition, clearly the work of one man, seemed to trace his progress as an artist. There was the early kitchen scene that was too deliberate, too rough. A nude came next, a black woman both innocent and erotic. Below her was a red-and-yellow parrot who seemed to have landed, just that moment, on the square of canvas. It, more than any of the other paintings, reminded her of Gauguin.

"Damned good, aren't they?" Max asked, coming in behind her.

She turned. He was wearing an open shirt, white trousers, brown and white shoes. "Good? They're great. And you leave your door open? These paintings shouldn't be here. They should be in a museum where people can see them." It was then that she made the connection. "That teakettle in the Bass Museum? That was by the same artist, wasn't it?"

He laughed. "Who would have thought it?"

"Who would have thought what?"

"That you would not only appreciate the paintings, but that you'd have the ability to identify them as well."

"Why? Because I'm a Miami Beach Bagel Beauty, I shouldn't know from art?"

"Most Miami Beach Bagel Beauties don't."

"Besides, I haven't identified them. I still don't know who the artist is. None of them are signed. Wait, I think I might know. There's a long, narrow painting of a mulberry bush hanging on the third floor of the Whitney in New York. I'd bet a dollar it's by the same artist as well. But I can't remember his name."

"Maxwell Rhoads."

"Your father?"

"Me."

"You?"

"I sign them on the back because I don't like my signature to get in the way. I've kept them—or most of them—because I like them. You see here, Miss Ruth, what I have chosen to call my late middle period. When I die, then they can go into a nice, air-conditioned, guarded room. In the meantime, I keep them around me. Old friends."

"What I should like to know is what comes after the late middle period?"

There was a draped easel in the far corner, facing the paned glass wall. He switched on an overhead spotlight, removing the cloth that hid the canvas. It was a nude. A lumpish figure, a woman, was resting on a gray plank. She seemed immobile, without personality.

"The colors," Ruth said, feeling she had to say something to disguise her disappointment. "They're too dull. I don't know. Maybe if I saw it in a museum, away from the others . . ."

"You're a very polite lady, Miss Ruth. But that painting would only look worse without the others. It's awful and we both know it. Truth is, I don't have a late period. I am what is popularly known as 'painted out.' "

He redraped the nude and, for that moment, in the harsh spotlight, looked old and beaten. "When my second marriage went bad, when gin became the first most important thing to me in the world, that's when I knew I didn't have it anymore." He took her arm and led her back into the main room, shutting the door on his paintings.

"So maybe you should give up the gin and get married again."

"I've stopped drinking gin. But I'll never marry again. Each time I've said I do, I didn't." He looked down at the two silver rings on his left hand. "I keep these as reminders in case I ever lose my head again. Not a likely possibility. You, Miss Ruth, have the distinction—dubious—of being the first lady I have voluntarily dated in almost ten years." He smiled at her. "And I'm starving you to death."

"I don't mind telling you, Max," she said, as they rode through Coconut Grove in the Jeep, "that I'm famished. I didn't eat a thing all day. Too nervous."

"About what?"

"You. This date. You think I'm used to going out to dinner with strange men I pick up on fishing piers? This is a new experience for me. Believe me."

"Enjoying it?"

"Immensely. You?"

"Immensely."

She liked the way he spoke, so soft, gently mocking himself, the South, the man-woman relationship. The restaurant was low and dark, candlelit. He ordered a drink she had never heard of, Tennessee whiskey, and she asked for a ginger ale.

"You should begin painting again," she said aloud, surprising herself. "If I'm being a *buttinsky,* tell me. But Max, you're too good to stop."

"Not anymore, Miss Ruth. I don't have it anymore. That's the plain and simple truth. I'm not the first painter who lost his art."

"You'll find it again. You have to look a little harder."

He laughed. "And what are you looking for, Miss Ruth?"

"Do I know? A little peace. A little quiet. No aggravation. Not much."

"You've given up, too."

"I have not. My career, whether I liked it or not, was marriage. Believe me, I was never an artist at it."

"Perhaps *you* should try again."

"I've had my offers."

"The gentleman at the pier who thought I was a waiter?"

"My brother-in-law, Meyer. A lovely man. Extremely comfortable . . ."

"If I might venture to say so, that old boy wants a nurse, not a wife."

"Whatever happened to southern courtesy?"

"Let's postpone the answer to that question, ma'am, while we dance."

They danced well together. She liked the smell of whiskey on his breath. She liked feeling his muscular arms around her. "I'm actually enjoying myself," she thought. *"Oy vey."*

"I can't believe it," she said, over coffee for him, Sanka for her, "that I'm sitting here with a famous artist, talking to him like he was a regular person."

"And he can't believe he's responding to you as a man to a woman. It's the first time in a long, long time, Ruth."

They had another dance. "Where did you learn to dance like this?" he asked her.

"After almost fifty years of weddings, *bar mitzvahs,* and what-have-yous, it's no miracle, believe me."

He took the long way back to Miami Beach. She told him about her youth, her marriage, her newly developed interest in art, Harry's death, her migration to Florida.

He stopped the Jeep by the Goodyear Blimp and he told her about his own youth in Florida ("Daddy owned a paper company") and how he had studied in Europe because he had always wanted to paint. He had lived in Paris for ten years with his first wife and, after that marriage had broken up, he had come home to Florida to work and had met his second wife. "Now she's up in Palm Beach, flashing her diamonds at the nabobs."

The smell of the night air was sweet as they completed the ride in silence, pulling up in front of the Monte.

Mae Weissman, who had her own future to think of and had devised a plan for it that very night, was keeping a lone vigil. "I was leaning over the balustrade of the Second Floor Balcony for a better view of the incoming tide," she told the girls the following morning, "which is how I happened to catch sight of them."

Mae's hearing wasn't what it might have been so she missed most of what was being said in the Jeep below her. But her eyesight, knock on wood, was twenty-twenty, thanks to the twin cataract operation she had undergone two winters ago, and the tinted glasses she wore helped wonderfully. "So, as I was gazing out at the mighty Atlantic, I happened to glance down and what did I see? That man she picked up, wrapping his arms around her and kissing her full on the lips." At this point in her narration, Mae had to stop to wipe her own lips, which had become wet with enthusiasm. "And the corker, girls, the icing on the cake, is that she did not resist! Not one little token protest, not one tiny demure 'stop it.' Her arms were right up there, around his neck, and her lips were smack dab against his. So much for the Snow White Princess Elizabeth New Jersey."

Mae called Armando over and ordered a black-and-white ice cream soda even though it was only ten o'clock in the morning. "One," she justified her action to the girls, "I refuse to be the kind of person who knows the calorie count of everything, the taste of nothing. And two, after sitting up so late last night, I personally feel I deserve it."

The girls agreed as one of them detached herself from the group around the pool and headed for the lobby telephone. Frieda had something to say to her brother Meyer.

 Eighteen

She understood when he didn't call the next day. "He has cold feet," she told herself. "He hasn't had anything to do with women in ten years and on the first date he's telling me the story of his life. Who wouldn't hold back a little?" On the day after, sitting by the pool, jumping a little each time the public address system went into operation, she thought that maybe he had more than cold feet. By the third day, when he still hadn't called, she decided he had a frozen heart.

She sat up in bed, staring at the black instrument, which looked as if it were a leftover prop from a Bela Lugosi movie. "Now, when I want someone to call, no one's calling." She lay back on the too-soft mattress.

"If these mattresses could talk," April had said.

"I wouldn't want to hear such language," Ruth had answered.

There was a shy knock on the door as Maria Carmen, the maid, put her kerchiefed head around it. "All right I come in now?"

"*Sí,*" Ruth said, getting out of bed, feeling guilty. The poor woman wanted to finish her work and here she was, lying in bed the whole morning, waiting for a phone call that would never come.

"Habla español?" Maria Carmen asked, smiling.

"Un poco," Ruth answered. *"Yo estudio en la escuela."* She couldn't remember the past tense but Maria Carmen seemed to get the general drift.

"Ud. habla muy bien."

"Muchas gracias."

Maria Carmen pulled out another one of her large repertory of smiles and set about her work, starting with the bathroom. Ruth put on her robe and sat at the blond wood desk, watching Maria Carmen mop the bathroom floor. Her hand rested on the telephone. "What makes me think he's going to call? We had one nice evening in which perhaps too much was said. Now he regrets opening his big mouth. So what? He could call and say, 'Thank you, how are you, I had a nice evening.' But he's not."

Her right hand moved away from the telephone and joined her left hand in her lap. She watched as Maria Carmen hauled herself up off the tiled floor and began to clean the washbasin.

"She's doing it backwards," Ruth thought. "She should be cleaning everything else first, then the floor." She didn't say anything. All her life she had known women like Maria Carmen, women who had washed and ironed and vacuumed for her. "Not that I really knew any of them." There had been more than a language barrier. "Something else. Something else kept us from talking."

She remembered as a child in Brooklyn, kneeling behind the privet hedges with her older brothers and sisters, jumping up when the new "girl" came running around the corner, wearing funny, old-fashioned clothes.

"Greenhorn / popcorn / five cents apiece," they had shouted. She was an Irish girl, a week off the boat, dressed in a long, green skirt and a thin coat, far too skimpy for the winter cold.

"Begone with you, now," she had said to them after she had caught her breath (they had scared her), running up the steps to the parlor floor of the brownstone they were renting on Avenue J, knocking on the door. It wasn't a timid knock and Ruth's mother, that perennially ailing woman, had answered it with a severe smile.

"A good morning to you, Mrs. Stone. I'm the new girl. Nora." She stood on the top step, barely suppressing that infectious grin of hers.

"Good afternoon," Mrs. Stone had said pointedly. Nora had been a half-hour late. "She stayed with us for years, that Nora. She even, finally, got Mother to love her. I wonder what become of that Nora. What we did to her."

She tried to remember her face but all that she could envision was Ann Sheridan in a film in which she played a spunky maid. She couldn't remember whether it was Ann Sheridan or Nora who had the husband who drank.

Maria Carmen, with her pail and her brush and her enormous haunches, had backed into the bedroom. Stepping around her, Ruth went into the bathroom and started the shower, thinking of the other women who had cleaned for her over the years.

"There was that Polish girl when we first moved to Elizabeth. God knows where Harry got her. She used to wrap her dress around her thick milk-white legs like a Japanese wrestler and get down on that kitchen floor and scrub it as if it were her lifelong enemy. She left one day to marry a butcher. I used to see her around Broad Street. Always asked about Nick and Audrey. A lovely woman.

"After her came a series of what we used to call (and who knew then it was wrong?) the *Schwartzers*. Lovely girls. Maybe a couple of stinkers but you'd find a couple no matter who you were dealing with. There was that entire family, the Evenings. Each of the girls had a peculiar name. Rhumella was the first and when she left to get married, Prumella came on. She wasn't such a hot cleaner, that Prumella, but she was good

with Nicky. Then she upped and got married. They invited us
to the wedding. We didn't go. We should've, but we didn't. I
think they were insulted, though I sent a check.

"Now I would go. What's the matter, when Selma's brother
died, I wasn't the only white person at the funeral?

"Selma. Six foot four and the color of stale caramel. The
troubles that woman has had. The troubles we've shared over
thirty some-odd years. But I always did right by that girl. I
paid her Social Security when no one was paying their girl's
Social Security. I never missed. Now, with her savings and the
Social Security and the pension that husband draws in, they're
very comfortable, knock on wood."

She stepped out of the shower carefully, suddenly missing
Selma. "Maybe I should put in a long-distance call? But what
would I say? 'I miss you.' Selma would think I've gone off my
rocker."

She heard the outer door close and went into the bedroom.
Maria Carmen had left it spotless. "I'll have to give her a bottle
of toilet water."

She went to the phone and had a revolutionary thought.
"Maybe I should call him? After all, he took *me* to dinner."
Then she moved away from the phone and began to dress.
"Over my dead body. The man is supposed to call the
woman." She stared at herself in the circular mirror over the
chest of drawers, trying to decide whether her new, accidental
hairdo was good or bad, got into her brown bathing suit, put
on her pool robe, had a cup of Sanka, a piece of matzah with a
dab of Fleischman's (no relation to Morris) margarine, put on
her sandals, and, still, the phone hadn't rung.

At the pool, she sat on the chaise next to the one April was
occupying. "So, April," she said, "how come you're not
getting your exercise?" Morris Fleischman was conducting
Simon Sez in the forecourt.

"Simon Sez wave to Madame Meyer," Morris shouted

through his unnecessary megaphone. Half a dozen ladies turned and waved at Ruth.

"I got my exercise last night," April said, winking and yawning. "I had a heavy date last night."

"I heard."

"Morris took me to the Boom Boom Room at the Fontainebleau and he paid for everything." She took a puff of her cigarette holder. "Did he call?"

"Not yet. Probably not ever."

"So it wasn't a match made in heaven, Draisal."

"What match? Don't start with a match. Before you know it, you'll have a fire."

"Did he mention marriage?"

"We only had one date, April."

"At our time of life, kid, you'd better move fast."

"He doesn't want a wife."

"What does he want?"

"He wants a woman."

"So what are you, a cheese *blintza?*"

"You don't understand, April. He wants a *woman.* You should've seen the way he kissed me good night."

"My darling dear, I don't want to shock you but hear this: you are a woman."

"April: he wants a *woman.*"

"If he ever does call you again, Ruth, you might mention the fact that you happen to have a friend who is a *woman.*" April flicked her ashes at the pool. "And Meyer?"

"He wants a wife. Anyway, after the socks incident, I don't think we'll be seeing so much of him."

"He'll be here right after lunch—so he won't have to buy you yours—full of apologies, with that I've-just-shit-in-my-pants look of his— begging to be kicked in the ass. I'd wait for the phone call from the artist, Godiva."

"You can stop with the Draisals and the Godivas, already, I have a name. And I don't think the artist is ever . . ."

April nudged Ruth with her knife-sharp elbow. Frieda was leading the Simon Sez ladies back to the pool under the direction of Morris Fleischman. "A quick, refreshing dip, ladies, in the Monte's specially chlorinated pool to complete our exercise program for the morning and to revitalize our skins. Good morning, again, beautiful *señora*," he said to Ruth. *"Bonjour, mon amour,"* he whispered to April, who looked up, fluttering new, blond eyelashes at him.

"Good morning, killer," she said.

By noon, Belle Fleischman and the public address system had made three announcements (one birthday, one anniversary, and one request that "if anyone finds a white bathing cap, please return it to the office"), none of them telephone calls for Ruth. Thus, when Meyer turned up, apologized, and (contrary to April's prediction) offered to take her to lunch, Ruth accepted. "I should sit here and wait for a telephone call that's never going to come?"

"Wherever you want to go, Ruthie," Meyer offered. "Your choice. Anyplace."

"The Boom Boom Room at the Fontainebleau."

"It's your choice."

The doorman took Meyer's Cadillac away and they went up a short flight of white steps and entered the Fontainebleau, walking through miles of black marble cherubs holding candelabras of entwined gold leaves to the Boom Boom Room which was, a sign announced, closed until five P.M.

They walked through another mile of fluted white marble columns, sculpted carpets, and crystal chandeliers until they found the stairs that took them to the lower level where the coffee shop, the Chez Bon Bon, was located.

This was a low-ceilinged room with gray-and-pink plaid Formica tables, a serpentine counter, canned mellow music emanating from speakers hidden in a three-dimensional mural at its far end. A bored hostess escorted them to a table for four located under the mural, whose elaborate mannequins were dressed in costumes of some eternal historic period and appeared to be comporting themselves in saucy frolic.

"Three dollars for a turkey sandwich," Frieda said, biting into hers with gusto. She and Saul had managed to slip into the Cadillac at the appropriate moment. "That's what I call nerve."

"The capitalist system," Saul said automatically, picking apart his club sandwich and removing bits of tomato, to which he was allergic.

"And you want to know something," Frieda went on, ignoring her husband, "this is not the freshest turkey I ever ate in my life."

"Plus the fact," Saul said, putting his sandwich back together again, *sans* tomato, "the portions are not generous."

After lunch, Ruth declined an invitation from Frieda to go shopping on Lincoln Mall and asked to be dropped off at the Monte. "Suddenly she's in love with the Monte," Frieda said.

By Saturday, it was clear that Max was definitely not going to call. "So he's not calling," April said over a shared meal in her apartmentette. "Big deal. You still got an ace in the hole."

"Meyer?"

"Well, a deuce in the hole."

"Okay," Ruth said to herself, alone, dressing for the Saturday-night dance. "I got the message. I'm never going to hear from him again. Big deal. He was a painter with a funny accent and green eyes. He wasn't really interested in me anyway and what difference does it make because where would it all lead? Nowhere. I'll stick to my own world."

At that moment the telephone rang and she rushed to answer it. Meyer was calling, wanting to know if he might escort her to the dance. She agreed reluctantly, putting the receiver back in its cradle, trying to forget the cottage at the end of Pinder Lane, the strength of Max's arms when he held her in them, and, perhaps most of all, his painting of the huge rose, spilling over onto the walls.

Piccolo Pete was singing as Ruth walked along the pier, Meyer at her side. There was a lone fisherman at the end of it but it was only Abel, dark and short and poker-faced.

"Ruthie," Meyer said, and she turned. He handed her one of Morris Fleischman's four-ounce paper cups. "Black cherry okay with you?"

"Fine with me, Meyer."

"Nice here tonight, no?" A sliver of silver moon hung over them in the black night.

"Very nice, Meyer."

"Ruthie," he said, taking the cup from her hand, resting it on the edge of the bench they had sat on, "I know I promised, but I have to know: you going to marry me, Ruthie?"

She looked into those sad, patient eyes, so reminiscent of Harry's. "Yes, Meyer," she said, retrieving the cup, sipping from it. "I'm going to marry you."

"I'll make you happy, Ruthie."

"I know, Meyer."

She pleaded a headache and concern for April ("It's not like her to miss a T.G.I.S. dance") and allowed him to walk her back to the Monte, promising she would name a date for the marriage within the next two weeks. She kissed him good night on the cheek, making a mental note that she would have to get him to change his after-shave, and allowed him to escort Mae Weissman back to the pier. Another chorus of "Making Whoopee" came from that direction.

April took several moments to come to her door. She was wearing the blond wig and an old flannel nightgown. "How come you're not at the dance?" Ruth asked, turning off the television, sitting down on the davenport, still covered with the Indian print fabric. "What happened to 'I'm-going-to-live-live-live-until-I-die'?"

"The gay life isn't all it's cracked up to be. I needed a breather."

"You're looking awfully green around the gills, April."

"I missed my B-twelve shot," April said, turning away from Ruth's inspection.

"You positive there's nothing else? That Morris Fleischman isn't treating you badly, is he?"

"He's an angel."

"Something's not kosher. You're not telling me everything, April Pollack. I smell a rat."

"As a matter of fact, Ruth," April said, turning to look at her friend, "I . . . Listen, is that your telephone?" The shrill ring came through the wall.

"I wonder who it is?"

"There's one sure way to find out, Draisal."

"I'll be right back. Don't go anywhere."

"Don't worry, the orgy doesn't start until midnight."

Ruth ran to her room, wondering what the bad news was, which of her children had had an accident, who was getting a divorce.

"Hello? Miss Ruth? It's me, Max Rhoads."

"You have some helluva nerve calling at this hour."

"I just this moment flew in from New Mexico. I wanted to talk to you."

"What's in New Mexico?"

"My grandson met with an accident in his hang glider."

"Is he all right?"

"One broken arm and a couple of bruises. He'll live. That boy's made of strong stuff."

"I knew someone had an accident when I heard the phone ring."

"I wanted to call you all the time I was out there, Ruth. I have to confess: I've been thinking about you some."

"They don't have telephones in New Mexico?"

"Not where Scott lives. He's a hippie."

"What kind of Jewish boy is a hippie living in New Mexico without a telephone?"

"He's not a Jewish boy."

"What is he, Syrian?"

"This year I hear tell he's an est."

"Very lovely."

"Ruth, come and have supper with me tomorrow night. I'm all fired up to make us a couple of platefuls of Max Rhoads's famous Southern Fried Chicken."

"Fried food doesn't agree with me."

"This will. I make it with polyunsaturated bread crumbs. Say you'll come."

"I'll come."

"I'll pick you up at seven, Miss Ruth."

"What should I wear?"

"Something comfortable."

She hung up the receiver and went back to April's apartmentette, wondering what she was doing, going to dinner with another man (in his house, yet!) when she was firmly engaged to Meyer, wondering what she owned that was comfortable.

Nineteen

In the end she put on her beige slacks and the off-white top. "Very virginal," she said to herself in the full-length mirror on the back of the bathroom door. She tried to rearrange her hair but it continued to hang straight. "Like Joan of Arc. After." She closed the bathroom door and picked up her big "sporty" beige bag which matched the sandals she was wearing. They had cost thirty-two dollars in Saks in nineteen seventy-six. She believed in good shoes.

She stopped at April's door. "One last inspection from an objective source," she said, wishing she weren't feeling nervous *and* guilty at the same time. She knocked again but there was still no answer. She opened the door thinking that if Morris Fleischman were there at seven o'clock on a Sunday night, he deserved to be caught with his pants down.

Only April was in the apartmentette, dozing on the davenport. Her blond wig was pushed back on her forehead, which showed a light film of sweat. Her purple robe was wrapped around her body, her arms around her chest. She looked green and ill and old. Ruth stared at her, noticing how deep the lines in her friend's face were. That face, Ruth thought, was so different in repose. When it was in action, the eyes lit up the pallid skin and the broad mouth, heavily lipsticked, smiled its clown smile and "you want to reach up and touch her so maybe some of that sour joy would rub off on you. But she hasn't seemed to have much joy lately, even with Morris Fleischman." Ruth turned down the air conditioner

("She'll catch her death of cold"), wiped April's brow, kissed it both out of affection and to see if she had a temperature, and, deciding she wasn't feverish, went down to the arched entrance of the Monte Excelsior to wait for her date.

Mae Weissman, more elephantine than usual in a dress made from some gray, shiny material, and Frieda were at their posts on the Second Floor Balcony. "Taking a little *schpitzeer,* Ruthie?" Frieda asked, leaning over the wrought-iron railing, looking down. "In your good sporty shoes and bag?"

"As it happens, I'm having dinner with a friend."

"I wouldn't want to butt in where I'm not invited," Frieda said, fanning herself with her hand. Ruth thought it probably made a very good fan: it was short and thick and stiff. "But I think I'd better warn you, darling, as one sister-in-law to another, that my brother Meyer is not going to take all of this lying down like a lox, while you keep him on a string like a yo-yo. First you say you do and then you don't. There are other fish in the sea for him to fry, Ruthie dear. You may think you're the queen of the Monte Excelsior, but there are other playgrounds in which a man like Meyer can swing. Do you get the drift of what I'm trying to say?"

"If you could only be specific, Frieda," Ruth said as the Jeep came whizzing around the corner, pulling up at the place where she stood.

"Hello, Miss Ruth, Fine evening tonight, wouldn't you say? Now if you just extend your pretty little hand, I'll help you into this vehicle."

A cough exploded above them. Max looked up. "I'd like you to meet my ex-sister-in-law," Ruth said. "Frieda Glaser and her bosom buddy, Mae Weissman."

"Evening, ladies," Max said, helping Ruth into the Jeep. "How do you do?"

"Very well, thank you," Frieda said, enunciating each

syllable. "Very, very well." She started to fan herself again, very quickly, as if she were attempting to slap her face but kept missing.

"I didn't know the Ritz Brothers were staying at your hotel," Max said, as he gunned the Jeep up to sixty.

"Are we in a race?" Ruth asked, watching the lights of Miami get progressively closer.

"Would you like me to slow down, ma'am?"

"Not especially. I was just asking." She wondered what her hair looked like and then forgot about it as Max put his hand against her cheek in that characteristic gesture of his.

"I thought you didn't like to touch people," she said, taking his hand, studying it. It was square and masculine with light blond hairs streaking across it. She even liked the rings.

"There are very few people in this world I enjoy touching and being touched by, Miss Ruth. I sure do like touching you."

She shivered.

"Are you chilly?"

"No. I'm fine, Max."

Shivers. Thrills. Like a seventeen-year-old chippie. But she liked his hand on hers and was sorry when he had to remove it to drive through downtown Miami.

When they reached the cottage, she suddenly felt over-whelmingly shy and embarrassed. "What on earth is wrong with me?" she asked herself. "I must be coming down with something." She sat on one of the sofas. Though the night was warm, Max had lit a fire in the giant fireplace. He then lit the candles on the dining table and put soft music on the stereo. "It's so romantic," she thought as he went into the kitchen, smiling that mysterious, private smile of his. "If it only had happened forty years ago."

He emerged from the kitchen with a tray on which sat two crystal glasses, a decanter filled with what looked like rust remover, a sugar dish, and a perfectly shaped silver bowl filled with ice cubes.

"Straight or on the rocks?" he asked.

"I don't drink hard liquor, Max."

"Oh, Tennessee sippin' whiskey isn't hard, Miss Ruth. It's soft and kind and helps people make friends easily. Now, say you'll try just a taste."

"I thought you gave up drinking."

"Tennessee sippin' whiskey isn't drinking. It's having a good time. Now, here's how I suggest, if I may, how you have your first taste. (You know, Miss Ruth, I envy you, drinking Tennessee sippin' whiskey for the very first time.) Some folks like to muddy it up with a touch of branch water and maybe a sprig of mint. Not me. I don't even like to dilute it with club soda to bring out, like some folks say, 'the flowers.' What I really like to do with Tennessee sippin' whiskey is to take a slug right out of the bottle, screw the cap back on, pass it to a friend, watch him slowly unscrew the cap, knock back a jolt, put the cap back on, and get him to pass me the bottle. Then we both get to grinning. Now, I can see you are not the bottle-passing kind. Yet. So we'll start you off with a cube of sugar in your glass and you just sip it real slow, letting that delicious ambrosia filter through the cube. Not too fast now. Sip it like you're stroking an old gray cat in the middle of winter. That's it."

Ruth looked up from the glass. "Not so terrible. I thought it was going to be bitter. It's not. It's mellow."

" 'Course it's mellow," Max said, sipping his whiskey neat. "Let me fix you another. Now sip it slow, Miss Ruth. And try grinning. If you have trouble grinning, concentrate on the image of a fat, happy hog."

She laughed. " 'A fat, happy hog.' " She sipped and held out her glass for more. "Am I going to have a hangover?"

"Not from Tennessee sippin' whiskey, ma'am. They filter it

through charcoal and that makes a big difference on Sunday morning in the size of the truck that hit you on Saturday night."

"You're going to make a *shicker* out of me," she said, putting another cube of sugar in her glass.

"*Shicker?*"

"A hard drinker. A drunk. You don't know basic Yiddish? You must come from some fancy family."

"Oh, I come from a very fancy family, Ruth. When I was a kid they used to send me to a farm every winter over in Lynchburg, Tennessee. They got three hundred people in Lynchburg and when I was there, the fishermen were still drowning worms in Mulberry Creek. That's where Davy Crockett built himself a cabin in eighteen hundred and eleven. And that's where I got my first taste of sippin' whiskey, from Mrs. Myra Lou Boland, aged ninety, who gave me a shot which damn near killed me. She looked at me and said, 'Max, does your heart good, don't it?' "

"Here's to Mrs. Boland," Ruth said, holding her glass up.

"No, ma'am. I've drunk enough toasts to Myra Lou Boland. Here's to us, Ruth." He looked at her over the rim of his glass.

"His eyes are biblical," she thought. "Fierce yet sympathetic. And so green. When he looks at me, I feel all funny inside."

A timer sounded in the kitchen. "Shoot," he said, getting up. "There's the blasted chicken. Let me fill your glass while I go see if it's dead yet."

She took the glass and went to the french doors that looked out on the back garden. "Look at me, Ma," she said aloud. "I'm about to sit down to dinner with man who cooked it himself. I haven't even lifted my pinky. I should feel guilty and terrible, but all I feel is happy and thrilled. *Thrilled!* That word. *Oy vey,* that's all I need at my age, thrills."

She stepped out into the moonlight, into a garden that looked as if Rousseau had painted it. "I feel as if I've just walked into another world. Ruth Through the Looking Glass." She sipped her whiskey and felt, for the moment, lithe and young and unafraid. She walked through the garden of huge red flowers to the pool that had been designed to look as if it were a mountain pond, filled with rippling blue water.

On the far side, facing the house, was a canvas awning stretched between two impossibly symmetrical royal palms. Under the awning stood a canvas-upholstered wicker couch of epic proportions. She went to it and sat down. The night was so magical, she hardly gave a thought to the possibility of soiling her beige trousers. She sipped her whiskey. "Why did I ever worry about my beige trousers?"

She laughed. She wondered when she had been happier. She had so suddenly found herself in the midst of the sort of beauty she had only seen in museum paintings. She was as far from the Monte Excelsior, from the places in which she had spent her life, as she could get. She took another sip, realizing that her glass was empty, that Max was standing over her, looking down, like a blond Tahitian god.

"You're looking damned lovely in this moonlight, Miss Ruth."

"You're looking pretty lovely yourself, Mr. Max."

He sat next to her and again she felt the thrill. She no longer worried that she might be ill. He poured more whiskey into her glass.

"To moonlight," he said, staring at her. "You feel it, don't you?" he asked after a moment.

"The whiskey?"

He shook his head, smiling. "No. The magic." He took her glass and put it on the ground next to his. Then he took her hand. "You know, I never thought I'd ever feel it again. I never thought I'd want to make love to anyone again. Suddenly I'm like a kid about to take his first sip of sippin' whiskey." He put his arm around her and kissed her. She resisted at first and tried to pull away. "You going to try and tell me you don't like this?" he asked, pulling her close to him.

"No," she said, "I can't tell you anything of the kind, Max." He kissed her again, his fingers working the back zipper of her blouse.

She pulled away again. "What do you think I am?"

"A wonderfully attractive woman."

"So that's why you like me."

"One of the reasons."

"Name one more."

He put his arms around her and kissed her cheek. "You're bright and sensitive and very feminine and totally alive. I'm hoping that maybe you and I can help each other get the most out of the rest of our lives."

"How much longer do we have?"

"Even if it's only three minutes, we should make the most of them. You're still very much a woman, Ruth."

"You're talking about making love, aren't you?"

"I'm talking about life, honey. Making love is part of it."

"You want me to go to bed with you, don't you?"

"Damn tooting." He kissed her and suddenly her blouse was off. She could feel how excited he was. "Tell me you're not feeling something, Ruth," he said.

"I'm feeling you," she said and laughed. "I'm feeling like a kid again and I'm getting something that feels like a hot flash and . . . Max, please, let's go inside before the chicken gets cold, before we both do something we'll be sorry for."

He started to unhook the back of her second best brassiere.

"I can't change the habits of a lifetime, Max."

The brassiere was off.

"Not tonight, Max."

"Tomorrow we may be dead. From what I hear tell, they don't make love in heaven."

"Not here, Max. Not out in the open."

"This is the best place, Ruth. Right out in the open."

Just as if someone had switched off the light, clouds moved across the moon. The only witnesses left were the stars. It was the first time, she realized, looking up at them, that she had ever made love with her eyes wide open.

Later, after they had finished the chicken and more of the whiskey, when they were lying on the wicker couch under a blanket he had gotten from the house, she asked him why she wasn't drunk.

"Oh, you don't get drunk on sippin' whiskey, Miss Ruth," he said, putting his hand on her cheek. "That's the beauty of it. You just get friendly."

"We certainly got friendly. I never been so friendly with anyone in my life, Max." She looked at him. "Max Rhoads. A nice name."

"Thank you, ma'am."

"What was it before?"

"Before what?"

"Before your family came to this country."

"The family came to this country in seventeen fifty-six as the result of some perfectly reasonable religious persecution. As far as I know, the name has always been Rhoads."

"You must have been one of the first Jewish families in America. You're a regular Yankee, Max."

He laughed and hugged her. "My family's not Jewish, Miss Ruth. Not as far as I know. The ones still alive and practicing are Episcopalians. High church at that."

She sat up. "You're not Jewish?"

"Not even a little."

"Vay es meehr." The look of dismay on her face was so genuine he had to laugh.

"You're laughing? Go ahead. Laugh. I've never even had a date with someone who wasn't Jewish and look at me now."

"God hasn't struck you yet."

She reached for what was left of the whiskey. "Wait till I get home."

"Miss Ruth, you saw all of me. I don't have horns and a tail."

"No," she said softening, "you don't have horns and a tail."

He put his arms around her and she kissed him. "When was the last time you made love, Ruth?"

"Years ago. Maybe ten, maybe more. Harry was the only man I ever went to bed with. Until now, and I don't suppose you could call this a bed. I haven't had much of a love life in the last years."

"I'm going to change all that."

"My mother was right about the gentile boys." She kissed him again and told him he'd have to take her back to the Monte. "I wouldn't want to be responsible for at least two heart attacks if I stayed out all night."

It was four A.M. when the Jeep pulled up in front of the hotel. Frieda, tapping her platinum-painted fingernails against the balustrade of the Second Floor Balcony, waited until they had kissed and Ruth had gotten out of the Jeep before she made her presence known.

"A very lovely time to be arriving home, Ruth. A very, very lovely time. I hope you had a lovely dinner. And I hope you had a very lovely time. A very, very, very lovely time."

"Ditto," said Mae Weissman, indignation incarnate.

 Twenty

"Back trouble, Ruth darling? At our age one has to be careful as to which extracurricular activities one chooses to engage in," Miriam Siegal was saying as Ruth lowered herself into the chaise April had been saving for her.

"Maybe she slept in a funny position," Belle Fleischman, taking a break from her duties, said.

Ruth smiled, though it was true she did feel an unusual and definitely painful twinge from the region just above her lower back.

The Monte Excelsior girls were gathered around the pool, each of them scrutinizing Ruth for signs of what Muriel Resnick liked to call "the wear and tear of senior citizen sex." None of them knew for certain that Ruth was having a sex life. Not even April. Mostly because "this is too good and too new and too private" to share with anyone but Max. She felt as if she were leading a secret and magical life. One word to anyone and the spell would be broken.

Two weeks had passed since she and Max had first made love. They had seen each other every night since. "Not that we've been to bed every night," she thought to herself. "However," and she maneuvered her body into a more comfortable position on the chaise, "we have been in bed a great deal. Indoors as well as out." The thought made her blush.

"Sun too strong, dear?" Mae Weissman—who studied her every move—asked.

"Not at all," Ruth said, closing her eyes. Her love life with Harry, even at the beginning, had been something quite different. With Harry, love had been like traffic on a city street: inexorable, bumpy, no detours, straight ahead. He had been stronger than Max, less polite, quicker. She had felt very much a woman when they had made love together.

"Actually," she amended, "we never really made love 'together.' Harry made love to me. When he was finished, he would roll over and instantly, annoyingly, fall asleep." The city street, after not so many years, had become a dark, punishing place, painful and boring.

"It's so different with Max. For starters, he takes his time. That may be a sign of age or a gesture of consideration. Either way, it makes me feel more of a co-owner in the enterprise instead of a silent partner. And then Max kisses and that makes some difference. And last, but certainly not least, he waits for me to have an orgasm, which, at this late date, I find I can have on a regular basis just like it says in *Cosmopolitan* magazine.

"When it comes right down to it, I guess maybe the major difference between the two men is that Harry expected it just as he expected dinner to be on the table, while Max understands that we're both doing each other a favor. Listen to me! Doing a man a favor! If my poor father, may he rest in peace, knew. And he's not even Jewish yet."

Breaking in on those thoughts with a similar one, Mae Weissman leaned her considerable bulk in Ruth's direction and waited for Ruth's eyes to open before she said, "And I'm given to understand, though I'm certain my informant was misled"—she looked in Frieda's direction as that woman clicked her knitting needles at a reckless speed—"that your new swain is not of the Hebraic persuasion?" She paused, lips pursed together like a mammoth Spaghetti-O, waiting for a rejoinder. None was forthcoming.

"Ah, here comes my brother Meyer," Frieda said, dropping a stitch, glancing at Ruth.

"Hello, Frieda," Meyer said, leaning over, giving her freckled and moist forehead a kiss. "Hello, Mrs. Weissman . . . ladies." He tried out a smile, sitting on one of the plastic folding chairs of which the Monte had a seemingly inexhaustible supply.

"Hello, Ruthie," he said finally, looking as if he were about to weep. Since their engagement, they had had but one telephone conversation, in which Ruth had disengaged herself.

"Hello, Meyer," Ruth said, telling herself: "I refuse to feel guilty. I will not feel guilty."

"How you been, Ruthie?" he asked, taking a fat, short cigar from the pocket of his white shirt, sucking it so that its tip was thoroughly wet, and finally lighting a match and holding it to the cigar's dry end. "You look terrific, Ruthie."

"Her back's not so hot," Belle Fleischman said, her tiny eyes the color of pink tea roses. "Ever since she began her late-night exercise program." One thing you could say about Belle, Ruth thought: she's prejudiced toward no one; she doesn't care who she's malicious about. "And gave up her girdle."

"You gave up your girdle, Ruthie?" Meyer, having a fairly keen awareness from his own married life as to what place a girdle held in a woman's wardrobe, was nonplussed.

"Yes, but she's holding on to her bra, Meyer," April said, waking up from yet one more nap.

"Thank God for small favors," Frieda said.

"You look wonderful, Ruthie," Meyer said. "You got such a nice color in your cheeks."

"Moon tan," Belle Fleischman offered, putting on her glasses, getting herself out of the chaise, and moving nonchalantly toward the office, where the switchboard had been buzzing for some time.

"You want to have a little dinner tonight, Ruthie?" Meyer asked.

"It's Saturday night again?" Ruth asked.

"Now she's losing track of the days," Frieda said, as if describing one more stage in an advancing illness.

"So what about it, Ruthie?" Meyer wanted to know. "You want to let bygones be bygones over a little dinner at the Royal Rumanian?"

Ruth was saved having to answer by an announcement being made in Belle's rasping voice over the public address system. "Phone call for Mrs. Ruth Meyer. Mrs. Ruth Meyer, phone call. There's a phone call for Mrs. Ruth Meyer in the main lobby."

There was a moment of silence as Ruth got up and went toward the lobby before Belle spoke into the public address system again. "Phone call, Mrs. Meyer. The *shagitz* from Coconut Grove, calling Mrs. Ruth Meyer."

"I like your kitchen," Ruth said as she peeled an onion. "Despite the fact it doesn't have modern conveniences."

"We aim to please at Casa Rhoads. What're you cooking tonight?" He was sitting in a bamboo chair, one leg over its fragile arm, eating a carrot.

"Ruth Meyer's Low-Cholesterol, Low-Fat, Low-Sodium, No-Sugar Meat Loaf. You won't be able to tell the difference."

"From what?"

"From Ruth Meyer's High-Cholesterol, High-Fat, High-Sodium, Pinch-of-Sugar Meat Loaf, reprinted in every New Jersey sisterhood cookbook since March of nineteen forty-seven."

She looked at the painting above the butcher block table as she diced the onion. It was the cauliflower, standing on its tray, waiting to be steamed.

"Such a poignant painting," she said, wiping the tears caused by the onion from her eyes with the back of her hand, reaching for a pan. They had an arrangement. Max would cook one night and pay for groceries. Ruth would cook the other night. And pay for groceries.

"You expect *me* to pay for groceries?" she had asked.

"You bet. That way I have no right to complain. Neither do you. It's what I call a right fair arrangement." He had put his hand against her cheek and tried not to laugh at the outraged expression on her face.

"I never heard of such a thing. Where I come from the man pays for the food, the woman cooks it."

"I hate to point this out, Miss Ruth, but where you come from is not where you're at now. Where you're at now—the way I see it—is that you're not getting paid with groceries to cook every night. Think of it in terms of wages and labor."

"You sound like my ex-brother-in-law." But she did think about it and finally agreed. "All I want to know is: who does the dishes?"

"I'm a very methodical man," he said, explaining that he'd do the dishes on the nights he didn't cook, and vice versa.

"If you're so methodical, why haven't you figured out a plan to begin work on your painting again?"

"First I'm working on you, honey. Then I'll think about my painting." He kissed her.

"I never been kissed so much in my life," she said, packing the meat loaf into the pan.

"You don't like it?"

She looked up through the onion tears. "Oh, I love it, Max. I love it." At least she said they were onion tears.

Later, after the sippin' whiskey and the meat loaf and the bliss of making love under the canvas canopy, she said, "You know, it's like night and day between the atmosphere here and

the atmosphere at the Monte. There, everyone's a big baby,
wrapped up in their towels, lying in their chaises, *cvetching* and
crabbing and concerned, really, only with their own shrinking
needs and expanding fears. They're all over sixty, yet every
single one of them is still looking for Mommy and Daddy.
When I'm there, that's the way I feel. Here, with you, I'm an
adult. I'm not afraid.

"You want to know something, Mr. Rhoads? I like paying
for my own groceries, cooking and washing dishes every other
night. At first, to tell the truth, I was insulted. But now I see
the point. I'm responsible for me. And you're responsible for
you."

"We could have a good life together, Ruth."

"*Oy.*"

"What's *oy* mean?"

"Yiddish shorthand for 'stop, you're making me nervous.' "

"Our courting days are over, honey. I want you to check out
of the Monte Excelsior and into Casa Rhoads."

"*Oy.* Don't say it again."

"It wouldn't be set in cement. We could have a trial."

"And I'd be sentenced to life. Do you know what my friends
and relatives would think if I moved in here?"

"What?"

"That I was a kept woman."

"Then they'd be mighty wrong. You'll be splitting the
taxes, the electricity, and the gas. Luckily, there is no
mortgage."

"I should have known."

"Unless, of course, you want me to pay the taxes,
electricity, and gas and you do all the housework, the cooking,
the shopping, the gardening . . ."

"You know something, big shot?"

"What?" he asked, kissing her.

"You're a women's liberationist in disguise."

"I'm not in disguise, Miss Ruth. Come on, say you will."

"Do you think we could play it cool for a while longer, Max? I'm still getting used to a lot of things. A lot of things!"

"All right. We'll play it cool for a while longer. But allow me to say life with me would be a lot more fun. You'd have someone to wake up with in the morning. You'd have someone to fight with. You'd get an awful lot of kisses. And think of your future as a nighttime fisherwoman."

"There's no doubt about it, Max. You could teach me a lot."

"You've already taught me something, Ruth."

"What's that?"

"That my late middle period is still appreciated by at least one human being in these continental United States. Here I thought I was the only one left and there were times when I wasn't all that sure about me."

"Your late middle period is already an established art fact, Max. Now what we have to get you started on is your early late period."

"You, Miss Ruth, may be able to do just that."

The Jeep arrived at the Monte Excelsior long after Piccolo Pete and his rumba band had played their last cha-cha-cha. "I've never been such a dirty-stay-out-late in my life," Ruth said, kissing Max good night.

"When we're living together in Coconut Grove and the bloom is off our romance, we'll go to bed every night at ten, and satisfy our lust early in the morning, like wild horses."

"Do wild horses . . . ?"

"*Madonna mío,*" a familiar voice said, and they both looked up to find Morris Fleischman standing above them on the Second Floor Balcony. "I wonder if you and your escort could lower your voices *un peu?* My guests retire at a seemly hour and we shouldn't want to disturb their nocturnal wanderings in the land of Nod, wouldst we?"

"Good night, Mr. Rhoads," Ruth said, kissing Max yet one more time and heading into the courtyard. "And good night, Morris Fleischman, cha-cha-cha."

"I can just see my daughter's face," she thought as she climbed the stairs, "when I announce I am moving in with a *goyishcha* artist. Nicky wouldn't be so bad. Knowing him, he'd probably think it was a good idea. Of course there'd be Frieda to deal with. And Meyer. Poor, dear Meyer. Maybe Mae Weissman could help him forget his troubles. Though if I do say so myself, she'd be a terrible replacement. Why that woman doesn't go on a diet . . ."

She stopped a few feet from April's door. "Oh, my God," she said. Below her, in the courtyard, Morris was having an argument with Armando.

"Are you crazy, you little punk—"

"No, *señor*, it is you who are *loco*. You told me . . ."

Ruth ran to the inert figure lying in front of Apartmentette One Two Four. "April! Are you all right? April?" She tried to lift her but couldn't. She went into April's apartmentette and picked up the phone.

"Good evening, *mon amour*," Morris's voice said after a few moments.

"For God's sake, stop that and get up here right away. Bring Armando with you. April's passed out in front of her door and I can't budge her. I don't even know if she's breathing."

Twenty-one

Armando and Morris, between the two of them, managed to get April into the apartmentette. Morris laid her on the davenport with surprising tenderness. "Light as a fairy feather," he said, standing over the bed, looking down at his "inamorata."

Armando was sent down to the switchboard to call Dr. Bellskie. "Get him here as quickly as you can, Armando," Ruth said. "If he can't come, you'd better call an ambulance. I don't like the way she's breathing."

Armando managed to get through to first the doctor's wife and finally the doctor himself. "He will be here in a quarter of an hour, *señora,*" Armando reported.

Morris stood over April, holding her hand, tears in his eyes. "She's the only woman I ever loved," he said, and for no good reason she could think of, Ruth believed him. "She's the only one who could dream as I dream, the only one who had the touch of true romance in her soul. Oh, beautiful, beautiful lady," he said, falling on one knee. "Don't desert me now."

Ruth put her hand on his shoulder and asked him if he could wait outside. She wanted to undress her friend.

"But of course, *madonna.* Of course." He went to the door, turned, took a final look at April, and left.

Ruth touched April's forehead with her palm, after loosening her robe. Not satisfied, she pressed her own cheek against April's forehead. "She feels cool. If only she weren't so gray." She stood up and turned away. "What the hell is the

matter with her?" She put her hands to her eyes. "I won't cry.
I will not cry. I am famous for being good in emergencies. I
will not break down now."

She turned back to the bed and began undressing April,
hoping she'd wake up with a customary, "What the hell is
going on here, anyway?" But she was as docile as a stuffed doll
as Ruth took off the robe and the matching negligee and got
her into her shorty nightgown and under the covers. The wig
had slipped forward on her head during the process. "That
goddamn wig," Ruth said, reaching for it, pulling it off
April's head.

"My God," she said. "My God!" Where once April's hair
had grown brown and unruly, there were only tufts and naked
patches of scalp. Ruth replaced the wig quickly, as if she were
covering some pornographic exposure, some terrible shame.
"What am I crying about?" she asked herself, stepping away
from the bed. "What's so terrible? So she has a minor scalp
problem. What's the matter, Isobel Shakin isn't as bald as a
billiard ball? It's not unusual. It's not the end of the world."
She sat in the uncomfortable chair facing the television set, her
hands folded into tight fists, as if she were preparing to fight
for April.

"I know," she admitted to herself. "I don't want to know
but I know. I know why April looked so green when she came
back from her supposed B-twelve shots and I know why April
is having an affair with Morris Fleischman and I know why
she's been even stranger than usual the last few months. The
funny thing is, I think I've known all along. I was too scared,
too silly, to allow myself to know I knew."

She stopped crying when Dr. Bellskie, the only thin doctor
she could remember knowing, came out of April's apartmentette an hour later, looking grim, like the suit he was wearing.

"She's up now," he said to Ruth and Morris, who had been

standing at the balustrade, staring down into the pool. "She wants to see Mr. Fleischman first." He waited for Morris to go into the apartmentette before he sighed and took his little black satchel and his five o'clock shadow down the steps into the courtyard, his head bent as if he were a defeated man instead of a good doctor in "the playground capital of the world."

Ruth watched him leave and then transferred her attention to the yellow sun making its first tentative move against the red sky. It was very quiet. All she could hear was the sound of the garbage truck in the service alley, the sound of someone snoring (Muriel Resnick?). Morris came out, his eyes red, his hands in the pockets of his trousers. He didn't say anything. He went down into the courtyard and sat on the edge of a chaise and buried his face in his hands.

"I've always been a chicken," she thought, forcing herself to go in to April, holding her hands together so they wouldn't tremble.

April was sitting up, two pillows propped behind her, the green cigarette holder clenched between her teeth. Her wig was in place. The rouge and lipstick she had applied only made her seem more sallow, more seriously ill.

"Now, get that scared shitless look off your face, Draisal, and sit down. Not there. Here, next to me. I'm not contagious."

"I'm not sitting down until you put that cigarette out."

"You really are a terrible pain in the ass, you know that?" April said, jabbing the cigarette into a Monte Excelsior ashtray. Ruth sat on the edge of the bed and April took her hand. "Do I really have to say anything, Ruth?"

"Do you think I want to hear it? But you have to say it. Aloud. To me."

"All right," April said, taking a deep breath, looking away

from Ruth. "I'm going to die. Not next year or in a couple of months but in a couple of weeks. I'm going to die, Ruthie, and I'm so fuckin' scared I don't know what to do. I'm so fuckin' alone, Ruth."

"Oh, no, you're not, April Pollack. Not by a long shot."

The two women put their arms around each other and cried.

Later, April told Ruth she had dismissed Morris Fleischman from her life. "We had a grand romance. I don't want him to see me disintegrate. Morris Fleischman is a man who is capable of making himself believe almost anything he wants, but even he couldn't watch me fall apart and still think me beautiful. Oh, yes, he really believes I'm beautiful. He's the only man who ever has. Let him keep thinking it. I told him I couldn't see him anymore and under all that affectation, he was able to understand.

"But I want you to know everything, Ruthie. My relationship with Morris was a lucky confection, a late plum God threw me. What you and I have, Ruthie, is the real thing. We shouldn't leave anything unsaid. We should talk about everything. You know what it is, don't you?"

" 'C'?"

"You hit it. The disease we never mention by name. Cancer."

"Can't they . . ."

"Sure. They could slit me open, stick a bag at my side, a piece of plastic where my tits should be. So I'd gain a month, a week, a few days. But I won't go through the pain, Ruth. I won't go through the indignity. I've stopped the chemotherapy. I want to die with a full head of hair on my head."

"Can't the doctor . . . ?"

"That's the first lesson you have to learn, Ruthie. Nothing Can Be Done. It's taken me a long time to believe that. But you know something? I'm ready. I've got only one reason for living and that's you."

"Morris Fleischman . . ."

"He loves me and he loves Lana Turner. He doesn't know either of us. What I always wanted was a man who would love me despite the fact I look like a Phyllis Diller doll. So I got him. We both had a little fun." She stopped and looked down at her left hand, at the wedding-band-engagement-ring set she always wore. "Herb didn't love me. He married me thinking, 'I'm no prize. She's no prize. We'll make the best of it.' You know something, Ruthie? I spent my entire early life getting ready to be a wife. I spent my middle years trying to be one. And I've spent my old age regretting it." She turned her head away but her hand stayed in Ruth's. "It's been some fuckin' life."

"How long have you known, April?"

"Since just before Harry died."

"And you didn't tell me? You didn't say . . . ?"

"You didn't have enough with Harry, did you? What'd you need, double agony? Besides, do you think I believed the cocksucker at first? Not this kid, I told myself. I'm not dying yet. They're wrong. I'll go to someone else, I'll find a better doctor. I went to Meiselman. To both Deehls. To Seltzer. Gittleman. Spivack. Weissberg. They all said the same fuckin' thing. I didn't care. I said it was a conspiracy. I denied it. April Pollack ain't dying, I said, over and over again. I said it for months. Then I got furious. Who the fuck was God, thinking He could do this to me? Just when you and I were getting ready to start a new life. He had to wait for that moment to take me? I used to go upstairs into the bathroom, lock the door, run the water, and scream.

"Don't think I didn't think of suicide. Get that little disapproving pissy look off your face. What difference would it have made? But there's always that tiny deceptive ray of hope. Maybe Florida sunshine would stop it. Maybe there'll be a new cure. A miracle. Who knew?

"Bellskie knew. Right away that smart motherfucker knew. First thing he did was get all the tests and diagrams from the doctors in Elizabeth. From that first day in his office, he didn't hold out any hope. That's what he said, the little shit: 'I don't hold out any hope, Mrs. Pollack. I'm sorry.' The chemotherapy would check it for a while but how long, he told me, was anybody's guess."

She stopped talking and looked at her friend. "What're you crying about? Stop it already. You think it helps?"

"Yes," Ruth shouted. "It does help. It helps me. Why the hell couldn't you tell me from the start, that's what I want to know?"

"Draisal, lower your *yenta* voice or Miriam Siegal will think we're killing each other."

"I don't give a rat's fuck what Miriam Siegal thinks, goddamn it."

April lay back and laughed. "Such language. This is almost worth it to hear you curse."

"Look at the time you've wasted, April. Don't you know I care for you? Don't you know that you've been a mother, a sister, and a friend to me? You've denied me precious time, April. Time we should have been spending together."

"There's still time, Ruth," April said, holding out her arms. "There's still plenty of time."

Ruth lay next to her and the two women embraced. "You know something," Ruth said. "I never told you how much I love you. I wasn't able to. I wasn't brought up to use words like *love*. So I'm telling you now: I love you, April Pollack. And for once in your life, you're going to let someone take care of you. Right?"

"Right. Take care of me, Ruth. I'm all yours, *mamala*."

In the morning, when she returned to her apartmentette, Ruth called the doctor. "How long has she got and what should I do?" He told her. April had anywhere from ten days to four months. She was to take pills to help with the pain. Only at the very end need she go into the hospital and that was to be avoided, they both agreed, if at all possible.

"I could recommend a psychiatric nurse," Dr. Bellskie said.

"She's got cancer, not insanity."

"The nurse would help prepare her to die. There's a special and relatively new branch of medicine devoted to—"

"April doesn't need any help dying."

"The nurse could give you support. Help you—"

"I'll help myself."

Morris Fleischman, looking gray and sad, said he would do anything he could. She had him have her bed moved into April's apartmentette. She told him not to tell anyone, that April "doesn't want anyone to know how ill she is. We plan to live our lives together as normally as possible until the time comes when she has to remain in bed. You can let the *yentas* believe she had a mild heart attack, which will explain why I've moved in with her."

Morris Fleischman burst out crying. Ruth touched him for the second time since they had met and went in to April. "You're going to get sick and tired of me if we live like this," April said. "Go put your bed back where it belongs."

"I'm sick and tired of you already and my bed belongs here. How are you feeling?"

"I'm in a little pain, if you really want to know."

"On a scale of one to ten?"

"Four and a half."

"With you that means an eight." Ruth went to the medicine cabinet and brought back two of the deadly yellow pills Dr. Bellskie had left for pain.

"I only want one."

"Suddenly you're a doctor? Why one? Why not two? Why did Bellskie say two if you're only going to take one?"

"I get too foggy on two. I want to know what's going on. If it still hurts I'll take the other one, believe me."

Ruth watched her as she swallowed the pill. She seemed, almost overnight, to have shriveled, to have new wrinkles, less skin, to have started growing inward.

Later, Ruth went back to her apartmentette (Belle had made it clear that she was still expected to pay her full rent, bed or no bed) and called Max. She told him that April, her best friend, was dying. He came that afternoon. Ruth asked Belle to leave them alone for a few moments, that she would mind the switchboard. The girls, from their chaises around the pool, sat in fascinated silence, watching Ruth and her gentile boyfriend talk earnestly behind the glass windows of the lobby.

"I won't be able to see you, Max, for perhaps a long time. I have to be with April."

"I don't want to question your judgment, Ruth, but do you really believe she wants you with her all of the time? Nursing her like a child? She might well want to be alone sometimes. I sure enough would."

"*I* want to be with her all of the time, Max. *I* want to nurse her. When she wants to be alone, she'll tell me to take a walk. I don't know how to explain it to you. April is the only woman in my life I have ever allowed myself to love. She comes first. I won't give up a second with her. I can't, Max."

"And what about us, Miss Ruth?" he asked, putting his hand against her cheek.

She took his hand and held it. "We have unfinished business, Max. To be continued. To be taken up where we left off."

"If it's still there," he said, looking into her eyes.

"For me it will still be there, Max."

"And in all honesty, I suspect it will always be there for me, too, Ruth."

She watched him—along with Frieda, Saul, Mae Weissman, Muriel Resnick, Belle Fleischman, Miriam Siegal, and
other assorted guests—as he walked across the lobby and out
the door, as he got into his Jeep and, looking back at Ruth
once more, waved good-bye.

"Good riddance," Frieda said, forcing her needles into a
new and intricate pattern.

Ruth ignored the girls as she went up the stairs to April's
apartmentette and let herself in.

It wasn't until two days later that April asked about the
painter.

"He won't be around for months. He has a commission."

"Hoo-ha. A commission. Where's this commission?"

"New Mexico."

"You didn't want to go with him?"

"I wasn't asked."

April looked at her friend busying herself at the sink. "I
don't like it."

"Then lump it. He's like every other man. His work comes
first. Now drink your tea and close your mouth."

"She's always asking for the impossible, that Ruthie," April
said.

 Twenty-two

In the early mornings, when they were indoors, April didn't
wear the wig though her hair was still patchy. "What I look
like," she said, every morning.

"You look fine to me. Now eat your breakfast."

"I'm not hungry."

"You have to eat, April."

"Why?"

Later, they would walk up to Lummus Park and sit on one of the benches, watching the older people playing cards, singing in Yiddish and sometimes Russian, practicing for the folk dance festival that never seemed to come. Sometimes they just sat in the sunshine, their eyes closed, listening to conversations.

"Someone told me they saw you in Florida when I was in New York."

"Who was it?"

"What difference does it make? Someone told me they saw you in Florida."

"So who was it?"

"Someone. I don't even think you know this person."

"Suppose I do?"

"Listen, Hannah, forget it. Someone told me they saw you in Florida when I was in New York. Let's leave it at that, shall we?"

"Who was it?"

"Someone."

"You know something," April said, as they walked back along Ocean Road, past the tiny, clean hotels and the blind man who played the "Anniversary Song" on his harmonica, day and night. "I've spent my entire life in Jewish ghettoes, just like my mother and my grandmother. They came to America to make their children Yankees. I'm about as Yankee as Golda Meir. I've never known any gentiles. Not intimately. I've had no non-Jewish friends. Not real friends. There was always that invisible line: they're *goyem,* we're Jews.

"Even in Elizabeth, it was the same goddamned thing. My social life revolved around the Hadassah and the sisterhoods, women just like me: born in America, raised in high middle

Yiddle traditions, traditions as empty to us as they are to the kids who come after."

"Suddenly she's a philosopher. You want to sit down for a minute?"

"I'm telling you something, Ruthie. Listen to me: you take away the mink coat and the Cadillac and the diamond-and-ruby cocktail watch and you know what you got?"

"What?"

"A peasant lady from Pinsk or Minsk or wherever the hell our ancestors came from. Is there anything sadder than a Jewish wife? At least the husbands had the Business. The kids have their colleges, their new professions. But what did we have?"

"Good times. A sense of family. A feeling of support, of security."

"That's not nearly enough, even if it's true."

"If you had it to do all over again?"

"I'd get a job, have a career, and fuck every man that walked into my office on the fifty-fifth floor of the Empire State Building. I'd make sure I was a somebody instead of a something."

Ruth reached over and touched April's forehead. Not that she ever ran a temperature. But it was something to do, a way to communicate. What was the good of talking about all that now? "You've had good things in your life, April."

"Thank you, Little Mary Moonshine."

"You have."

"Early on. My expectations. They were the best things. I believed that once I got away from my parents and that terrible smell of my mother's cooking, I was going to have a wonderful life. Marriage was going to solve everything.

"And in the beginning, Ruth, I did love Herb. And he loved me. We would've done anything for one another. But how can two people continue to be in love for forty years when all he could think about was the price of rubber for that goddamned tire company of his and all I could think of was what pin Deborah was going to give me for being on the contribution committee: the plain gold heart or the one with the infinitesimal diamond."

"You've had good friends. That doesn't count?"

"I've had you. That counts for more than you'll ever know, Ruth."

They spent their afternoons watching reruns on television ("When they took Mary Tyler Moore off, that's when I lost my will to live") and the evenings playing rummy and, inevitably, talking.

"You're not tired?" Ruth would ask.

"I look tired, don't I?"

"You don't look so tired." She looked awful. A wicked witch in a child's fairy tale. She had lost so much weight.

"I'll have plenty of time to sleep," April said, and smiled. She was not, Ruth realized, afraid to die anymore. She wasn't even bitter. "It's me," Ruth thought, "who's afraid now."

"I want to talk about Herb tonight," April said, as if she were announcing the topic of her sermon for the evening.

"So who's stopping you?"

"I haven't really talked about him since he died ten years ago next month. I don't miss him. I never did. By the time he died, we had stopped caring for each other in almost every way. I have to admit it: by the time he died, a piece of me was glad he was dead.

"He ate so much. Such a *chozer*. No matter what the doctors told him, he still shoveled it in, as if every meal was his last. That's the way he approached life. Only I happened to be the dish he shoved aside. I understood. I wasn't much good to him. I couldn't give him a kid, and that would've made the

difference. I certainly was no help to him in the business. Who
the hell could work up an interest in tires?

"And his other preoccupations, besides eating, wasn't what
you might call riveting. Pinochle with the Boys. In the
beginning it was every Friday night. Later, it got to be every
Tuesday night, too. Who the hell did that cocksucker think he
was fooling? I knew her name, address, and Social Security
number. You remember when I flew out to Vegas to get my
divorce . . . ?"

"Could I forget an event like that?"

". . . and he came out and promised and pleaded and
begged and I let my arm be twisted? The very first Friday
night, where was Herb? 'Pinochle with the Boys. Don't wait
up, April.' By then I really didn't give a hot shit.

"How many times did you ever see us laugh together, Herb
and me? Maybe, if the TV was loud enough and Milton Berle
was vulgar enough, we'd both work up a chuckle. There was
no mutual joy, no understanding, no respect, and no interest."

"I never knew it was so bad, April."

"Who you trying to fool, Draisal? It was just as bad for you.
What about Harry and his Miss Frazer? What about Charlie
Silverman and that *curva* checkout girl from Foodtown? What
about Teddy Cohen and Al Paskow and Mark Zimmerman?
They all had them. And when you think about it, who could
blame them? They were out in the world, making big money,
driving big cars, smoking big cigars. They were living. Why
do you think every single one of them dropped dead the
minute they retired? Bored to death.

"We were safe. We had developed Boredom Immunity. We
were bored the whole fuckin' time! Cleaning houses (or
overseeing the maid) isn't exactly mentally stimulating work.
No one could call going to sisterhood meetings a life-enriching
experience. We were dumb and boring and none of us ever got

any younger or prettier except for the desperate ones who ran
and had nose jobs and face lifts and checked into milk farms
and a helluva lot of good it did them.

"I tell you, Ruth, our generation of women was screwed
from the beginning. What was the happiest period in your
life? Don't tell me. Mine was the same. When I was nineteen
and working, bringing home twenty-three fifty a week,
assistant to the assistant buyer of aprons in Macy's basement. I
loved it. I loved the screaming and the shouting and the
subway ride home and how tired I felt all of the time and the
terrible luncheonette food I ate and the corns on my toes
because I pushed them into heels two sizes too small because,
as you know, I don't exactly have pigeon's feet.

"Herb used to sing 'My Feets Too Big' to me when he was
just getting started. How the hell did they get into those
businesses, I'd like to know? How did he come to choose
tires? How did Harry decide on cigars? How come they all
made so much money? The war?

"You know, my mother-in-law used to touch wood every
time someone mentioned World War II? 'Thank God for
the War,' she'd say. What an awful bitch that woman was.
When we invited her out to our new house in Jersey, she'd
bring food for her and her second husband. 'Just a little soup
for Sam and me.' I wanted to kill her. She was high kosher.
'A barren woman,' she told me, 'has no right not to be
kosher.'

"I don't think the next generation has a chance, either. So
they don't go to sisterhood meetings. They go to the club. So
their husbands aren't pushing tires. They're putting in new
teeth. Oh, maybe they read a little more because they belong
to Book-of-the-Month and twice a year they go to a matinee
but they're all still locked in the same prison, the same dead
end: husband goes to work; wife stays home.

"It's their daughters who have a chance. Don't tell me I'm a Women's Libber. You're damned right I am. Let the wives go out and work and feel some respect for themselves. Let them throw a few bucks into the household pot. That way they won't be their husbands' maids, their kids' nurses.

"Can you imagine Herb or Harry or any of them lifting one finger to help with the housework? 'Go get me a cold glass of water,' Herbie would say to me seven times a week as he lay in bed in his undershorts, looking like a yellow marshmallow, hypnotized by the television. Not just a glass of water, mind you. A *cold* glass of water. Like a fool, I went and got it for him. Which meant I had to *schlep* down to the kitchen, wrestle the ice-cube tray, run the water, and bring it all back upstairs, by which time he was asleep. 'A hostile act,' Ann Landers said when I wrote in. 'You should seek help from your clergyman.' Can you imagine Rabbi Roger Pincus Hairtoff offering help? He'd turn to Herbie and ask if perhaps the glass shouldn't have been chilled.

"Oh, Herbie. Herbie! Unlike your mother, may you rest in peace. If there is a heaven (which I seriously doubt) and if I do join you, let me tell you something, kid: things are going to be different up there. A helluva lot different." She stopped talking and took a breath.

"Talking my head off, huh? Nice thing about knowing I'm going to die is that I can say anything I want. Death is making an honest woman of me."

"It's good to hear it all said out loud, April. But you must be tired. You want to go to sleep now?"

"A few more minutes. I had a dream about Herbie last night, Ruth. Scared the shit out of me. But it wasn't a bad dream. Herbie was standing on a hill, whistling. You know how his whistling used to drive me crazy? It was like being married to a Musak speaker. He could whistle the entire scores from *Sound of Music, Oklahoma,* and *Man of La Mancha.* Every time I hear 'The Impossible Dream,' I get a big, fat knot in my stomach.

"Anyway, there was Herbie, whistling his little heart out. But somehow it didn't make me want to go for his jugular the way it used to. For one thing, I liked the song he was whistling. Nothing I could identify but at least it wasn't the crap he learned from standing around too many elevators. Something old, with charm. It made me feel good about the man, the way I felt when he first picked me up at the Knights of Pythias dance on Pitkin Avenue.

"I stood there, listening, and finally I realized he was whistling for me. It was a signal. He wanted me to come to him on that hill. I said, 'Listen, Herb, I'm not your dog any longer. Don't whistle for me.'

"He stopped and said, 'I'm not whistling for you, April. I'm whistling to you.' And he started again. A medley of April songs. You know the kind of thing. 'April in Paris.' 'Those April showers / May come your way.'

" 'I'm scared, Herbie!' I shouted up to him. 'I'm afraid to come.'

" 'Don't be afraid, kid,' he said. 'I'm here, waiting for you.' So I went to him. I was young and not bad-looking again. And that hill, it was nothing. A snap. I can't walk down the fuckin' balcony steps, Ruth, but that hill was so easy, so goddamned easy." She closed her eyes, too big for her emaciated face.

Ruth whispered a question she had thought of asking ever since she had found out. "April, you want to talk to a rabbi?"

"Nope. The only thing being a Jew ever did for me was to make me feel I belonged. But belonged to what?—that's the question. If I hadn't felt I belonged, I might have broken out, done something else with my life. It was too easy and too hard. Belonging."

She opened her eyes and tried to sit up. "You know something? I've always wanted a sister named May. Get it? April. May. You're my May. 'Those April showers / They bring the flowers / That bloom in May.' You're still blooming, Ruthie-May. I want you to promise me something. Promise me you'll live your life. Promise me you'll take chances. Promise me you won't be safe and frightened, that you won't stick yourself in this ghetto for the rest of your days. Promise me you won't be a coward."

"I promise, April."

"And one last request."

"Yes?"

"Don't you dare let them put 'Beloved Wife' on my tombstone. As a matter of fact, don't let them give me a tombstone. I don't want to be stuck in the ground. Have them put my ashes in a nice little *shisel* somewhere. And, if you get a rabbi, at least get a good-looking . . ."

"Stop, April. Please."

"Why stop?"

"You're making me cry so terribly."

On a perfect Sunday morning, two weeks after she had found April passed out in front of her door, Ruth woke with a dry throat. "I feel as if the Russian Army marched through my mouth," she said to herself as she tiptoed across the room to the kitchenella, moved the flowers Morris Fleischman insisted on sending daily to a more convenient spot, and poured herself a glass of apple juice.

She drank it while she looked at April, all curled up against the wall, her big feet sticking out from under the blanket. "That April," Ruth said, finishing the juice, rinsing the glass, placing it on the miniature drainboard. "She can never keep her feet under the covers."

She went into the bathroom, urinated, washed her hands,
brushed her teeth, shook her head at the image in the mirror,
and went back into the other room, with the intention of
covering April's feet.

April was all curled up. One hand, closed in a fist, was
pushed up against her lips, distorting them. Ruth reached
down and pulled her hand away. It was cold. So cold. Too
cold. She lost control for a moment and began to shake her
friend's body. "Wake up, April. Wake up."

It was clear, after a moment, that April would never wake
up. Ruth lay down on the bed and put her arms around April's
body. She held her like a mother comforting a sleeping child.
Finally, she felt she could cry. She didn't think she could ever
stop.

Nick wanted to fly in and "take care of things."

"That's not why I called you, *yonkle.*"

"So why did you call me?"

"Because I needed someone to talk to who wouldn't think
that I was asking for someone to come and 'take care of
things.' "

"Ma, please. Let me come and help you."

"Definitely not."

"I'm coming anyway. I know you. This is one of your
famous SOSs."

"Nicky, if you come flying out here, so help me God, I'll
never—"

"Ma! Your best friend just died. She had no one else in the
world but you. You cannot do the whole thing by yourself."

"Why not? Because you say so? Nicky, please, listen to me:
let me do this by myself. I want to. I need to. April is my
responsibility. My sole responsibility. Can you understand
that?"

There were a few moments of coast-to-coast silence. "I think I can, Ma."

Morris Fleischman wanted to help, too, but couldn't. "Beautiful lady," he would say each time he saw Ruth, and burst out crying.

She arranged it all. She talked to the funeral director Belle (who was, oddly enough, being very helpful) recommended, a short man with a waxed mustache. She told him to keep it simple. "Simple is expensive, Mrs. Meyer."

"Keep it simple and not expensive, Mr. Gorell."

She talked to several rabbis Belle had lined up and finally chose the youngest and best-looking. "Keep it secular and sincere."

"Will do, Mrs. Meyer."

She wavered between inviting the girls and not inviting them. She finally decided to invite them. They sat in the row behind her in their most somber pants suits, talking in what seemed to them appropriately sepulchral whispers. Morris and Belle sat a row behind them, Morris looking ten years older. Belle had her arm around his narrow shoulders, attempting to comfort him.

They were in the smallest chapel of the Mount Ararat Final Resting Assemblage in downtown Miami. The walls were a combination of beige plasterboard and ersatz stained glass. She sat not listening to the rabbi (how she would've liked to have Rabbi Kauffman there and for a second had thought of calling him, of asking him to come) who, after all, hadn't known April and wasn't likely to say anything meaningful. But still, as April had said, she had "belonged" and certainly it was too late for her not to belong now.

Later, after Belle had taken Morris away, after Ruth had refused an invitation from Frieda and the girls to a "quiet luncheon," she returned for a last view of the genuine sterling silver urn and its final resting place. She had the feeling that April was with her, having a pretty good time. "If you think it's difficult to die a dignified death in this country," she could hear her friend saying, "just try and get a simple, serious funeral."

"Well, April," Ruth said as she walked along Biscayne Boulevard, past the old hotels being torn down and the new ones going up, "you did have a dignified death. And your funeral was, with the exception of some of the mourners, fairly serious. You got your niche and you got your handsome rabbi."

"All I want to know is, was he well hung?"

"Oh, April. April. How I miss you already. That filthy mouth. That *yenta pisc*. What am I going to do without you?"

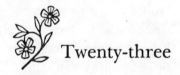

Twenty-three

She spent the two weeks following April's death walking the streets of South Beach, sitting in Lummus Park. It was so quiet in the early mornings, she could hear the tap-tap-tap of an old man's walker as he made his way up Ocean Road on some daily pilgrimage.

"You're not sitting *shiva?*" Frieda asked as they met in front of the El Morro bodega where that woman surreptitiously did her shopping. "For your best friend?"

"They're moving the davenport out of my room and putting in the orange crates at this very moment, Frieda."

"You're getting very sour in your old age, Ruth. Very sour."

She enjoyed walking past the *"shalom"* shops. It was April who had pointed out that a tenth of the little stores in South

Miami Beach were named Shalom. "The Shalom Bakery. The Shalom Barbershop. The Shalom Shoe Store. The Shalom Medical Center. It's a very popular name."

"It means 'peace and hello' in Hebrew," Ruth had said.

"It also means 'good-bye.' "

The Shalom Bakery on Washington featured humantasshen, challah, onion bread. "Close your eyes and you're in Brooklyn," April had said.

Ruth went into the shops they had gone into together and found herself buying miniature crates of candy oranges, pirate heads carved from coconuts, stuffed baby alligators. "Seven months of the year I'm dead," one shop owner told her. "Then the guys with the money come down. If I didn't own my own home, if I didn't have my Social Security, to tell you the truth, I'd be dead twelve months a year."

She avoided the Hebrew Home for the Aged on Collins ("such a final place," April had said) and made it her business to pass the Paris Theater at least once a day.

"Look, there's a live show there, Draisal," April had said during one of their walks. "And there's a two P.M. performance. Let's go. When's the last time you saw something live?"

"It's a burlesque theater, April."

"We'll have a few laughs."

They crossed the street, going under the marquee of the theater and up to the booth where a young man with suspicious hair sat, chewing gum.

"So what's the show?" April asked.

"You wouldn't like it, missus."

"If it's because there's a dirty word or two, believe me, that wouldn't bother me, sonny."

"Take it from me, missus, you wouldn't like it."

"And why not?"

"Boys," the cashier said. "Boys are up on the stage, taking off their clothes."

"Jewish boys?"

"Jewish, black, white, green. All kinds of boys. You wouldn't like it."

April marched over to the pictures displayed in the outer lobby. They were of young men, posing in athletic supporters. "Just what I need to see after my lunch, a bunch of kids wearing jock straps."

"They don't wear them on stage," the cashier said.

April looked at the pictures again, then at Ruth, who was standing out on the sidewalk, wanting nothing to do with the enterprise. "What do you say, Ruthie? Want to have a little fun?"

"Are you out of your mind, April?"

She'd have lunch in the delicatessen they had both liked because it was so dark and reminiscent of New York and then go to the bench they had shared in Lummus Park during the last days of April's life.

April's words ran through her head as she watched the older people playing cards, singing in Yiddish, gossiping, fighting, living. "Everyone calls this part of Miami Beach the Jewish Graveyard," April had said. "That's not true. Look, these people haven't come here to die. They're here to live, kid, and don't let anyone fool you. They're the survivors. They're the ones who had the guts to pick up fifty or sixty years ago and get their asses out of Poland/Russia. Half a century later, they had the guts to pick up and get out of New York.

"Look at them. Look at the shape they keep themselves in. Look at the armory of anti-sun equipment they *schlep* around. Caps and hats, green visors, blue nose protectors, orange umbrellas. They take care of themselves.

"You know something, Ruth? I envy every single one of them, every little lady with pink hair who keeps kosher in her two-room pullmanette. They at least believe their traditions;

they have something to fall back on. Me, I'm falling back on thin air."

Throughout April's illness, throughout her own days of mourning her friend, Max had always been there, in the background of her thoughts. "All I have to do is pick up the phone," she said to herself as she looked up at the much-plastered ceiling of her bedroom. "But to call a man on the telephone! I never in my life called a strange man. A simple little call and I'm afraid to pick up the receiver. What am I so afraid of? I went to bed with the man. I can't call him? And what's the matter, all this time and he hasn't picked up the receiver, spent a few cents on a postcard? I know what I told him but still, he could have called."

In the end, she waited for the evening, put on her light summer yellow dress, a little makeup, and went to the pier. "Maybe he's fishing," she told herself, hoping.

No one was on the pier except some kids passing marijuana cigarettes around ("Such a terrible odor") and two fishermen she hadn't seen before.

"I'll call tomorrow," she said to herself. But she didn't. She couldn't bring herself to call. Instead she went back to the pier. Toward the end of the week, she found his fishing pal, Abel.

"How are you this morning?" she asked the short, dour man. He nodded his head. She waited a few moments. "Catch anything today?" He moved his head from side to side impatiently. She thought she'd better come to the point. "Have you seen Max Rhoads lately?"

"Not hide nor hair. Ask me, that fellow's given up on the fish. Now, if you don't mind, lady, I haven't."

"Suppose he's sick?" she asked herself as she walked back to the Monte. "Suppose he's lying there in that godforsaken cottage with a broken leg and no food? Tomorrow morning, I'm going to call him come hell or high water."

That decision made, she began to prepare lunch for herself in the kitchenella. With a certain amount of maneuvering, she was able to reach into the back of the half refrigerator where she kept that mainstay of the poor, the dieting, and the unimaginative, a can of tuna fish. "So maybe I'll call him this afternoon," she thought, as she was about to make the decisive step of inserting the can opener into the can. "I have a phone phobia. I'll get over it." There was a knock on the door, a calling out of her name. "Ruthie? It's me. You decent?"

For reasons she didn't have to make clear to herself, Ruth didn't want Frieda to know she ate tuna fish for lunch. She put the can back into the refrigerator and went to the door.

"You have a spot on your trousers, darling, just above the knee. Looks like maybe V-8 juice. Want me to get it out for you? A drop of milk . . ."

"That's all right, Frieda."

Frieda sniffed. "Do I smell a new perfume?"

"Youth Dew by Estee Lauder."

"Saul brought me back something from the drugstore called Wild and Wet and you almost can't tell the difference."

"Saul has quite a nose."

"Speaking of Saul, he and Meyer are downstairs in the Caddy, waiting for us. I was deputized to come up here and ask you, politely, if you would do us the honor of gracing our table at Wolfie's for lunch this afternoon. You've been avoiding everyone long enough. Time to break out and have some fun. It's Meyer's treat. What do you say?"

"I say I'd love to." She suddenly wanted to see Meyer, to bask in the warmth of his never-changing, solid personality.

She regretted her decision once she was seated in the front seat of Meyer's Cadillac, the real power of Frieda's new perfume only making itself felt in that enclosed space. It was, she reflected later, an afternoon of smells. Frieda's perfume. Meyer's cigar. Saul's body odor. The delicious delicatessen smells of Wolfie's. The constant stale suntan-oil aroma of Miami Beach.

"You feeling better, Ruthie?" Meyer had asked as she had gotten into the car and waited for Meyer to depress the button that would lock them all in.

"Much better, Meyer. It's very kind of you to invite me to lunch."

"Think nothing of it." He looked at her with his pale-brown plaintive eyes, smiling his familiar boy smile. She touched his arm. He did remind her of a watered-down Harry, more mild and even-tempered. She did feel affection for him. There was no doubt of that.

They waited under the sign at Wolfie's that said, "Groups of Three or Four," while the ultimate odors of the day attacked their salivary glands. Corned beef, pastrami, turkey, liverwurst, salami, frankfurters, onions, red peppers, pickles, sweet rolls, hot roast beef sandwiches thick with gravy, french fries as thick as a man's finger, bowls of cole slaw, potato salad, cabbage soup, and borscht, danish and assorted pastries and cold drinks of every flavor and color made themselves temptingly known in an orchestrated symphony of olfactory music.

"This is the way Marx envisioned it," Saul said once they had been seated, once they had committed the menu to memory. "Society for Golden Agers. He saw the whole thing. Senior citizens banded together in tight, mutually cooperative groups, fed and clothed by the state, enjoying each other in convivial, comradely circumstances."

"We're not fed and clothed by the state, Saul," his wife informed him.

"Let me tell you something a little bird told me, Frieda: Social Security can go very far in a place like Miami Beach."

"So what's everyone going to have this afternoon?" the waitress asked. They ordered sandwiches, potato salads, diet black cherries.

"You look like maybe you lost a few pounds, Ruthie," Meyer said above the noise from the competing tables. "You'd better take care of yourself if you know what's good for you."

"You know about that new fat farm up in Hallandale?" Frieda asked, her mouth filled with corned beef. "Mimsi Gadeemer spent a week there and came back looking like a metal hanger."

"Hallandale?" the waitress, who had dyed black hair and wore a pin that said "Gloria" on her uniform, asked, setting down the platters of sandwiches. "I live in Hallandale."

"*You* live in Hallandale?" Saul asked, incredulous.

"In a trailer court," Gloria said, putting her hand in the pocket of her uniform and coming out with a pack of photographs. "Here's what it looked like when I moved in. And here's what it looks like now."

"You like living in a trailer?" Frieda asked, her mouth now filled with unchewed pieces of kosher pickled tomato.

"Just take a gander at this trailer and see what a beautiful home I've turned it into with only my own ingenuity and guts."

Meyer moved closer to his sister to get a better view of the snapshots. Ruth let her attention wander around the room. Sitting under the blown-up portrait of Spencer Tracy was a woman wearing a hat. It was a black straw hat and not exactly out of place but there was something about the tilt of the brim, the shape of that crown, that made it look like a Madison Avenue hat and an expensive one at that.

The face under it was lean and dark with high cheekbones

and jet-black hair streaked with white. It was a hard New
York face, and, in its way, beautiful. The woman was in her
mid-fifties and there were tears in her eyes which did nothing
to make her seem more sympathetic or less hard-edged.

The man, whose familiar back was to Ruth, reached across
the table and, with a clenched hand, touched the woman's
cheek. (Ruth felt, for no good reason, she later told herself, as
if her own face had been slapped.) He pushed his chair back
and moved to the seat next to her, putting his arm around her.

Ruth placed her lean pastrami sandwich back on its plate
and stood up. "Ruth, where you going?" Meyer asked,
looking up, concerned.

"Back to the Monte. I just remembered something I have to
take care of. Don't move. I'll take a taxi."

"Your sandwich," Saul said, eyeing it.

"You eat it, Saul."

She stopped at the door and turned and looked at the table
where Max and the woman in the black straw hat were sitting.
She had stopped crying. And once again, incredibly, Max
made that intimate gesture Ruth knew so well: he put his
hand against the woman's cheek. And just as Ruth had once
done, the woman grasped his hand and held it.

"So now I know," she said to herself later that afternoon,
sitting on the edge of the davenport. "Or do I? Maybe it was a
relation of some kind? Maybe it was perfectly legitimate?
What did I see?

"So why hasn't he called me or tried to get in touch with
me?

"So why was he touching her every two minutes when he's
from the famous non-touchers?

"So maybe I should ask him point-blank? So maybe it's
time."

She reached for the telephone, realizing that seeing Max in a banquette with another woman at Wolfie's had cured her phone phobia. Armando put through the call in record time. The telephone rang twice and was answered by a crisp, insinuating voice. Ruth had no doubt that it belonged to the woman in the black straw hat. She replaced the receiver very gently.

"So now I really know. He's a Don Juan. She's better-looking than I am, fifteen years younger, and she's not embarrassed to cry in public places. Let them live and be well. I should never have gone to bed with him. Nobody wants the cow when they can get the milk for free. I'm probably more embarrassed than I am hurt. That's why I'm crying. I'm embarrassed. And I'm a fool. A sixty-six-year-old fool. I'm getting what I deserve. Everyone knows you can't be old and in love, too. Love is for the young. I'm a foolish old woman." She reached for the mock tortoiseshell Kleenex box, grabbed a tissue, blotted her eyes. "Enough with the crying already."

She stood up and went out onto the landing and stared at Apartmentette One Two Four. "April, if you were only here." She tried the door and found it was open. A short, fat woman in a pink slip and brassiere looked up from her sewing, surprised.

"I'm sorry," Ruth said, backing out. "I didn't know someone new had moved in. A friend of mine used to be in this room."

"Don't let it upset you," the woman said in a high-pitched voice. "I'm used to people barging in. When you have four daughters, believe me, you get used to people barging in." She put down her sewing and held out her hand. "I'm Mrs. Lillian Lustig of Newton, Massachusetts. How do you do, dear?"

Ruth gave the requisite short biographical sketch and

returned to her apartmentette. She lay down and tried not to think. There was a knock on the door.

"Who is it?"

There was no answer, only a persistent knock. "Could it be?" she asked herself. "Maybe he saw me at Wolfie's. Maybe he's come to explain."

She opened the door. Meyer stood there, a brown paper bag in his hand. "More socks?"

"I thought you might want your sandwich," Meyer said, giving her the bag. "The waitress gave me an argument but I gave her a little something and she threw in a fresh bottle of diet black cherry."

"Thank you, Meyer."

"You should eat, Ruthie."

"I will, Meyer."

"You want to tell me why you left like that? Frieda spotted that artist fellow as we walked out. Was it because of him? If so, I'm sorry, Ruthie . . ."

"I'm the one who should be sorry, Meyer."

They stood staring at one another for a few moments, Meyer holding his two hands together, Ruth holding the brown bag. "Ruthie, I want to ask you for the very last time: will you marry me?"

"Yes, I will, Meyer."

"Next Sunday, Ruthie?"

"That will be fine, Meyer."

"I'm looking forward to it." He stepped in and awkwardly kissed her. "I'll make you happy, Ruthie. I may not be a great romancer but believe me, I won't give you any trouble, either."

"I believe you, Meyer."

He kissed her again with more assurance and said, "I'd better go tell Frieda, no? She'll make all the arrangements."

She watched him run down the stairs and approach Frieda, who was holding court by the pool. She closed the door and went back to the davenport. "Of all the things that were going to happen to me in this life," she said aloud, "I would have thought the least likely was my having Frieda for a sister-in-law twice over."

Twenty-four

There were a great many long-distance telephone calls.

"It's what Ronald and I have wanted for you from the start, Mother. Uncle Meyer is a good man. He can give you the sort of security and comfort you have always known. I must say Ronald and I were a trifle upset when you upped and went down to Miami Beach to live in a hotel neither of us had ever heard of and what we hadn't heard of couldn't be good. But I have to hand it to you, Mother, you knew what you were doing."

"Audrey . . ."

"No, let me finish, Mother. I owe it to you. And it's after five o'clock so no one's worried about money. I have to say that it was terribly clever of you putting yourself in that second-rate hotel, playing poor so Meyer would take sympathy on you. Who says feminine wiles are dead?

"You can imagine what we thought when we saw you in that dump, all by yourself. All the way to Key West Ronald swore you were going to do something reckless. One hears all those stories of new widows signing everything over to the first man they meet. And all the while you were setting your perfect trap for Uncle Meyer."

"Audrey . . ."

"And I do want to say, Mother, that you're doing the right thing by your family, the memory of Father, and your new husband in waiting as long as you have to get Meyer to pop the question. All I can say is, we're all very happy and pleased with you. You're doing exactly what I would do if Ronald (God forbid) ever passed away and his brother, Morton (God forbid), became available.

"In the sisterhood encounter groups we're encouraged to communicate our good feelings as well as our bad to our loved ones and to our children. That's what prompted this phone call. Mother, I am very proud of you."

"Thank you, Audrey."

"Ronald and I and hopefully the girls are planning to fly down on Saturday . . ."

"You don't have to Audrey. Really."

"Mother! What would people say? Of course we'll be there. And if you happen to speak to your son and he is planning on attending, be sure to impress upon him the fact that he must wear a tie and a jacket. I know that Linda will be properly attired. Even if she isn't Jewish, she has a nice sense of time and place. Odd that I like her more than I like him, isn't it?"

"*Odd* isn't the word I would use, Audrey. Thank you for your call. I appreciate it. Now, if you don't mind, I have to urinate."

"Mother, I wish you wouldn't use that word . . . "

"You want I should do it on the phone?"

"I know he's a terrific old guy, Mother, good of heart and strong of body, but what the hell are you marrying him for? It's not going to be what anyone would call a meaningful relationship, you know what I'm saying?"

"Nicky, he's comfortable, he's nice, and he loves me."

"Mother, you're already comfortable. Who needs nice? And the real question is, do *you* love him?"

"I'm not going to discuss my love life with you, *yonkle.*"

"All right. Just putting my two cents in. Linda and I will be arriving Saturday morning unless that's against some religious law passed by the city of Miami."

"You know, Nick, you don't really have to . . ."

"Please! Don't go into your self-effacing it's-only-little-old-unimportant-me-getting-married act. Besides, Linda's never been in Miami Beach."

"In her life?"

"Well, in this life. She wants to see the Fontainebleau."

"It'll cost you a fortune."

"What's the matter with you?"

"Nothing's the matter. What should be the matter?"

"When you start talking about money and your voice gets all angry and taut, something's the matter."

"Nothing's the matter, believe me. I'm just sick and tired of everyone giving me their personal evaluation of my forthcoming marriage. It's not such a big deal. I'm tired of being alone. Since April died, I've felt very lonely. Meyer isn't exactly scintillating company, it's true. But he is company."

"I don't think that's a reason to get married, Ma."

"No? Maybe not for you. You're young. When you get to my age, it's about the best reason there is."

"I don't believe it, Ma."

There was a moment of silence before Nick said, "Ma, listen. Why marry Meyer? Why not live with him for a while. Say, six months. That way—"

"Can you imagine your Uncle Meyer agreeing to an arrangement like that? He gets a mild coronary when he's five minutes late for the parking meter. Anyway, the whole thing is set."

"Not in concrete, Ma."

"You know something, Nicky? You're impossible. Just plain impossible."

"You crying?"

"Why should I be crying?" she asked, crying.

"You should be crying because you're taking the god-damned easy way out. You should be crying because you're doing what you think they want you to do. You should be crying because for the first time in your life you've got the money and the freedom to do whatever you want to do. Go to Europe, go to Tahiti—you can go anywhere you want, do anything you want to do. And what are you doing? Opting for Meyer Meyer, the one-dimensional man with the double name and the triple-threat sister. You're making a major mistake, Ma. That's why you should be crying."

"You don't know anything about it," she shouted. "I'm alone and I'm old and I'm scared. You don't see any of that, do you? You're just like your father. Sure, you got the money, you go. It's not as easy as that. You can't understand that, can you?"

"I can and I do, Ma," he said, his voice going quiet. "But you're not bedridden or senile. You could still live a life."

"I'll be living a life with Meyer, Nicky. You'll see."

"Okay, Ma."

There was another uncomfortable silence. "This phone call is costing you a fortune," she said, breaking it.

"Ma, you know I only said what I did because I love you, don't you? If I didn't care about you, I wouldn't try so hard."

"I realize that, Nicky. And you want to know something? I love you, too."

"Now I know, Ma."

"Why only now?"

"Because you told me. Listen, I'll see you on Saturday."

"Be sure and bring a tie."

*

"I understand from impeccable sources that you're getting married again, darling," Leona LeVine said. "And as I happen to be at my condo here in Hollywood, Florida, I thought I would give you a call and wish you all the luck in the world. You and Meyer will have a lovely little life together, I'm certain of it. If you ever get bored with all those *alta cockers* in Miami Beach and would like a fresh and innovative view, step onto a bus and come and visit. I'll take you to the club. It's exclusively for professional men. Your doctors, your lawyers, your attorneys. Not even pharmacists are allowed to join. I'd love for you to see it, Ruth, and my new condominium home. It's been divine talking to you, darling, and lots and lots of luck on your forthcoming nuptial celebration."

"Hold all phone calls," she told a greatly recovered Morris Fleischman at the beginning of the week. "Especially local ones." Suppose Max decided to call? "I wouldn't know what to say to him. And I don't want to speak to him," she told herself.

"Very good, *madonna*. You're beautiful when you're being strong and determined. Has anyone ever told you that?"

"And I'm not at home to any unexpected guests."

"That is what we call a *fait accompli,* Madame Meyer. Your adoring sister-in-law put in your request for privacy over a month ago. 'No calls for Ruth Meyer that originate in Miami or thereabouts. No surprise visitors who arrive in red Jeeps.' I had been given to understand you were in mourning for our mutual friend and . . ."

"Were there any local calls or surprise visitors?"

"Ah, that would be telling, my dear," Morris said, putting his skinny fingers around her wrist, pulling her close to him, looking around the lobby to make certain they were alone. "What's to stop us now, my darling? I was a broken man when April left us. You can make me whole again, *cara.* Who would know? You're getting married for what one has to believe is the last time. Permit yourself this one final charitable act, this one final *noblesse oblige* gift. Allow me to enter your chamber tonight, *madonna*. I will appear in the guise of your eternal slave, a faded silver rose clenched in my teeth, an aphrodisiacal potion in a flagon at my belt. We can forget, together, *mon vie. She* would have wanted it this way."

Ruth pushed him away but not with as much force as she might have. "You really are despicable, Morris Fleischman." She reflected, as she walked across and out of the lobby, that, as awful as he was, he was better in his lecherous role than he was when he was in mourning, looking as if he had lost his reason for living. She didn't know why, but she was concerned about Morris. She wished he would put on a little weight.

"You don't know what love is," he called out after her, "until you've tasted bondage."

After some thought, she decided to forgive Frieda. If Max had genuinely wanted to reach her, neither the Monte's switchboard nor Morris Fleischman would have stopped him, she reasoned. And the only possible reason he might have wanted to talk to her was to inform her about the woman in the black straw hat. "My life is set. I'm going to marry Meyer. So Frieda helped a little by playing Cupid, by being a *buttinsky*. She meant, God bless her, well."

Thus she was able to get through the many conferences Frieda, as architect of the wedding, called. "We've taken the Marie Antoinette Suite at the Fontainebleau," Frieda announced, her yellow tent dress newly pressed, her face red with importance. All available undamaged ears belonging to the ladies sitting around the pool perked up.

"You had to pick Marie Antoinette?" Saul asked, chomping on what might have been a salami sandwich.

"The Leon Trotski Suite was booked," Frieda said, turning

away from her husband and addressing Ruth and the girls. "You have no idea what it's costing."

"I don't want to know," Ruth said. "Let it be a surprise."

"Usually," Mae Weissman said, "the bride's family pays for the wedding."

"We do things differently here in America," Ruth said.

"Now we have to get down to the particulars," Frieda said, pulling several sheets of thin paper from her Diet Pepsi cooler bag. "Do you have a preference as to baby franks bathed in a glow of buttery pastry à la Alsace or delicately spiced Meat Balls Romanesque?"

"Frieda," Ruth asked, "do I have to be involved in choosing the menu? In matters of food, I trust you implicitly."

"Sure, then it will be all my fault when you don't like something."

"I'll take total responsibility."

"What about the dress?" Miriam Siegal wanted to know.

"I have here," Frieda said, at the top of her voice for the benefit of those girls at the far end of the pool, "a check to the tune of one hundred and fifty dollars which your intended asked me to discreetly hand over to you in order that you should go out and buy yourself, in that good man's own words, 'something snazzy.' "

"Give it back to my intended," Ruth said. "I can afford to buy my own dress."

"Good," Frieda said. "Because Meyer said that if you didn't use it, I could."

"You're so very lucky, Ruth," Mae Weissman burst out fervently. "What a generous soul that man has. What a generous, generous person. If I were you, I'd be *cvelling* instead of sitting there with that *marooky* expression plastered all over your face, looking as if you swallowed something that wasn't dead yet. If I were you, Ruth Meyer, I—"

"If you were me, you'd be getting married to Meyer on Sunday and happy as Amy Carter." Ruth got up from her chaise. "But you're not. So you're not."

"What do you want to do about flowers?" Frieda asked. "Mums, lilies of the valley, or baby's breath?"

"Black orchids," Ruth said over her shoulder.

She had several quiet dinners with Meyer, all (at Ruth's request) without Frieda and Saul, most at Meyer's favorite restaurant, the Royal Rumanian. One was prepared by Ruth in Meyer's practical kitchen (at his request).

"You're a great cook, Ruthie." He managed to get a goodly amount of Ruth's high-fat meat loaf into his mouth along with half a boiled potato.

"No, I'm not," she said. "I'm an okay cook."

He finished chewing, laid his fork down, and put his hand over hers. "Tell the truth, Ruthie: you getting used to the idea?"

"Yes, Meyer. The truth is, I am definitely getting used to the idea."

"And I am," she thought, as he drove her home in the Cadillac. "Not the idea of cooking and sewing and taking care of a household and a husband. But the idea of being with someone. I'm not the kind of person meant to be alone. Even when things were at their worst with Harry, it was better being with him than being by myself. I suppose that's not good. Always having to depend on someone else. I should be able to be by myself. But I'm not. I need someone there for me.

"April was always there for me. She wouldn't want me to marry Meyer. I can hear her now. 'What're you doing to yourself, Draisal? Sticking yourself in the same situation you were in for most of your life? Go out and swing a little before you commit yourself. Tell Meyer to play with himself for a couple of years.' "

As patient, as dogged as he was, Meyer wasn't going to wait a couple of years. Or a couple of months. She watched him as he drove his car. He was wearing glasses, a new development. His expression was set at Very Earnest. He was intent on getting where he was going. He had never, he told her, had an accident or committed a traffic violation in his entire life.

"And what about the other one?" she could hear April saying. "What about the artist who happens not to be Jewish?"

"He threw me over."

"You don't know that."

"I'm pretty certain."

"You do know that he's been trying to call, that your sister-in-law has set up one of her famous blockades?"

"I know what Frieda did. I don't know Max tried to call."

"You've always had a convenient way of knowing what you want to know, Draisal."

She told April to go away as she asked Meyer to repeat what he had said. They were in front of the Monte Excelsior. "Maybe lunch tomorrow, the day before the big day?"

"Not tomorrow, Meyer. Tomorrow I go to the beauty parlor for the full treatment."

She reached for the door handle but he took her hand and held it. "I got something for you, Ruthie." He handed her a blue velvet jeweler's box and switched on the car's interior light. "Every bride should have an engagement ring. But since you already got one, this is for your little finger."

She opened the box. A platinum ring set with tiny rubies and pavé diamonds was there. "A cocktail ring," Meyer said, as she put it on her pinky. "Don't ask me why, but that's what the man said. Go no? A cocktail ring."

She kissed him on his beautifully shaven cheek. "Thank you, Meyer."

"And for your information, Frieda had nothing to do with picking it out."

"That's nice to know, Meyer. I love the ring." She kissed him again. "I'll see you on Sunday."

"Good night, Ruthie."

She looked at the ring as she climbed the stairs. It was a nice gesture for Meyer to make. "It's not bad," she said, holding it out before her, trying to convince herself she liked it. It was then she heard the telephone ringing inside her apartmentette. She struggled with the key, reached the telephone, and picked it up. "Hello," she said. "Hello?"

"Beautiful lady, I was wondering if you would be interested in a good-nightcap in the privacy of your own room. . . ."

She put the receiver down, supposing Morris missed April almost as much as she did, looked at the ring in the dim light provided by the reading lamp, and then made preparations to go to bed. "It's not bad," she said. "Not bad at all."

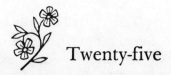 Twenty-five

"When am I ever going to learn the first time?" Ruth asked herself as she studied Ricky Lizzardi's "far out" hairdo in the mirror. Her experience that morning at his salon had been very much a repetition of her initial visit. She turned on the shower and began to wash out the set and as much of the turquoise rinse as she could.

Toweling her hair, she thought she heard a knock at the

door. "Just what I need. Tourists dropping in to see the Old Lady with Turquoise Hair." She replaced the damp towel with a fresh one, wrapping it around her head. She went to the door and opened it.

"Happy bachelor day to you.
Happy bachelor day to you.
Happy bachelor day, dear Ruth Meyer.
A happy bachelor day to you."

Frieda, Mae Weissman, Miriam Siegal, Lil Lustig, Belle Fleischman, Muriel Resnick, Myrna Wenk, and Mimsi Gadeemer came rushing into the apartmentette, each carrying a platter of food. "Would I let you be married without a little shower, Ruthie?" Frieda asked.

"You think we'd let you leave the Monte without a proper sendoff?" Belle Fleischman wanted to know, picking the yellow cellophane wrapping from the platters, revealing Sloppy Joe sandwiches held together by toothpicks mounted with olives.

"That's an exquisite shade of turquoise," Mae Weissman told her.

"Ricky Lizzardi calls it 'Israeli Blue,'" Miriam Siegal informed everyone.

They toasted her half a dozen times with various diet sodas, forced her to taste a slice of the Shalom Bakery's Mocha Melba Peace Cake Supreme, and gave her several presents: a pink slip, a black slip, and a nylon see-through kimono imprinted with transparent scenes of long-ago Japan.

"Just pretend you're a virgin, Ruthie," Belle Fleischman advised her. "Meyer will never know the difference."

After they had finally left, Frieda reluctantly taking the remainder of the cake to Saul, Mae not so reluctantly taking the leftover sandwiches to her room, Ruth went back to the shower and shampooed again. "I'm going to miss them," she thought. "Awful as they are, I'm going to miss them. Though I'm sure there'll be another group of girls at Meyer's condominium. Maybe a touch swankier. But still, the girls."

By the time she finished playing with her hair, it was almost seven o'clock. "My last free night," she said, turning on the television. She found a Marlene Dietrich film called *Knight Without Armor*. Dietrich was playing a Russian duchess condemned to die during the Revolution. "It's the way I feel about tomorrow," Ruth said.

Meyer called during one of the commercials. He was watching the same film. "That's a good sign, no, Ruthie?"

"A very good sign, Meyer."

"No cold feet about tomorrow?"

"Not one cold foot," she lied.

"So I'll pick you up at three-thirty P.M. on the dot."

"I'll be ready."

During another commercial (they were coming fast and furious), she tried on the wedding dress. She had bought it on Lincoln Road and wasn't at all sure about it. "You look not a day over one hundred and five," she could hear April saying. "If the neckline were any higher, it would qualify as a ski mask."

"That's what I get for taking Frieda shopping with me."

Sitting in the apartmentette, watching Dietrich confront a crowd of several hundred extras got up to look like Russian revolutionaries, she felt profoundly unhappy with the dress. "Dietrich's going to her execution wrapped in fifty yards of French chiffon and I'm getting married in baby-blue satinette from Korea. Maybe I have something else."

She waited for another commercial. "Show your devotion to Elvis," the announcer said. "With this once-in-a-lifetime only-time-on-TV offer: the Elvis Keepsake Bracelet, Necklace, and Anklet combination . . ."

She went to the closet. "There's my good black but that's only appropriate for the way I feel. The white and the pink are a little sporty. Maybe I should call Meyer and we could elope?" The visual of Meyer carrying her down a ladder made her laugh. She put her dresses away. "I'll wear the blue satinette. Everyone will be pleased. Meyer with my modesty. Frieda with the money it cost me. Mae Weissman with how awful I look. They'll all go away happy."

She returned to the film, thinking that it was a relief that neither Nicky nor Audrey would be able to attend the wedding after all that fuss. Nicky had to finish a film, Audrey was being installed as the president of her sisterhood. "I've had enough of them. I don't want recriminations, congratulations. I don't want to think. I'm going through with it and that's that."

Dietrich had managed to get herself rescued from the revolutionaries and was now dining with the commander in chief of the White Army in the banquet hall of a Russian castle. She was wearing a low-cut sequined gown trimmed with feathers. "She needs feathers like I need feathers. Maybe I do need feathers. Maybe I should wear my stole. The Fontainebleau will probably be over-air-conditioned. It's over-everything else." She stood up and went back to the closet.

"Even though I swore to April on my Jewish word of honor that I would never wear my stole again, maybe just this once." She put on the blue satinette dress, matching shoes, and the mink stole. She studied her image in the bathroom door mirror. "I look like Rose Kennedy's maid."

Hugging the stole, she went and sat on the davenport as Dietrich once again fell into the hands of the revolutionaries. There was a knock on the door. "Maybe it's the revolutionaries coming for me. More likely it's Frieda, coming to annoy me with last-minute advice on how to prepare her brother's breakfast cereal."

She adjusted her mink stole and opened the door. "Now listen, Frieda," she began as Max pushed by her. She shut the door. He turned off the television. They stood staring at each other.

"What in tarnation do you think you're doing?" he asked, looking at her outfit. "Playing Baptist?"

"You want a little something cold to drink?"

"What I would like is to find out why your blasted phone has been disconnected for the past month. 'Sorry, old bean,' was all I heard, four times a day. 'Madame Meyer is not taking any calls.' "

"There's some dietetic cream cheese in the icebox if you maybe feel like a little nosh."

"Ruth, tell me why that five-thousand-year-old fancy boy has been telling me you weren't here? I have a right to know, don't you think?"

"There's an onion bagel, maybe a trifle stale . . ."

He backed her into the corner between the door and the bed. He put his arms around her and the stole and the dress. "What the hell's been going on, Ruth? Why didn't you call me after your friend died?"

"I tried."

"Not damned near hard enough. I only found out that she did die when I got a phone call from that fat gal, Mrs. Weissman, telling me I had better get my tail over here tonight or it would be 'too late.' She's a real pal of yours. And mine. She showed me how to get up here without having to walk through the lobby."

He pulled her close to him. "I've missed you so much, honey, I just can't tell you." He kissed her. It was a long and deeply satisfying kiss.

Trembling, she pushed him away, pulling the stole more tightly around her. "I'm engaged to be married, Mr. Rhoads. I'll thank you to take your hands off me and stop talking at me in that tone of voice."

"You're marrying the fellow who needs a nurse, right?"

"If you're referring to my late husband's brother, yes."

"When?"

"Tomorrow afternoon. Four or five P.M. sharp."

"You're not going to do it, Ruth. You can't."

"Oh, yes, I am, Max. And stop holding on to me as if I were the toy duck in your bathtub."

"Then you had better stop talking like a toy duck." He pulled her to him and she allowed the stole to drop to the floor. "Don't you know I love you, Ruth? More than anything else in the world."

She allowed him to keep his arms around her. "Yes? And I suppose you love that *curva* I saw you all over in Wolfie's?"

He laughed. "What's a *curva?*"

"A lady who sells her favors."

He laughed again and led her to the davenport, sitting her down, sitting next to her, touching her cheek with his hand. "That lady only sells other people's favors, darling. She's an agent from New York. An artist's agent. Eleanor de Vries. She owns a gallery, a very fancy, prestigious gallery."

"She was crying and you were petting her. She answered the telephone when I called."

"Eleanor's a very dear and very old friend who has her own problems. A sick husband, kids who aren't much help . . ."

"They never really are."

"Eleanor came down here to see my paintings."

She sat up and looked at him. "Your late middle period?" His green eyes were happy.

"Not my late middle period, Ruth. My early late period.

I've begun to paint again. Seems I found my muse once more. In the last couple of months—actually, since the day I met you—I've started all over again. I've finished one painting, half a dozen sketches."

"They're good?"

"They're great. Leastways, Eleanor thinks so. She wants me to try and get ready for a show next year. She wouldn't take no for an answer."

"She didn't look like she was getting no for an answer."

"My daddy always said a woman wasn't really in love until she showed a little jealousy. I reckon, honey, that you're in love. You just don't want to admit it."

"You're painting again," she said, not listening. "Max, that's wonderful. It makes me feel like sunshine. I have this big burst of happiness inside of me for you."

"It's because of you, Miss Ruth."

"Stop."

"You're my muse, Ruth."

He pulled her closer to him and kissed her again. This time, she responded. "What about a little glass of sippin' whiskey? For old time's sake?" He pulled a pint bottle from his jacket pocket.

"I'm not sure I have any sugar," she said, going to the kitchenella. "Saccharine do?"

"I don't think, Miss Ruth . . ."

"Nope, I was wrong. Here's two cubes I stole from the Royal Rumanian."

They sipped their whiskey. "To your early late period, Max," she said.

"To our early late period, Ruth."

She looked at him over the rim of the glass. Then she made an uncharacteristic move. She put her glass down, reached over, put his glass down, and kissed him. As they kissed, he began to unzip the back of the baby-blue satinette dress. "How the Sam Hill do I get you out of this pillow case?"

"Keep zipping. But be careful. I have to wear it tomorrow."

"Allow me to say, Miss Ruth, that I have serious doubts about that." His hand began to undo the hooks on her brassiere as she forgot the dress and the wedding and everything else save the joy she and Max were able to give each other.

"I've got to get up," she thought, looking at the luminous dial on the clock radio. "Seven A.M. I've got to make decisions, actions, moves. My God, have I got to get up." Max, still asleep, put his arms around her and she allowed herself to be held, to fall into a comfortable limbo, reassured by the warmth of his body. "One of the nice things about him," she decided, closing her eyes, nestling in, "is that he doesn't smell old. No Palmolive Gold. No Johnson's Baby Talc. He smells like a man."

Two hours later, she became conscious, just, of the sound of the door opening. It alarmed her, but only for a moment. It would be too dark to see anything other than the fact that the bed was occupied. Against the damp cold of the air conditioner, Max had pulled the covers over his head. Maria Carmen would take a look, shut the door, and go on to the next room (where she really had her work cut out for her, Lil Lustig being a terrible *schloomper*).

But the door didn't close. Instead, it opened halfway, allowing a shaft of bright sunshine to enter the room.

"Maria Carmen," Ruth said, "come back later. Give me an hour or so, if you don't mind, *por favor*."

The door stayed open. With a sinking heart, Ruth realized it wasn't Maria Carmen entering the room on tiptoes, finger to her mouth, loudly shushing. It was Frieda, opening the wooden Venetian blinds, allowing the sun to fully illuminate the room. Behind her, also tiptoeing, came Saul. Then Audrey and Ronald, their two daughters and their two husbands. Nick and Linda brought up the rear.

They assembled themselves around the bed. At a signal from Frieda, ten people shouted, in unison, "Surprise. Surprise."

"What the hell . . ." Max said, emerging from the covers like a jack-in-the-box.

"Oh, my God," Audrey said, clutching her husband's arm for assistance. "Oh, my God."

"Max," Ruth began, pulling the sheet and the thin blankets around her. "I'd like you to meet my daughter, Audrey . . ."

But it was too late to introduce Audrey. She had gone running out of the room, followed by her husband, her children, and their mates.

"That was my daughter, Max," Ruth said, with a control she felt was about to break. "This is my son, Nick . . ."

"Ma, for Christ's sake," Nick said. "Ma . . ." And he burst out laughing. Linda joined in, then Max, then Saul, and, finally, Ruth.

"Well," she said, "I suppose from one point of view, it is kind of funny." She proceeded with the introductions. "Where's Frieda?" she asked, while Max was shaking hands with Saul.

"Downstairs in the lobby," Saul told her. "Using the pay phone to call her brother Meyer."

Twenty-six

"There's absolutely no alternative. That's perfectly clear. Ronald's out right this minute making inquiries at Autumnal View's Miami office. I mean," Audrey went on, lighting another cigarette, "there's something very wrong with a woman your age engaging in that sort of behavior."

"Yes," Nick said, "we all know the sex urge withers and dies at age forty-three."

"It's amoral and unbelievably immature," his sister went on, ignoring him. "She has to be put where she'll be properly supervised. Believe me, there's none of that sort of thing going on at Autumnal View . . ."

". . . Yeah, all inmates are carefully monitored . . ."

"Mother, do try and look at it on the bright side. Ronald and I will only be a few minutes away. We'll be popping in and out—"

"Would you please shut the fuck up?" Nick said. "And put that goddamn cancer stick out. I don't care if you want to commit suicide; there's no reason for you to contaminate all of us."

"I was waiting for you to say something like that. So typical of you, Nicky. Now, listen to me: I'll smoke if I choose to. Still a free country, last I heard. And I'll thank you very much to stop using that sort of language in front of my children. They're not exactly used to . . ."

Nick stood up and took a few steps across the small nylon carpet which took up much of the Monte's lobby floor.

"Nicky," his wife said, putting her hand on his shoulder.

"She's so fuckin' irritating."

"That's not the issue," Linda told him. "And punching her in the face won't help."

"Really," Audrey said, taking several furious puffs on her cigarette.

"It may not be the issue," Nick said to his wife, "but I think it would help." He looked at his mother, who was now sitting on a once-pink sofa wearing her blue satinette wedding-day dress. Her neat, pretty hands were folded in her lap. She was staring out the window. At the pool, the girls were gathered around Belle Fleischman, who was regaling them with details of the morning's events. Max was pacing back and forth across the courtyard, his hands behind his back, his eyes staring at his feet. He had been asked to remain outside, to give Ruth "a little time with the family."

"I've been with them nearly an hour," she said to herself. "That's enough time with the family." She looked at Max, who, at that moment, looked at her and smiled, and then she looked at Nicky and his kind eyes and tried to listen to what he was saying to her.

"You don't have to go to Autumnal View, Ma. And you don't have to marry Uncle Meyer. Why can't you just stay here? Go on as you are. You seem happy enough."

"That's a possibility."

"Or come and live with us, Mother," Linda said.

"The truth is, I hate California."

" 'It's cold and it's damp,' " Ivy, the granddaughter who had embraced Zionism as a mother substitute, quoted.

" 'That's why the lady is a tramp,' " Sheri, the one who had opted for wifedom with a dental surgeon in Philadelphia, sang. Realizing its implication, she blushed. "Sorry, Gran."

"Think nothing of it, Sheri."

There was a silence while they all looked at Max pacing in the courtyard and then at each other. "What are we going to do?" Audrey asked the ceiling, which was covered in white acoustical tile. "What *are* we going to do?" She alternated, between cigarettes, from a deft assurance to a nervous uncertainty. She lit one, inhaling deeply, as the door from the street swung inward, revealing Meyer with Frieda standing behind him.

"Meyer has something to say," Frieda announced over his shoulder. Through the open door they could see Meyer's Cadillac parked, for the first time, illegally. "Go ahead," Frieda said, propelling him into the lobby. "Go ahead, Meyer."

Meyer moved into the center of the room, stopping at the sight of Max trying to open the door which led into the lobby. Audrey had locked it. "Okay," Meyer said, as if he had just been asked a question. "Okay, I'm still willing to marry you, Ruthie. That's it in a nutshell. Not as much as before, I admit. But still, I'm willing. One little chapter for me doesn't add up to an entire dirty book. There's still time. We'll start all over again. From the top. Like they say on TV." Suddenly he looked at Ruth. "But don't you ever, don't you ever, expect me to act like the Sheik of Avenue B. Maybe, once in a while, when and if the mood strikes me and I don't have indigestion, maybe then . . ."

Audrey jumped up, kissed her uncle, and turned to Ruth. "Well, Mother, what are you waiting for? Run upstairs and redo your makeup . . ."

"Don't start ordering me around, young lady. No one ever said I was willing to be forgiven," Ruth said, staring at Max.

"Are you crazy? He's normal, Mother. He's Jewish. He's well-to-do. What more do you want?"

"Mother," Nick said, sitting down next to Ruth, taking her hand. "Tell me something. Would Max marry you?"

"Absolutely not," Max said. He had come around through the street entrance. "I don't believe in marriage, son."

"Thank God," Audrey said.

"However," Max went on, "I have asked your mother to come and live with me."

"Oh, my God," Audrey said.

Nick looked at his mother looking up at Max. "Not much security, Ma," Nick said.

"I'm not sure security is what I want, Nicky."

"Mr. Maxwell Rhoads doesn't have any security whatsoever," Ronald announced, entering the lobby with a sheaf of papers in his hand. "I got a good friend of mine off the golf course to run a credit check on you, Mr. Rhoads. You're broke, Mr. Rhoads. You haven't got the proverbial pot. Social Security is your only income. You live in a house that is on loan to you. And get this," Ronald said to his mother-in-law, "only for life."

"For how much longer should he want it?" Ruth asked.

" 'An artist who hasn't worked in years,' " Ronald read from the papers he was holding, using his public speaker's North Jersey monotone, " 'he owns a number of his own paintings which could command a sizable amount, especially given today's market. Mr. Rhoads, however, has refused all offers.' "

"Why should he sell them?" Ruth asked. "He likes them."

"He's only after your money, Ma," Ronald said, handing her the papers.

"Don't call me 'Ma,' Ronald," she said, pushing the papers from her, feeling tears behind her eyes. She stood up, saying, "Excuse me," and went into the ladies' room.

"Well, of course," she could hear Audrey saying, out in the lobby. "What else would he be after? My God, here's a man who's evidently well-educated, who was an artist of some little fame before he went over the hill, gentile yet, and suddenly he wants a little old Jewish lady to come and live with him. For her company and irresistible sex appeal, I suppose? I mean really."

"Shut the fuck up, Audrey." Nick looked at Max apologetically.

"That's all right, son. She's entitled to her say."

"I mean, here's a man . . ."

She examined herself in the mirror, dabbing cold water on her eyes. "Look at the lines in your face. Look at the old, *alta cocker* stranger staring back at you with faded eyes and stretched skin around the neck or what you can see of the neck in this dress. What could he want with me?"

"Mother, are you all right?" Linda asked, coming into the ladies' room.

"Think about it, Mother," Audrey said, following her sister-in-law into the cramped space. "What on earth have you got to offer a man like that? I mean *think about it,* for God's sake. Use your head. You've got a nice, comfortable income. You'll pay the rent, do the cleaning, cook the food, and change your will. What has he got to lose?"

"Max isn't like that," Ruth said, feeling the tears again, holding them back, looking down at the ugly shoes that matched the ugly dress.

"Of course he is. All men are."

"And what about that young chippie he was wining and dining in Wolfie's?" Frieda asked, pushing her way in.

"She's his agent."

"That's what he told you."

"Come on, Mother," Audrey said, sensing victory, putting her hand under her mother's elbow. "I'll come and help you freshen up."

"You stay here. I want to go to my room for a moment and think."

She escaped out into the lobby. "Ruth, honey, why don't

you put an end to all this horse manure being flung around this place and come home . . ." Max made a movement in her direction but she held up her hand.

"Ruthie," Meyer began, from his place on the faded pink sofa, "Ruthie . . ."

She held up both her hands, silencing them both. "I need a few minutes to think," she said, walking across the lobby, out the door, and up to her apartmentette.

When Audrey and Linda were sent to inquire as to how her thinking was progressing, they found the door to the apartmentette open but Ruth wasn't there. Her Avon lady carryall as well as her toiletries and some of her clothes were missing. The satinette wedding dress and shoes were in the closet. On the air conditioner was taped a note, addressed to Max and Meyer: "I need a few days to think. Just a few days. Please do not worry. I'm sorry to be the cause of all this heartache and expense. Ruth."

"Call the caterer," Frieda shouted when the contents of the note was made public. "Call the hotel. Cancel everything."

"Where you going?" Nick asked Max as he left the lobby, heading for the red Jeep.

"To find her, son. Where else?"

He didn't find her.

It was not until four days later that Frannie Meiselman, Rabbi Kauffman's married daughter, called an on-the-verge-of-a-nervous-breakdown Audrey from Key West, Florida. She told her that her mother was safe and finally sound, that Ruth had come to her father to ask his advice.

"Which was?" Audrey wanted to know.

"My dear, he couldn't tell her what to do. No one could. She had to decide for herself."

"May I speak to my mother?"

"She says she doesn't want to talk to anyone from the family just yet. She says that the wedding is on, that she will see you all at the Monte Excelsior first thing Sunday morning, that Frieda is free to make any plans she wishes, that someone should have her blue satinette wedding dress pressed. She sends her regards to Meyer and asks that Mr. Rhoads not be informed of her plans. She is writing to him."

"Do you think I could possibly speak to my mother?"

"I'm sorry, dear," Frannie Meiselman said. "Your mother just left the room."

Rabbi Kauffman, eighty and frail, with watery blue eyes, led her into the room he called his study. It was long and cool and tropical, with louvered windows, rattan furniture, and a Sydney Greenstreet electric fan in the center of the ceiling. It was the last place in the world Ruth expected to find a five-foot-one man wearing a black yarmulke and a navy-blue suit. She had been in Key West nearly two days before she had worked up the nerve to call him. She wasn't certain she wanted an answer. Not at all certain.

The rabbi, in his sweet, singsong voice, told her he couldn't give her one.

"Not in a situation like this, Mrs. Meyer. No, no. You must make your own decision. I cannot tell you what you should do with your life." He put one trembling, pale hand on her shoulder. "I will, however, make a suggestion," he said, as he led her into the dining room, where his sympathetic daughter was serving lunch.

"Think what your father would've wanted you to do, Mrs. Meyer. Think what your father would've wanted for you."

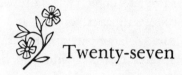

Twenty-seven

"Are you ready, Ruthie?" He held his big hand out to her. She took it and felt—that word they all used—secure.

"I'm ready, Meyer." It was Sunday. She had returned on the early-morning flight. She was in her blue satinette wedding dress. Meyer wore his gray silk suit with a Harry Truman handkerchief. They were in Meyer's Cadillac, headed for the Fontainebleau. She rested her head against the familiar upholstery, told Meyer she wouldn't mind if he smoked a cigar ("As a matter of fact, I'd enjoy it"), and felt not only secure but comfortable.

"The comfort of the familiar," she said to herself. "This is what I've known for most of my life. Big men. Big cars. Security. Comfort. 'Nothing fancy.' But everything secure, comfortable. That's why our parents came to America. So we should all be secure and comfortable. And we are. There's no doubt about it. Look at me. Look at Meyer. Look at my children. The fact that perhaps I've lived a narrow life shouldn't bother me. Think what my grandmother had to go through eighty years ago in a *shtetl* in Russia. I should be very happy with my life."

She glanced over at Meyer with genuine affection, touched his arm, and smiled. He smiled back but immediately returned his attention to the car. "The comfort of the familiar," Ruth repeated to herself as the Cadillac turned into the driveway of that most familiar, most comfortable of hotels, the Fontainebleau.

"Everything's under control," Freida announced, opening

the doors of the Marie Antoinette Suite, allowing Ruth and
Meyer to enter. The suite was decorated in several shades of
blue wallpaper, carpet, and upholstered hotel French furniture. A large portrait of Marie Antoinette looking like Norma
Shearer had been hung in the foyer. Decorative license had
been taken in the other rooms where copies of Van Gogh,
Whistler, and Botticelli vied for attention. Frieda stood under
a small study of Bonaparte.

She seemed to have assumed some of that general's
managerial air. "Nicky is waiting for you in the Pompadour
Room," she told Ruth. "Please go there at once and, if he's not
too nervous, get him to pin the orchid corsage (white) floating
in the bathroom sink on your dress *after* he dries it off, one leaf
at a time. Meyer, you come with me to the DuBarry room,
where the rabbi wants to have a few words with you, man to
man. Now, who do you suggest should discuss the musical
selections with Mr. Baumgarten? Or would you prefer that I
handle the music?"

Mr. Baumgarten, Piccolo Pete, stood at a small upright
piano, smoking a tiny cigar, pulling on the sleeves of his
dinner jacket. It was agreed that Frieda should handle the
music. "Nothing too *schmaltzy*. Classics. Your Irving Berlin
and that school. Okay? Good. Now go to your places whilst I
go to the kitchen and calm down the caterer, who's *cvetching*
about the size of the oven. You'd think they'd give you a
decent-sized oven. In this one a toothpick would have trouble
getting broiled. Now, please. Go!"

Nick was lying on the king-sized bed watching the news on
a giant-sized television when Ruth entered the Madame
Pompadour Room. "Get your feet off that bedspread," Ruth
said automatically.

"Ma, you're allowed to rest your feet on the bedspread if
you're not wearing shoes. It says so on the back of the door."

"Where's Linda?" she asked, sitting in a chair upholstered in gold floral lamé.

"She volunteered to come up with Sheri and Ivy and their husbands, the two *schlemiels*."

"Michael's a *schlemiel*, I'll grant you. Gary happens to be a very religious person."

"He happens to be a pompous, neurotic nut, searching for the parents he never had in the tribal rites of the Chosen. He's as judgmental as his mother-in-law."

"Do you mind if we don't discuss it, Nicky?" She pulled at the top of her dress.

"Ma, how you feeling?"

"Don't start with me, Nicky. Everything's been arranged."

"So was World War I. There was no reason they had to go through with it. Ma . . ." Nick began as Frieda thrust her head into the room.

"Is that corsage dry yet?"

"Tell you the truth," Ruth said getting up, going into the bathroom, "I forgot all about it."

A great deal of noise came from the direction of the living room. *"Oy vey,"* Frieda said, looking over her shoulder. "Everyone came at the same time. You should see the getup Mae Weissman has stuffed herself into. Green velvet! In this climate! She looks like a giant olive with that pimento-red face of hers.

"Nicky, now listen to me: when I knock on the door three times, and you hear the Wedding March, you should start walking with your mother on your right arm. I just hope you've been practicing."

"How long have we got, warden?"

"Give them a half-hour on the meatballs and say fifteen minutes on the franks."

Ruth reentered the bedroom as Frieda shut the door. She

was holding the orchid by one of its petals. "Do you have to wear that thing?" Nick asked.

"I suppose so. Anything on TV, Nicky?"

"You look. I'm going to mingle. Unless you want me to stay and hold your hand?"

"I've done enough hand-holding. Find out what Mae Weissman is wearing."

"Green velvet."

"In this climate?"

Linda was standing under the Botticelli, sandwiched by two of the Monte Excelsior girls. "So my dear," Lil Lustig was saying to Miriam Siegal, "we went to my great-grandnephew's *bar mitzvah* in New Rochelle. I do not exaggerate when I tell you that the hot-and-cold table was as big as . . ."

Nick, from across the room, made motions indicating he would rescue her if she wanted. Linda smiled and said, in their private language, no. She was enjoying herself.

Audrey was at the far side of the room, sampling the food as if she were testing for poison. Finishing a meatball, she placed the toothpick it had been speared on carefully in an ashtray. Then she straightened a tablecloth. It was as if, Nick thought, neatness counts. As if a straight tablecloth guaranteed a straight, upright life.

He turned, speared himself a frankfurter, avoided Uncle Saul, who had that I'm-going-to-tell-you-a-dirty-joke look in his eye, and made his way through the room filled with polyester organdy and fifty percent nylon chiffon. The girls had "put on the dog," gotten out the rouge and the lipstick and the yellowing diamonds and the superhold hair spray. The main room of the Marie Antoinette Suite looked like a rehearsal hall for a Broadway revival in which old stars were trotted out to do their thing.

Nick watched them with mixed emotions. Exasperation.

Affection. They *were* old stars, the Greek chorus of naysayers who had always been in the background of his mother's life.

"They don't change," Nick said to his mother, back in the Pompadour Room. "Those *yentas* never change."

"You want to pin this on me?" she asked, handing him the limp corsage.

"You want the truth?"

"Anyone ever tell you, Nicky, that you've got a little of the *yenta* in your own nature?"

"I'm my mother's son," he said, taking the orchid, pinning it to his mother's dress.

"You're such a bad boy, sometimes."

"Who's responsible for that?"

"You. By this time, already, you should be taking responsibility for yourself. Me and your ex-psychiatrist have been doing it long enough."

"You always have to have the last word, Ma?"

"With you around I never get it."

The knock came, three times. "The precursor of doom," Nick said.

"Let's go, *totela*. I hear the Wedding March."

"You one hundred percent certain you want to go through with this, Ma?"

"Ninety-nine and three-quarters."

Frieda opened the door, saying in her well-known stage whisper, "Come on, already. What're you waiting for?"

Ruth put her hand on her son's arm and they began to walk to the strains of the Wedding March, slightly jazzed up, into the Grand Salon of the Fontainebleau's Marie Antoinette Suite.

"I finally have an inkling," Ruth said to herself, looking up at the portrait of the French queen, "of how that lady felt on her way to the guillotine."

Twenty-eight

The rabbi, so unlike Rabbi Kauffman, looked as if he were auditioning for a place on Mount Rushmore. He cleared his throat portentously as he followed the progress Nick and his mother were making through the aisle the guests had reluctantly made. The Wedding March, with its Kay Kyser lilt, competed with the voices of the guests.

"She looks lovely," Miriam Siegal was saying. "Absolutely lovely. I don't care what anyone says. So blue's not her color. I think she looks lovely. Absolutely lovely." Miriam Siegal wiped an imaginary tear from a false eyelash.

Piccolo Pete, Mr. Baumgarten, brought the Wedding March to a close as Ruth joined Meyer in front of the rabbi and the marbleized mock fireplace.

The rabbi sighed, put his hands together in a gesture of prayer, and began his seventy-five-dollar service in carefully enunciated words. "We are gathered here today . . ."

Ruth's attention wandered. By moving only a little to the left, she could see the portrait of Marie Antoinette. In school Ruth had been a reluctant, silent admirer. "Such a selfish woman," she thought, recalling the "Let them eat cake" quotation. "But strong. Immune to public opinion. She didn't give a damn what anyone thought."

". . . marriage is a sacrament at any age," the rabbi was saying. "Not a convenience but a mutually agreed-upon venture of love."

"That's a nicely expressed idea," Ruth thought to herself.

She repeated the phrase. " 'A mutually agreed-upon venture of love.' "

The rabbi was asking Meyer if he had understood what had been said.

"Sure," Meyer answered.

"And you, Ruth?" the rabbi asked, turning to her. "Have you understood the meaning of my message? That marriage should not be a business partnership, but a love relationship; that marriage should not be a matter of pragmatism, but of romance and affection . . . no matter what age that marriage is embarked upon."

She looked into the rabbi's ordinary brown eyes. For a moment he was no longer a pretentious man with a seventy-five-dollar sermon in his pocket. For that moment, he was a spiritual adviser who understood. She gave him her full attention and it was then that she saw—miraculously, it seemed to her—the Gauguin copy of *The Moon and the Earth,* hanging to the right of the fake fireplace, above Miriam Siegal's head.

"Do you promise to love, honor, and cherish Ruth?" the rabbi was asking Meyer.

"I do."

"And you, Ruth: do you promise to love, honor, and obey Meyer?"

She tried but she simply could not get the two requisite words out of her mouth. All she could see was the Gauguin. Her mouth was dry, her tongue paralyzed. She wondered if she were having a stroke. She asked herself what would have happened to Gauguin if he had thought about what his father would have wanted him to do before he left for Tahiti. "He'd still be sitting in a bank behind a little cage, adding up things," she said aloud, startling everyone within hearing.

"Somebody get her a glass of water," Meyer shouted.

The crowd parted as Ronald went toward the kitchen. He met Max coming through the service door, tried to stop him, was pushed aside, and stood helplessly by the sink as Max, in khaki trousers and alligator T-shirt, barreled his way through all the finery gathered in the Marie Antoinette Suite to the place where Ruth stood.

"Ruth, come with me, honey. I need you. I want you. I love you so much."

"You don't have any money."

"You do."

"You won't marry me."

"Darn tooting. I been married twice and in my book that's twice too often. Ruth, you need me as much as I need you. You can't hide that, honey. There isn't any doubt about it, is there?"

She looked up into his green eyes. "Oh, there's plenty of doubt, Max. Plenty."

"Would you please say something, you big ox," Frieda told her brother.

"Ruthie," Meyer said slowly, "you can't go and live with some *shagitz* artist in a hippie house. You're not made that way. If you were younger I'd say go, try it. But there's not so much time you can afford to experiment. Stay here with me. Be comfortable. We'll have a good life together."

"Oh, you're all making me crazy," she said, taking one more look at the Gauguin, running into the bedroom.

Max and Meyer got to the door at the same time. They tried to squeeze through simultaneously, Max finally inching in first, Meyer tumbling in after him.

Frieda tried to follow but Nick put a restraining arm around her. "Let them work it out, Aunt Frieda."

"Listen," the rabbi said, distracting her, "if you want me, Mrs. Glaser, you know where to find me." He started to take off the robe.

"Oh, no, you don't. You were paid for two hours, you stay here for two hours. That's the agreement. You don't like it, sue me."

"Godless woman," the rabbi said resignedly, attempting to break through the crowd circling the meatball platter.

"I'm going in there," Audrey said after a few impatient moments. "Come on, Ronald."

"Leave them alone," Nick said.

Audrey tried the door. It was locked. She put her ear against it. So did Frieda, who reported, "It sounds like singing. They couldn't be singing, could they?"

Nick, with Audrey behind him, other interested parties behind her, ran through the kitchen (startling the already near-catatonic caterer), through the bathroom, and into the Pompadour Room.

Meyer was sitting on the bed, holding the orchid corsage and his cocktail ring, watching Betty Grable sing, "I Wish I Could Shimmy Like My Sister Kate" on the television. "She decided to go with him," he said.

"You poor man," Mae Weissman said, sitting next to him, putting her ample arm around his shoulder, bringing his head close to hers. "What you need is a little motherly comforting, don't you?"

"Yes," said Meyer. "I do."

Nick let himself out onto the terrace. Below him he could see two figures—one in baby blue, the other in army khaki—running down the steps of the Fontainebleau, climbing aboard a red Jeep parked illegally in the middle of the driveway, speeding off. If he hadn't known better, he would have said they were youngsters starting off on some great adventure. For a moment, he felt old.

He went back into the Grand Salon. Almost everyone had gone. Linda looked at him, smiled, and reached out for him.

As he hugged her, he could hear Frieda arguing in the kitchen with the caterer. Saul was eating the last meatball.

"Best affair I've been to in a long time," Saul said. "No?"

Epilogue

He led her directly to the wicker couch under the awning supported by the two royal palms. A tablecloth, china, whiskey glasses, silver had been set up as if for a picnic.

"How did you know?" she asked.

"That Mrs. Weissman is a real good friend of ours and right handy with the telephone. She called in the nick of time." He touched her face with his hand. "Now you stay here, Miss Ruth. I'm going to prepare our non-wedding dinner. Won't take but a moment."

"He doesn't know me very well if he thinks I can sit out here and wait around for him to serve me," she thought, following him into the cottage through the french doors, stopping in the studio to admire his paintings.

"*Oy vey,*" she said, shocked. The studio walls were bare with the exception of one painting and several sketches.

The painting was of a woman—an older woman—with her back to the viewer. She was lying on a grass bed in the middle of a clearing in a jungle of red flowers. Her face was half turned as if she had only that moment stopped looking backward and begun looking forward. The sketches were of the same woman. She was nude in all of them.

Max came in and stood behind her, setting the sippin'

whiskey on a table along with the sugar bowl. "What do you think?" he asked, putting his arms around her.

"I think it's wonderful, Max."

"You don't mind it's you? That you're in your birthday suit?"

"You kidding? You're immortalizing me and now you're asking if I care whether or not I have a dress on?"

"It's a combination painting: your fantasy and mine. Eleanor de Vries wired me that a major museum is interested. Knowing Eleanor, that could be the Aurora, South Dakota, Museum of Tribal Art but . . ."

"Where are the others, Max? Where is your late middle period?"

"I put it in here, Miss Ruth," he said, handing her a small, flat package tied with a red bow. "Consider it my non-wedding present to you."

She opened it, feeling odd and nervous. "I didn't bring you a present," she said, her hands fumbling with the bow.

"Oh, yes, you did, honey. You brought me a present the first time you walked into this house. Now, open that damned thing."

It was a savings-account book made out to her name. There were two hundred and fifty thousand dollars in it.

She looked up at him. "You sold your late middle period? Every single painting?"

"I had to get rid of the ghosts."

"You could've put them in the attic."

"And I wanted you to have what your family wants you to have, Ruth: security."

"Deep down, Max, I've always felt I had security with you."

He leaned over and kissed her. "Now you have a little more."

She allowed him to take her out to the picnic dinner under

the early evening moon. Placing sugar cubes in the bottom of
their glasses, he poured them each a couple of fingers of sippin'
whiskey. Then he uncovered a tray of crackers and foie gras.
"Now, sip your whiskey, Miss Ruth. Eat that pâté. You're
going to need your strength."

"My darling Max, you may have taken a nice, comfortable,
Jewish widow and turned her into a rich woman living in sin
with her artist lover, but I have to tell you one thing: to you
this may be pâté. To me it's still chopped liver."